## He wouldn't re

Keeping her eyes steady on Nick's, she ~~~
towards her. Andie's mouth was so close that he
could feel her breath on his lips. 'When Rose
first asked me to check you out, she gave me a
picture of you,' she whispered. 'Your mouth
fascinated me. I dreamed of kissing you even
then. Kiss me now.'

For a moment he hesitated. Then he touched her,
gliding his fingertips over her throat, her shoulders,
then slowly down the sides of her breasts. Leaning
forward, he took her mouth with his.

In the tiny cabin the moonlight grew brighter. But
Nick was only aware of Andie. He was utterly
lost, completely trapped in the hot, ripe passion
they were creating between them. She murmured
his name, and the sound pushed him over the
edge. And suddenly he knew that his life would
never be the same again...

Dear Reader,

Rebels have always appealed to me in a very special way. I admire their courage in daring to be different and their honour in accepting the consequences of their actions. So I guess it was inevitable that I'd choose to make my hero, Nick Heagerty, a true rebel—in every sense.

Nick is a rebel *with* a cause. When he was sixteen he was accused of causing an accident that cost a child her life. And he's been paying for that act ever since, giving up his home, his family and even his heritage. He's determined to remain a loner, never being responsible for anybody but himself. That is, until he meets beautiful private investigator Andie Field.

I hope you enjoy the sparks that fly between Nick and Andie. It takes a strong woman to capture a rebel—but it's always worth the effort.

All my best,

Carolyn Andrews

P.S. I love to hear from my readers. You can write to me at Harlequin Mills & Boon Limited, Eton House, 18-24 Paradise Road, Richmond, Surrey TW9 1SR.

# THE BLACK SHEEP

BY

## CAROLYN ANDREWS

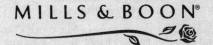

MILLS & BOON®

*All the characters in this book have no existence outside the imagination
of the author, and have no relation whatsoever to anyone bearing the
same name or names. They are not even distantly inspired by any
individual known or unknown to the author, and all the incidents are pure
invention.*

*MILLS & BOON and MILLS & BOON with the Rose Device
are registered trademarks of the publisher.
TEMPTATION is a registered trademark of
Harlequin Enterprises Limited, used under licence.*

*First published in Great Britain 1998
by Harlequin Mills & Boon Limited,
Eton House, 18-24 Paradise Road, Richmond, Surrey TW9 1SR*

© Carolyn Hanlon 1997

ISBN 0 263 80813 01

In loving memory of my cousin,
Julianne Langton Maxwell.
Thanks for enriching my life.

And a special thank-you to my editor, Brenda Chin,
for suggesting that Nick have a 'secret' in his past.

21-9803

*Printed and bound in Great Britain
by Caledonian International Book Manufacturing Ltd, Glasgow*

"DID MY UNCLE NICK forget about us?" Sarah asked.

It was her own thought exactly, but Andie managed to mask her anger with a smile as she turned to wink at the young girl. "No way. We're unforgettable."

Sarah didn't look entirely convinced. She appeared as she always did, perfectly composed and much too serious for a nine-year-old girl. The four-hour train ride from Boston hadn't left even one wrinkle in her white linen suit.

Andie didn't bother to waste time checking her own attire. The moment they'd stepped off the train, the muggy August heat had slammed into her. Her slacks stuck to her legs the same way her blouse was clinging to her back. And she was sure that her blazer had that trendy rumpled look that had faded from the fashion magazines about five years ago. Not that she was a big fashion magazine fan. But during her ten years on the Boston police force, she'd read everything she could lay her hands on to keep herself awake during stake-outs.

As the train behind them hissed and groaned and then lurched forward along the rails, Andie stood on the station platform scanning the parking lot once more for a gray sedan. That's what Nick Heagerty's assistant, a gravelly voiced man named Grady, had said they'd be driving. But there was still no sign of it.

Taking a deep breath, Andie shoved down the surge of temper. To say that she was unhappy with Nick Heagerty was understating it by a mile. It had annoyed her when he hadn't found the time to attend his sister-in-law's funeral. But after thinking it over, she'd decided to cut him some slack. The last time he'd seen his niece had been five years earlier. And the occasion had been another funeral—her father's, his brother's. Perhaps he'd been right to postpone this first meeting with Sarah. The Heagerty Vineyards on Seneca Lake was a much more cheerful place to renew an acquaintanceship than the Boston mausoleum where Rose Heagerty had recently lost her battle with cancer.

But to be late in picking up the little girl who'd been entrusted to his care—a girl who'd just lost her mother! Andie took another deep breath and exhaled on a count of ten. She had to keep her emotions under control, not only for Sarah's sake, but also for her own. If she were going to keep the promise she'd made to her friend Rose on her deathbed, she had to keep a cool head. Sarah's entire future hung in the balance.

As the heiress to an estate worth millions, Sarah had a number of relatives who wanted to be her guardian. Of course her maternal grandmother and her uncle Conrad believed they had the inside track. But in her will, Rose Heagerty had surprised everyone by naming her brother-in-law Nick as Sarah's guardian. Now all Andie had to do was to make very sure he was the right man for the job.

The initial background check she'd run on him had raised as many questions as it had answered. Nick Heagerty was a man of curious contrasts. There was the rebellious teenage runaway who'd served his country for ten years as a navy SEAL. And then there was the laid-back captain of a charter sailing business in the Caribbean who'd come home when his brother died and saved his family's winery from financial ruin. Any lingering doubts she'd had about Nick's qualifications as a father had faded in the face of Rose's complete trust in her brother-in-law.

With a frown, Andie glanced at her watch. It just didn't

make any sense that he was late. A man with a military background should be punctual if nothing else. As she searched the parking lot again, she quickly went over in her mind everything that Grady had said to her on the phone.

His instructions had been very precise. Nick had a meeting at the state fairgrounds and so she and Sarah were to get off the train in Syracuse. That way he and Grady could be waiting on the platform to make Sarah feel welcome when they arrived.

The platform had been deserted when the train had pulled in. The station had been empty, too, except for the man behind the counter, and he'd had no message to pass along from Nick.

She and Sarah were essentially alone now. In front of them, the parking lot held a few vacant cars. Behind them, beyond the tracks, fields choked with tall grass and wildflowers spread to a distant line of trees. The only sound was the steady drone of insects.

Andie felt a shiver of unease. It was too quiet, and she and Sarah were too isolated. For the first time the weight of the gun in the pouch she wore around her waist gave her some comfort. Not that she thought she'd need it. In fact, she'd debated whether or not to bring it with her at all. As a cop, she'd long ago come to terms with using her gun. She made a point of never firing it carelessly or unnecessarily.

But delivering Sarah to her uncle was more than a favor she was doing for her best friend. Rose had hired her to investigate Nick Heagerty, to make sure he was the right person to raise Sarah. And she always took her gun when she was on a job. In the end, she'd decided to bring it for backup. Better to be safe than sorry.

And for some reason, right now, she didn't feel exactly safe. As a cop, she'd also come to terms with trusting her instincts.

Squeezing Sarah's hand, she said, "Your uncle Nick's

probably running late at that meeting. How about we give him five more minutes? Then we'll call a cab, check into the best motel in Syracuse and order up pizza and movies."

Sarah's expression brightened. "Really? Grandmother never let me watch movies. She says they're filled with trash."

"Of course they are. That's why they're fun." Out of the corner of her eye, Andie saw a gray sedan turn in off the highway. "Oh, hold on. I think Grady and your uncle Nick are here." She brushed Sarah's long, honey-blond hair off her shoulders. "There, I think you'll pass inspection."

Sarah reached for one of Andie's hands. "I think I'd rather watch movies."

"Listen." Andie cupped the little girl's chin with her free hand. "Your mom loved you very much. And she put a lot of thought into choosing the very best person to be your guardian. I think we have to trust her on this. But just in case she was wrong, remember our deal?"

Sarah nodded. "You'll stay for two weeks."

"And if Uncle Nick turns out to be a jerk, or a dweeb..."

Sarah giggled.

Encouraged, Andie rolled her eyes. "Or even worse, if he's a nerd, we're outta here." She held up her hand and waited for Sarah to give her a high five.

"What if he doesn't like me?" Sarah asked.

Andie's eyebrows rose. "That would make him a real dunce cap. I don't think your mom would have wanted your guardian to be a dummy, do you?"

Shaking her head, Sarah slapped Andie's hand. Then they both turned to watch the gray car pull into a spot near the center of the parking lot. A heavyset woman climbed out of the passenger side. Her blond hair was pulled back into a bun, and she was wearing a white pantsuit that fit like a second skin.

A nurse? With a frown, Andie turned her attention to the

man circling around the front of the car. Medium tall and thin, he was wearing a chauffeur's uniform. Andie's frown deepened. Could this be Grady? She'd guessed from the deep voice with its hint of a brogue that Grady'd be older, with a little more girth. But the odd-looking couple was walking straight toward them. Andie edged slightly in front of Sarah as they drew close.

"You must be Sarah." Beaming a smile at the little girl, the woman extended her hand. "I'm Elaine, your new nanny."

Andie reached over and gripped the woman's hand. "And I'm the old nanny," she lied. "Where are Grady and Nick?"

"I'm Grady," the thin man said in a high-pitched voice that matched his physique.

In a pig's eye, Andie thought as she watched him pull a fat envelope out of his pocket.

"Nick's tied up at the fairgrounds. He sent Elaine in his place. That way she and Sarah can start getting acquainted, and we won't have to trouble you any further." He handed her the envelope. "This should more than compensate for any inconvenience."

Andie glanced at the neat stack of bills inside the flap. Then, slipping the money into her pocket, she smiled at Skinny. "Very generous. Why wasn't I informed of the change in plans?"

"When I called, you'd already left for the station."

Shifting her weight to the balls of her feet, Andie reached behind her back to give Sarah's arm one quick squeeze. "Run! Get help in the station!"

Elaine grabbed for Sarah as she dashed past and got a fistful of air. Then Andie launched herself into the woman and together they tumbled to the ground, rolling over and over. At the edge of the platform Andie managed to scramble on top of the larger woman, but then she was jerked to her feet and the thin man pinned her against his chest.

"Don't move."

Andie gasped as his arm tightened around her throat.

"I have a gun." He shoved it into her side, then swore at the chubby, blond woman. "Get up, stupid. Get the girl."

As soon as Elaine struggled to her feet, Andie went perfectly still. Sarah had covered half the distance to the station, but precious seconds would be lost when the little girl reached the door. Already Elaine was picking up speed.

Andie brought her foot down hard on the man's instep at the same moment that she jabbed her elbow into his stomach. Then pivoting, she gripped both hands together and slammed them into his jaw. The gun hit the platform a second before the man did. Andie kicked the weapon onto the tracks, then raced after Sarah.

"To the car, Elaine!" The hoarse shout came from behind Andie as she gained on the nurse. Elaine didn't bother to glance back. She merely veered right and headed for the sedan. Andie didn't change direction until she saw Sarah disappear through the station doors. Then, satisfied that her charge was safe, she skidded to a stop and whirled in time to see the chauffer jump the small hedge that bordered the parking lot.

As she raced after the man, Andie unzipped the pouch she wore around her waist and pulled out her gun. She fired a shot into the air. The woman picked up speed and the man ducked low as he dodged behind a car.

So much for persuading them to stop, Andie thought as she lowered the gun and leapt over the hedge. Other than as a means of persuasion, she would only fire her gun to save a life. And Skinny was not posing a sufficient threat. Narrowing her eyes, she focused on overtaking him as she followed his zigzagging path through the parking lot. He still had twenty yards on her when he yanked open the car door and threw himself behind the wheel. Elaine barely managed to join him before the car peeled into reverse.

Andie was ten yards away, close enough to be sprayed

with gravel as the gray sedan shot past her. For the next few seconds she concentrated on running. And breathing. Keeping clear of the dust that the car stirred up as it accelerated, she focused all her energy on a final sprint. Just before the car squealed onto the highway, she made the license plate.

Then she slowed, gasping for breath, and circled to begin a slow jog back to the station. She'd just caught a glimpse of Sarah through the sliding-glass doors when a second gray sedan pulled up beside her. Signaling the little girl to stay where she was, Andie turned to face the man getting out of the passenger side. Nick Heagerty.

She'd spent hours studying the picture she'd clipped to his file. But the photo hadn't captured the essence of the man standing in front of her.

Oh, the features were similar enough. Thick, dark hair that curled a bit over the ears, strong, angled cheekbones. The scar beneath his left eye hadn't shown up in the photo, though it looked old. And the mouth was different, too. The photographer had captured it curved halfway between a grin and a smirk. Appealing and annoying at the same time. But at the moment Nick Heagerty's lips had thinned into a grim, disapproving line.

Then there was the sheer size of the man. Though he wasn't that tall, perhaps not even six feet. Still, there was something about him—a solidness, a strength that testified to his military background and contrasted sharply with the playboy image that the picture in the charter sailing brochure had projected. Face-to-face, Andie knew that this playboy was no one to play around with. And he was certainly not a boy.

She stepped up to him. "You're late."

"And you are?" Nick asked.

"Andie Field. Someone just tried to kidnap your niece." It was only as she lifted her hand that she remembered she was still holding the gun. The instant Nick's fingers clamped on her wrist, Andie's throat went dry. Not because his grip was painful. No, it was the look in his eyes. The photo hadn't done them justice, either. They were caught somewhere between green and gray, piercing, fascinating. For a second her mind went completely blank.

In that same second Nick slipped the gun from her hand.

"Is there a problem?" a man approaching them asked.

A *big* problem was the first thought that popped into Andie's mind, though she was sure she hadn't spoken the words. With some difficulty she tore her gaze away from Nick. The voice had been deep, gravelly, and it fit the large man with iron-gray hair who now stood at Nick's side.

"Someone tried to kidnap Sarah? Where is she?" Nick asked.

"She's safe in the station." Relieved at how normal her own voice sounded, Andie continued. "And if you don't mind, I'd like my gun and my hand back."

Through the glass doors, Nick saw a young girl with long blond hair. He switched his gaze back to Andie with a frown. Absolutely nothing that he saw reminded him of the cool and rather terrifyingly efficient letter she'd sent him outlining Rose's instructions for Sarah's new guardian. He'd pictured Ms. Field as a more matronly type, someone he could have sent packing, along with her charge, without a second's hesitation.

Not that the slender waif standing in front of him was going to make him change his plans. Sarah, his niece, was the only one he was concerned about, now even more so, if what Ms. Field said was true. She certainly deserved better than what life was dishing out to her, and he was going to make sure she got it. Rose, of all people, should have known better than to send Sarah to him. Heagerty Vineyards was the wrong place to raise a child. And he was the wrong man to do the job.

And if Ms. Field chose to argue with his decision? For a

moment he studied her. She wasn't at all as he'd imagined. For one thing, the woman packed a gun. And her hair, instead of being iron-gray and clamped back in a bun, was dark as night and mussed as if a man had just run his hands through it... But something had happened here, he reminded himself, and Andie Field had been in the middle of it. Ten years in the navy had taught him to never underestimate a possible opponent. His hand tightened briefly on her wrist before he released her to examine the weapon. He intended to find out what was going on here.

"Why are you armed?" he asked.

"I'm a private investigator. I have a license to carry it."

"It's been fired."

"I shot into the air to frighten them."

Satisfied, Nick handed her the gun and watched her slip it back into the pouch she wore around her waist. "What exactly happened?"

"A couple in a gray sedan arrived about five minutes ago. They claimed to be your assistant Grady and a nanny, and they tried to pay me off and kidnap Sarah. Why were you late?"

"A flat tire," Grady said as he strode to the car.

"You'll never catch them," Andie said. "The police will have a better chance. I got a plate number and hopefully a set of prints. I kicked his gun onto the tracks."

Nick stared at her. "The man was armed?"

"Briefly," she said.

He removed a cellular phone from his pocket and tossed it to Grady. "Call Mendoza." Then taking Andie's arm, he pulled her toward the station doors. Sarah stepped through them as they opened automatically.

"I called the police," she announced, looking from Andie to her uncle Nick.

"Good girl." Nick rested his hands on her shoulders, then stooped down so that his eyes were level with hers. "You're coolheaded, just like your father. Your dad always knew exactly what to do in a crisis." He rose, leading her into the station. "C'mon. We'll wait for the police inside where it's cool. You and Ms. Field can tell me what happened."

AN HOUR LATER Sarah was still telling her story, this time to a brusque, solidly built police lieutenant in a rumpled sport coat. Lieutenant Mendoza.

Though she was grateful that Grady's call had summoned someone of Mendoza's rank to the scene, Andie wasn't entirely comfortable with the bear hug Nick and the lieutenant had exchanged amid much back thumping. She would have preferred that the lieutenant be totally objective when it came to the Heagerty family. The attempted kidnapping could only have been plotted by someone who'd known of the plans she and Grady had made. That suggested it was an "inside" job.

Still, Andie couldn't find any fault with the way Lieutenant Mendoza was handling the case so far. He'd been gruff when he'd questioned her, and more impressed with her previous job on the Boston police force than he was with her present one as a private investigator. For her part, she was pleased that he'd asked all the right questions and listened to the answers. He was visibly disturbed when he'd learned that Sarah was an heiress. The wrinkled jacket worked in his favor, too. It meant he did more than sit behind a desk and push paper.

She'd even seen a hint of approval in Mendoza's eyes when he'd learned about the gun on the tracks and when she'd handed him the envelope the chauffeur had given her. "Skinny" hadn't been wearing gloves. If he had a record, they'd have a name.

"Mendoza's a good man. He works hard."

Andie turned to find Grady at her side with several soft drink cans clasped in his large hands. Nick's assistant had been serving up refreshments from the vending machine ever since the police had arrived. Standing well over six feet tall with the build of a linebacker, the "real" Grady, even at forty-something, looked more like a bodyguard than a butler or chauffeur. Andie knew from Nick's file that the two men had been together since their navy days and that Jeremiah Grady was a full-fledged partner in the charter sailing business. Carefully, she plucked one of the soda cans free. "Plus, he's an old friend of the family."

Grady chuckled. "Old rival is more like it. But he helped us out with some problems at the winery."

"What kind of problems?"

Grady's grin faded, and Andie could have sworn that his face flushed as he shot a quick look at Nick. Then he cleared his throat. "Some vandalism. More annoying than anything. A month ago some visitors got sick on wine in the tasting room. Mendoza got a friend of his to design our new security system."

She stared at him as he moved on to offer drinks to the two uniformed men who had responded to Sarah's phone call. There'd been no hint of *problems* at the winery when she'd done a background check on Nick. And she'd have bet her old shield Grady was sorry he'd brought the subject up.

Flipping up the metal tab on the soft drink can, Andie took a long swallow and shifted her gaze to Nick. She hadn't looked at him since they'd walked into the station. All because of her reaction when he'd touched her. She could still recall how weak she'd felt, breathless, and her train of thought had evaporated into thin air. No man had ever made her feel that way before.

And he'd taken her weapon. She might have been transformed into a statue for all the protest she'd made. It was only when the soda can suddenly snapped in protest that she realized how tightly she was gripping it. Slowly she relaxed her fingers.

Instead of worrying about Mendoza's objectivity, she might better worry about her own when it came to Nick Heagerty.

She studied him through narrowed eyes. Since he'd first taken Sarah's hand in his, he'd been acting the role of the caring and concerned uncle. But Andie had learned that Nick Heagerty was a man who'd played many different roles in his life.

He'd aroused her curiosity ever since Rose had announced that he was her choice for Sarah's guardian. At first glance, Nick seemed a highly unlikely candidate for a Dad. Even Rose admitted that his family considered him a "black sheep." He'd been sent away to a fancy prep school after his junior year in high school. The details concerning the incident that had plunged him into disgrace had been vague, and then he'd chosen not to redeem himself. Instead he'd run away before graduation to join the navy. Ten years later, with a college degree and an honorable discharge on his résumé, he'd used an inheritance from his grandmother to purchase a sailboat, which he'd christened *Nomad*. And until his brother's and parents' untimely deaths, he and Grady had run a successful charter business in the Caribbean.

In the first report from the operative that she'd hired in the Virgin Islands, Nick's sailing bum persona had checked out. However, when she'd asked the investigator to check further, he'd come back with more.

Not that Nick had been involved in anything illegal. No, it was the investigator's opinion, based on the number of blank walls and dead ends he'd run into, that Nick had been involved in some secret work for the government. Andie hadn't pursued it any further at the time because, since Nick had taken over the reins at Heagerty Vineyards, he'd been a model citizen and become a respected winemaker. With several gold medals won at prestigious wine competitions, sales had doubled, and for the first time in ten years, the family business was operating at a profit.

Andie's gaze dropped to his hand still so protectively clasped around Sarah's. Strong hands, she thought. Even now she could recall the pressure of each one of his fingers when he'd gripped her wrist. His other hand rested on Sarah's shoulder. The palms were wide, the fingers long and lean. In addition to strength, they were capable of offering comfort. And pleasure.

Andie blinked when she realized where her train of thought had led her. Her head snapped up, and she met Nick's gaze. The little tingle of awareness that had begun when she'd started looking at his hands grew until she felt a pull, sudden and strong. What in the world...

"Ms. Field?"

It was only when she found Lieutenant Mendoza blocking her path that she realized she'd taken a step forward.

"There's nothing more we can do here," Mendoza said. "I told Nick I'll be in touch just as soon as we get any information on the license plate or the gun."

"And in the meantime, what are you going to do to protect Sarah?"

"The safest place for her right now is at Heagerty Vineyards. They have a state-of-the-art security system." He gave her a reassuring smile. "A good friend of mine designed it. He's an ex-cop just like you."

The second that Mendoza and the policemen left, Andie walked over to Nick. "I have a few questions."

He met her eyes squarely. "So do I, but I think that they can wait until we get Sarah safely settled at Heagerty House."

MUCH TO ANDIE'S SURPRISE, the forty-five-minute drive to Sarah's new home passed very quickly. Once inside the gray sedan, she'd expected the atmosphere to be strained. But

Nick managed to diffuse the tension almost immediately by keeping up a steady stream of conversation with his niece.

Sensitivity wasn't a quality that she'd expected to find in Nick Heagerty. She studied him over the top of Sarah's head. Perhaps she hadn't given enough consideration to the nomadic existence he'd lived since he'd been sent away from home at sixteen. Maybe he was just the kind of man who *would* understand the kind of turmoil his niece was going through right now. This was the second time in Sarah's short life that she'd been uprooted and faced with adjusting to a new home, a new family. The little girl had barely been four when her father had died in a boating accident and her mother had made the decision to live with her family in Boston.

But four was old enough to be frightened by the change, old enough to be almost overwhelmed by the challenge of making new friends. Andie knew the feelings very well. As the daughter of a happy-go-lucky gypsy who'd believed that all of life's problems could be solved by pulling up stakes and starting over again in a new town, Andie had never known what it had meant to feel "at home" until she'd shared a room with Rose in college.

Rose. As her eyes misted, Andie turned and tried to focus on the blur of trees whipping past the window. It still hurt to recall those happier times with her friend. She and Rose couldn't have been more mismatched as college roommates. The rich girl with her last name carved in granite above the massive library doors and the poor girl who'd been lucky enough to get a full financial aid package.

Sarah's sudden laughter brought Andie's attention back to the present.

"You got thrown off a horse? You're kidding!"

"Scout's honor," Nick said. "And it gets worse. I landed on a barbed-wire fence. I had to get a tetanus shot, and I couldn't lift my right arm for days."

"Nasty," Sarah said.

"Not nearly as nasty as the black eye I gave your father when I found out he'd put a burr under my saddle."

"He did that?" Sarah asked, wide-eyed.

"Confessed the whole thing. Under pressure, of course." He paused to flex his arm. "Maybe that's why my arm hurt so bad."

For a second Andie's eyes met Nick's. His were filled with laughter. Even as she smiled in response, she was suddenly as aware of him as she'd been when he'd touched her. She stared at him. Could minds meet, thoughts mingle?

Nick was the first to break the contact. Shifting his gaze out the window, he leaned forward. "Slow down a little, Grady." Then he pointed. "See those two piles of stones over there?"

Both Andie and Sarah looked at the piles, turning to keep them in view even after the car whipped past.

"That's one of the old Erie Canal locks. You'll have to get Grady to tell you about them. He claims one of his great-great-uncles helped build the canal." For one moment Grady's hearty laughter filled the car, but the instant it faded, Sarah had questions. As his niece and Andie leaned forward to hear Grady's story, Nick took a moment to study the formidable Ms. Field. Within twenty-four hours he intended to know everything about her. Already he knew she was competent. Mendoza had been very impressed. And why shouldn't he be? He'd left the train station with a gun, several sets of prints, a detailed description of the two suspects and a license plate number. She was probably telling the truth about her ten years on the Boston police force. It was Mendoza's job to check that part out.

They had discussed that his own job would be to keep a close eye on Andie Field, until Mendoza could report back. "Tough job, but somebody's got to do it," was Mendoza's low-voiced comment as he'd left the station. And it wasn't bad work, Nick thought as he watched Andie push her hair back. Under other circumstances, he would have thoroughly enjoyed it. Her skin was pale, and the delicate line of her cheekbone added to the fragile look she had. Except for her chin. It showed strength. The skinny chauffeur probably hadn't noticed her chin. Nick had to prevent a smile as he thought of the confrontation. She'd given very few details, but he could picture it quite clearly. And it gave him a good deal of satisfaction to imagine the frustration the skinny chauffeur must have felt watching his weapon sail out of reach onto the tracks.

It was the one image that had helped him control the icy mixture of anger and fear he'd been feeling since Andie and Sarah had described what had happened on the platform.

He had to hand it to her. She was clever, too, kicking the gun out of play. That part of her story alone had nearly convinced him that she was telling the truth. A cop who'd spent time on the streets would know the danger of a gun going off. And she hadn't pulled her own weapon until Sarah was safe in the station.

It occurred to him that he already knew quite a bit about Ms. Field. She was competent, tough and clever. Clever enough to have come up with a foolproof plan to kidnap his niece for money? That was the question. The would-be kidnappers had known exactly where and when Sarah would arrive. As far as he knew, that information had been shared by only Grady, himself, and Ms. Field. Foiling the first attempt to snatch Sarah might be a part of her strategy. Who would suspect her the next time?

She glanced up at him then, her eyes brimming with amusement over something Grady or Sarah had said, and for a moment Nick lost his train of thought completely. His suspicions slipped away, and he was aware of no one but Andie.

"There it is, Sarah. Heagerty House." Nick heard Grady

speak. The words began to make sense only as he felt Sarah's hand slip into his.

"It's big," she said.

"Huge," Nick said as he tugged her closer. "We'll have to put a bell around your neck so that you don't get lost."

As they turned off the highway, he pointed out the winery and the wine-tasting store, nestled close to the driveway.

Heagerty Vineyards was indeed very impressive. The house itself sat on the top of a hill overlooking Seneca Lake. Fanning out from it on three sides were acres of vines forming a criss-cross pattern on gently sloping hills. Andie noticed that Grady pressed a button in the car to open the wrought-iron gates that marked the entrance to a tree-lined drive. Less impressive were the low rock walls that surrounded the estate.

As if reading her thoughts, Nick explained to Sarah that the walls were wired and tied into a security system. "You'll be perfectly safe here," he said, squeezing the little girl's hand.

A woman was waiting for them in the foyer. She was almost as tall as Nick, thin, and meticulously made up. Not one curl of the silver-gray hair that framed her face was out of place. And her eyes, framed in designer glasses, almost exactly matched the icy blue color of her dress.

"You're late," she said, addressing Nick.

Nick ignored her comment and made the introductions. "Sarah, meet your great-aunt Maggie."

"Aunt Marguerite," she corrected, aiming a frown at Nick.

"And this is Ms. Field," Nick continued, "Rose's dear friend who has been kind enough to bring Sarah to us."

Marguerite's ringed fingers barely brushed Andie's, and her gaze never left Nick. "How much longer should I hold dinner? Or should I have trays sent to their rooms?"

"No," Nick replied. "Ms. Field and Sarah will dine with us as long as they're our guests. Grady—" he turned to the older man "—show the ladies to their rooms while I explain to Aunt Maggie why we were delayed."

"We dress for dinner," Marguerite said over her shoulder as Nick accompanied her down the hall.

"Relax," Nick said. "They're not going to show up naked."

Andie had to bite down hard on the inside of her cheek as she followed Grady up the stairs to the suite of rooms that she would share with Sarah. She didn't dare look at the girl until Grady had closed the door behind him. Then she drew in a deep breath and assumed a haughty expression. "We dress for dinner."

Sarah giggled. "She reminds me of Grandmother."

"Well, she certainly ruined any thought I had of changing into my jeans. Thank heavens your mom filled in some of the gaps in my wardrobe. But you..." She walked to the little girl and brushed her hair back over her shoulder. "You have so many clothes. How will you possibly make a decision?"

"I'll wear my blue dress. I think it's the same shade as Great-aunt Marguerite's."

Though Sarah's expression was perfectly serious, Andie didn't miss the glint of mischief in her eyes. "Way to go! Show 'em you're not a pushover."

"What do you think of Uncle Nick?"

Andie gave the little girl's shoulder a squeeze. "The important question is, what do *you* think of him?"

"He's funny."

"Yes." Without even wanting to, Andie could picture the fan of wrinkles at the corners of Nick's eyes when he smiled.

"Do you think he likes me?"

Andie's heart turned over at the hint of uncertainty she saw in Sarah's eyes. "Absolutely." And if he didn't.... "I'm going to stay until we're certain of that. Remember our deal?"

They were interrupted by a knock on the door.

"Our luggage," Andie said, moving to the door. "Last one dressed is a rotten egg."

NICK STOOD on the deck of the *Nomad* and watched the crimson streaks in the western sky fade to pink. He'd promised himself thirty minutes of solitude before he kept his ten o'clock appointment with Andie Field. He'd hoped to postpone their meeting until after Mendoza had checked her out. But she'd cornered him in the dining room and pinned him down to a time and a place before he'd had a chance to escape.

Determination was a quality he admired. And it went with the competence he'd already noticed. As for her loyalty to his niece and to Rose, he could admire that, too, if it turned out to be real. But if he'd learned one thing from life, it was not to trust the persona a man or woman presented to the world. It could be put on and discarded as easily as a Halloween mask.

One thing he didn't need Mendoza to tell him was how Sarah and Andie felt about each other. The affection between them was almost palpable. Nick's lips curved as he recalled the way they'd walked hand in hand into the parlor, a ready-to-do-battle set to their shoulders and smiles on their faces as if they'd made a secret pact to win over the enemy. Not only had Marguerite stopped pontificating in midsentence, but she'd actually smiled when Sarah curtsied in front of her. Since he was sure that Andie was the brains behind the battle plan, his admiration for her had shot up several notches.

Shutting Marguerite up was a trick Nick hadn't often accomplished himself. Tricking her into a smile was an even bigger challenge.

On the other hand, the fact that Andie loved Sarah didn't mean that she didn't like Sarah's money, too. Frowning, Nick began to pace back and forth across the deck of the *Nomad*. What he needed from Mendoza was confirmation that the very bright and competent P.I. hadn't been behind the attempted kidnapping. If Ms. Andie Field did check out to be everything she appeared to be, and she truly cared about his niece, it should be even easier to stick to his plans. So why in hell was he worried?

No. Not worried. Just restless. He'd stayed too long in one spot. If it hadn't been for the problems at the winery, he'd have been back in the Caribbean six months ago, and Rose would never have sent Sarah to him there.

With a sigh, Nick leaned against the railing. Sarah was a complication, something he had to take care of before he left. He looked out over the water. The lake's surface was as smooth as tinted glass, not a ripple anywhere. If there was any sign of wind, he'd have gone for a sail. Instead he'd had to settle for sitting on the deck of the moored boat. Too bad, because sailing always cleared his head.

Turning, he glanced up at Heagerty House. His niece and her companion had been assigned to the corner suite of rooms above the sloping roof of the back porch. The lights were still on. The sound of a laugh—Sarah's, he was almost sure—carried through the open window and over the water. In a moment it came again. He could picture Sarah and Andie quite clearly, their heads close, giggling over something.

Women rarely took him by surprise. But Andie Field had certainly done that. And it was more than her appearance. Though there was nothing to complain about in that department. Those long legs. He'd noticed them right away when he'd spotted her racing across the parking lot at the train station. Then there was her hair. Mussed, it made a man's hands itch to straighten the tangles out. Smooth and shiny, the way she'd worn it at dinner, it tempted a man to mess it up.

Oh, there were all sorts of pleasurable possibilities that he might wish to explore with Ms. Andie Field if she weren't a gun-toting private eye, who'd appointed herself both advocate and guardian angel to his niece. As it was, the lady spelled *trouble*, and they were headed on a collision course. Just as soon as he was sure she hadn't masterminded the kidnapping attempt on Sarah, he fully intended to send her packing.

"You still here?" Grady asked, ducking his head to clear the overhang as he climbed up from the galley. "I thought you had an appointment with Ms. Field."

Nick glanced at his watch. "In fifteen minutes. I told her to come out here as soon as Sarah fell asleep."

"If you've got some time to kill, how about giving me a hand with the cookies?"

"Cookies?" Nick's brows rose as he followed Grady down a short flight of steps.

"Cooking clears my head." Grady poured a bag of chocolate pieces into a bowl of dough. "Same way sailing clears yours."

"Cut the crap. You're making chocolate chip cookies because my niece happened to mention that they were her favorite."

Nonplussed, Grady began to drop spoon-size dollops of dough into neat rows on a cookie sheet. "It's a cinch your aunt Marguerite isn't going to ask that fancy French chef of hers to whip up a batch."

Nick pulled two beers out of the refrigerator and handed one to Grady. "We've discussed this before. It's not going to make it easier on any of us if Sarah starts to feel too much at home here."

Grady met Nick's eyes squarely. "Miss Sarah belongs with you, lad. Sooner or later, you're going to have to accept that. And don't waste your breath trying to convince me otherwise."

Nick didn't. Sarah was a subject on which they'd agreed to

disagree. Instead he asked, "What do you think of Ms. Field?"

"I like her."

"You always were a sucker for a pretty face."

Grady settled a filled tray in the oven and twisted a timer. "She's a bit more than a pretty face, I'd say. Single-handedly, she kept your niece from being kidnapped."

With one finger Nick traced a line through the condensation on his bottle of beer. "What if she set it up?"

Grady stared at him. "You don't believe that."

"Sarah's a very rich little girl."

"Why should she set it up and then prevent it?"

"So no one will suspect her the next time."

"You've got a suspicious mind, lad." Grady frowned. "I'm not saying it hasn't served you well in the past. But you're wrong about Ms. Field. Unless..." Suddenly, Grady grinned.

"What?"

"You're attracted to her!" Grady's grin widened. "That would explain why your brain's gone a little mushy. But at least there's nothing wrong with your taste."

Footsteps overhead prevented Nick's reply. Seconds later Andie climbed down the steps to the galley.

Still grinning from ear to ear, Grady unfastened his apron and lifted it over his head. "Evening, Ms. Field. I know you'll want to speak privately with Nick. I'll just go on up to the house and keep an eye on Miss Sarah. That way you won't have to worry about rushing back." Turning his head, he winked at Nick. "When the buzzer goes off, take the cookies out. I'll finish this up later."

Andie let her gaze take in the small, fully equipped galley. The last rays of the sun slanted in through the porthole, intensifying the rich gleam of wood and the duller shine of stainless steel. "Nice boat." She climbed up on the stool across from Nick. "You couldn't have sailed her all the way from the Caribbean."

"Most of it. Grady and I came up the coastline and then down the St. Lawrence and through the canal locks. We only had to transport her over land for about the last fifty miles."

Andie glanced around the galley again. "I can see why you wouldn't want to leave her behind."

"It's home," Nick said.

She shot him a quick look. "You prefer this to the house?"

"As I said, it's home. I haven't felt that way about Heagerty House in a very long time."

"Why not?"

"It's a long and very boring story, Ms. Field."

"Andie, please. Between your aunt Marguerite and Grady I've been Ms. Fielded to death."

She was wiped out, Nick suddenly realized. Not that the fatigue was easy to spot. But it was there in the smudges under her eyes and in the way her shoulders sagged just a little. She hadn't eaten much at dinner, but he'd blamed that on the undercurrents in the room. Not that she hadn't handled herself well with Aunt Maggie, but he'd often felt his own appetite slip away in the older woman's frigid presence. "Would you like a beer?" he asked.

"Sure."

He moved to the refrigerator, then glanced back over his shoulder. "Unless you'd rather have wine. We do happen to make a very nice Chardonnay."

Andie wrinkled her nose. "I'm not big on wine."

"We'll have to educate your palate," Nick said as he opened the bottle and handed it to her.

"Before we do that, I'd prefer to talk about who might have tried to kidnap Sarah this afternoon. If it will set your mind at ease, I didn't do it."

The lady was full of surprises, it seemed. Nick was grateful that the buzzer went off. As soon as he silenced it, Andie went on. "In your shoes, I'd have put me on the top of the suspect list. You were certainly at the top of mine."

She had guts, too. He had to admire that. To buy himself some time, Nick took the tray out of the oven and began to transfer the cookies to a wire rack. Above the rich, sweet aroma, he could still catch her scent. Spring flowers.

"Are those chocolate chip cookies?"

Nick glanced at her, distracted by the mixture of accusation and longing in her voice. "Grady's idea. He thinks the quickest way to a woman's heart is through her stomach."

"He could be right."

"Go ahead, take one," Nick offered.

"Oh, no. I can't. If I eat one, I could easily eat a dozen. Or more."

Nick grinned. "A weakness?"

"Of catastrophic proportions."

She was sitting with her hands clasped tightly in front of her, and it was only as she finished speaking that she dragged her gaze away from the cookies. So she wasn't as self-contained as she appeared. It occurred to Nick that he might be developing a weakness of his own for a delicate-looking brunette with soft, brown eyes... But there were things he needed to know about Andie Field besides her weaknesses. "You said I *was* at the top of your list of suspects. You've eliminated me?"

Andie took a sip of her beer. "When Rose died, Sarah inherited a lot of money. Nothing I turned up in the check I ran on you suggests that you need any. Plus, as Sarah's guardian, you already have control of her fortune until she's twenty-one. And then there's the fact that it was a very sloppy kidnapping attempt. From what I know about you, if you'd wanted to kidnap Sarah, you'd have succeeded."

Nick studied her for a moment. Could she possibly be as ingenuous and straightforward as she seemed? Experience led him to doubt it. "I don't yet know enough about you to eliminate you from my suspect list."

"I assume that Lieutenant Mendoza is running a background check on me. What he'll find is that I resigned from the Boston police force and recently opened my own private investigations office just outside of Boston. I'm in debt, but not more than I can handle. And if I had tried to kidnap Sarah, I wouldn't have failed, either. But of course, you have to take my word on that."

"What I'm really curious about is why my sister-in-law hired a private investigator to escort Sarah to Syracuse."

"Rose and I were roommates in college. Mismatched to be sure. We joke'd that her family was probably paying my way. But we became friends. When she learned she was dying, she asked me to help her out."

"And just what was it she asked you to do?"

"Rose had decided that you would make the best guardian for Sarah. I think what she wanted at first was a stamp of approval."

"And you gave it?"

"No. First, I ran a check on you."

She sat very still, he noted. No nervous gestures. But when she reached for the bottle of beer, her hand shook slightly. So she wasn't as cool as she appeared. "You must have missed some of the good stuff."

"Parts of your career with the navy were classified. That in itself answered some of my questions about your real business in the Caribbean. All in all, I was able to give Rose a fairly accurate picture. She called you the prodigal son."

Nick's eyes narrowed. He was impressed that she'd discovered or guessed as much as she had. "And the reason I left Heagerty Vineyards in the first place? Did Rose fill you in on that?"

"Not the details. But she seemed to think that you'd more

than paid your debt." Andie leaned toward him with a smile. "She was so pleased with your success here."

"The prodigal son only wasted his inheritance, as I recall. I'm guilty of much more than that. I'm the last person she should have assumed would take on the responsibility of raising a young girl. The least she could have done was ask me."

"She did. She told me...she must have."

When he merely shook his head, Andie opened her mouth, then closed it. Slipping from her stool, she began to pace.

It was the first time Nick had seen her control slip, if only slightly, but it gave him little satisfaction.

"I know she told me she asked you." She walked back to the table as she searched her memory, recalling bits and pieces of her conversations with Rose. Of all the problems she'd expected to face, this wasn't one of them. "I asked her right at the beginning if you'd be willing. She said..." Andie paused trying to remember Rose's exact words. "Making a home for a child would be your salvation."

"Not exactly a direct answer," Nick commented.

"But it seemed... I assumed—"

"Much more than you should have. Not that I'm blaming you. Rose surely would have anticipated my answer."

"What do you mean?"

"You're going to have to give Sarah to Rose's second choice."

"I can't." In the space between the table and the wall of the galley, she began to pace again. "Maybe I should describe the runners-up. There's her grandmother, a clone of your aunt Maggie. Rosamund Forrester believes that children should be perfectly behaved little dolls. She won't even let Sarah watch movies! And Conrad, Rose's brother! He's a real beauty! He has a slight gambling addiction and views Sarah as a temporary respite from his financial difficulties, just until his mother dies. Damn it!" She slammed her hands down on the table. "Sarah's a wonderful little girl. You can't send her away."

"I mean to do just that."

"I won't let you. She's lost both her parents. And she's just nine. Not that you'd notice, because she tries to act older. Too old. Have you even taken one minute to think about how she must feel? Betrayed. Deserted. And a little guilty, perhaps, because her mother died and she's still alive." Andie raised her hands and dropped them. "You can't send her away. She thinks you're funny, and her biggest worry right now is whether or not you like her."

"Whether I like her or not doesn't matter. I'm not fit to be Sarah's guardian. And do you want to know why?" He took a deep breath. "Because twenty years ago, I was responsible for a little girl's death."

Andie simply stared at Nick. Before a single word came to her mind, a phone rang. Nick took it out of his pocket and flipped it open. "Yeah?... She'll be right there." He glanced at her. "Grady says Sarah's having a nightmare. She's asking for you."

Halfway up the galley stairs, Andie turned back. "We're not finished yet, Nick Heagerty."

# 2

ANDIE SCANNED the lake from the window seat in her room. The *Nomad* had disappeared. Two hours ago when she'd first awakened, it had been tied to the buoy, its shadowy outline just visible in the breaking light. According to Grady, Nick slept on the boat unless the weather prevented it. She'd planned to take the dinghy out there and finish her discussion with Nick Heagerty just as soon as Sarah was awake. But the wind had picked up first, and he'd gone for a sail. The Finger Lakes, aptly named, were narrow and long. He could be gone for hours.

Patience, Andie reminded herself. Because she wanted to pace, she pulled her knees up and wrapped her arms around them. A breeze sent the curtains billowing into the room and carried the scent of roses. Andie shifted her gaze to the garden.

Directly below her window, the porch roof sloped steeply away, and just beyond it was a rose garden, complete with a winding path and a gazebo overlooking the lake. On this side, the house was fringed by only fifty yards or so of land before the earth fell away in a sheer drop to the water. The only way to the beach was down a zigzagging set of wooden stairs that had given her pause the night before. But Grady had assured her they were inspected and reinforced regularly.

Thinking of Grady made Andie smile. Out of all the people at Heagerty House, he alone seemed to have a genuine affection for Sarah. Before the little girl had drifted back to sleep last night, Grady had promised to take her on a tour of the entire estate this morning, starting in her mother's rose garden.

Andie was going to pass on the tour. The first thing on her agenda was to deal with Nick Heagerty.

During a long, sleepless night she'd had plenty of time to consider his statement that he'd caused the death of a little girl. Not deliberately. She knew that instinctively from the way he treated Sarah. And there'd been no mention of it in the check she'd run on him. But being involved in something that resulted in a child's death left scars. She carried her own.

Even now, a year later, she could see quite clearly in her mind a figure at the end of the alley pointing a gun at her partner. She could still smell the rotting garbage from the Dumpster at her back, feel the cold steel of her gun pressing against her palm as she called out a warning. And she could still see the slender figure jerk back and then pitch to the ground as her bullet found its target.

She'd saved her partner's life, but Freddie Jones, age fourteen, was dead.

Andie unclenched her fingers one by one. She couldn't afford to empathize too strongly with the guilt Nick must be feeling. If she let her emotions creep in, she could jeopardize Sarah's future. She had to remain objective. Rose had decided that her daughter's future should be with her uncle Nick. Surely a mother had to know what was best for her child. And if Rose had kept some secrets? Well, she must have had her reasons.

So Andie had formulated a plan. Step one was to convince Nick Heagerty that he was the best choice as Sarah's guardian.

With a frown, she rested her chin on her knees. Somehow her plan had seemed better in the middle of the night than it did in the light of day. If Rose had still been alive, Andie would cheerfully have strangled her best friend.

"Do I look all right?"

Turning, Andie saw Sarah standing in the connecting doorway wearing one of her perfect outfits, pink linen shorts and a flowered blouse. It tugged at her heart to see how much the girl wanted to be loved and accepted.

"Pretty as a picture," Andie said with a smile. "But I think you need some play clothes. You know, something you could get dirty and not have to worry about." Rising, she pushed the curtain aside and ran her fingers along the drape. "If I were as clever as Maria Von Trapp in *The Sound of Music,* I'd be able to whip something up out of this. Even Scarlett O'Hara was good with drapes. As it is, I think you'll have to settle for jeans."

"Really?" Sarah walked toward her. "Grandmother says ladies never wear jeans."

"Your mom wore them all the time in college. And she was the best lady I knew." Andie tilted her head to one side. "If you were bigger, I'd let you borrow a pair of mine. As it is, I guess we'll have to bite the bullet and shop for some."

"Shop?"

"'Til we drop," Andie promised as she led the way to the door. When she opened it, Marguerite was standing there with her hand raised to knock. Andie noted that even at nine in the morning, the woman was dressed for success in a cream-colored linen suit with a pearl choker and matching earrings. "Mrs. Heagerty. Maybe you can help us. Where's the nearest mall?"

When Marguerite repeated the word—*mall*—as if it were a disease, Andie heard Sarah turn a giggle into a cough, and she found herself struggling to keep her smile merely polite. "It's a place where we can buy Sarah some clothes, eat some horribly nonnutritious fast food, and maybe take in a movie."

Marguerite's gaze shifted quickly from Andie to her great-niece. "Sarah's clothes look perfectly fine to me." Though her expression never wavered, she did give Andie's jeans a pointed glance before she continued. "I never purchase anything locally. Maybe Sandra Martin could be of some help. She's my personal assistant. Right now, she's on a business trip with my son Jeffrey, but they'll be back this afternoon. In the meantime, I'd like to have a word with you, Ms. Field. Privately."

"Perhaps while Sarah's having breakfast?" Andie suggested.

Less than ten minutes later Andie found herself following Marguerite across Persian carpets and gleaming oak floors to the huge fireplace at the far end of the formal parlor. A private talk with Marguerite Heagerty wasn't on Andie's agenda, but with Sarah happily eating French toast with Grady and the *Nomad* still missing from its mooring, she had time to kill. Besides, she was curious about Nick's aunt Maggie.

It didn't surprise her at all when the older woman chose to sit in the same wing-back chair she'd held court from the evening before. During the long cocktail hour before dinner, no one had sat in the matching wing-back on the opposite side of the fireplace. Not even Nick. Andie settled herself into it without waiting for an invitation.

Then she waited. And so did Marguerite, folding her ringed hands in her lap and making no move toward the silver coffeepot that sat on the glass tea cart between them. Nick might have the final say at the winery, but it was clear that his aunt reigned supreme over the household. Why? Andie couldn't help but wonder. Nothing that she'd learned about Nick Heagerty or experienced firsthand had led her to believe that he would allow himself to be intimidated by anyone.

She smiled at Marguerite. "I take mine black."

"I beg your pardon?"

"The coffee. You can hold the cream and sugar."

"Oh." The eyes behind the designer frames blinked. Then Marguerite raised one hand and lowered it. "My arthritis. It's always worse first thing in the morning. Would you mind?"

"No problem." Andie reached for the pot.

"I take cream and sugar."

As she filled the order, Andie glanced up at the portrait that hung over the mantel. The painting of a distinguished-looking, gray-haired man had drawn her gaze more than once the night before. The patriarch of the Heagerty clan, she'd assumed at first. Except he didn't look anything like Nick. Instead he bore a strong resemblance to Marguerite. After passing the cup to the older woman, Andie looked back at the portrait. "He's a very handsome man."

"My father." Marguerite didn't glance up at the likeness. "He brought the vines for the Manetti Vineyards from Italy, and he built this house. That was before the Heagertys bought him out."

"You must be very proud."

"I'm even prouder of my son."

Andie didn't doubt it as she studied the woman across from her. Marquerite's voice had been devoid of emotion when she'd spoken about her father, but not when she spoke about her son.

"Jeffrey is following in his grandfather's footsteps. He was trained in winemaking at Cornell, and now he'll take his rightful place...." Marguerite paused and took a careful drink of her coffee. "But I didn't ask you here to discuss my family. I'm concerned about Sarah. Rose made a mistake in sending her here."

"Rose didn't think so."

"Nick tells me you're more than an old friend of Rose's. You're a trained private investigator. You, of all people, should be able to see that he's a totally inappropriate choice as a guardian. I don't know what Rose could have been thinking. Was she... I mean, she must have been very ill near the end."

Andie set her cup down on the cart. "If you're suggesting that she was incompetent, you're mistaken. I was with her until the end. She was quite lucid."

"I see. Well, I can only assume that she wasn't fully informed about Nick's background."

Andie felt a quick spurt of anger and shoved it down. "I did the investigation myself, and I told her everything."

For the first time Andie saw Marguerite's lips curve. But the smile never reached her eyes. "But then, you were her best friend. How could you possibly have been objective? You must certainly have had some doubts about Nick's qualifications. And when Rose insisted on ignoring them, you finally went along because you trusted her judgment."

It took a great deal of effort for Andie to keep her hands from balling into fists, to keep from giving any sign of the anger she felt. If only Marguerite's description hadn't so accurately given voice to her own greatest fear.

Marguerite took another sip of coffee. "Perfectly understandable. Letting your feelings get in the way of your better judgment. Or perhaps you just didn't do a thorough enough job of investigating Nick."

The woman should have stopped while she was ahead, Andie thought grimly as she felt her rage turn cold and settle icy in her veins. "If you're trying to tell me about Nick's 'secret,' that he was responsible for the death of a child, I know all about it."

"What do you know about that?" Marguerite spoke the words in a whisper. "It was an accident." Her cup rattled in the saucer, and she gasped as coffee spilled onto her lap. "My skirt." She set her cup on the tea cart.

"Are you all right?" Andie asked.

"Fine." She dabbed at the stain with a napkin, then rose. "I'll have to change." She took three steps, and when she turned back, she had regained some of her control. "The accident's in the past...unfortunate and best forgotten. It's the future you ought to be worried about. Sarah's future. Nick's going to leave Heagerty Vineyards. He'll run away just as he did before."

Andie watched Marguerite hurry out of the room. Curiouser and curiouser. The thing that fascinated her most about detective work was how the answer to a question often gave birth to other questions. And at the top of her list right now was why the secret "accident" in Nick's past scared the wits out of his aunt Maggie. There wasn't a doubt in her mind that what she'd seen flicker in the eyes behind those designer glasses was fear.

But why was a question for another day. Andie followed Marguerite's route out of the room. Right now she had several questions to ask Nick Heagerty. A quick look in the kitchen brought her a scowl and several phrases in French from the chef.

She beamed her best smile at him. "Hi, I'm Andie Field, and I want to thank you for making French toast for Sarah this morning. It's her favorite breakfast, and it was just the thing to make her feel at home."

She had already turned to leave when the chef said, "If you're looking for her, Ma'm'selle, I believe she's in the rose garden. The quickest way is out the back door."

"Thanks," Andie said as she hurried across the room. With her hand on the knob, she turned back. "You know, she loves French fries, too."

The chef's brows snapped together and his breathing became rapid. "How dare you? Those soggy strips of potato! They are *not* French!" He lapsed into his native language then, but Andie managed to catch the word *sacrilege*.

When he finally sputtered to a halt, she shook her head sadly. "You're absolutely right. Poor Sarah. Those soggy

American things are all she's ever had. No one's ever exposed her to how the French can fry a potato."

As she pulled the door shut behind her, she could hear the chef muttering in French again, but the tone was calmer. Sarah's laugh had her turning in the direction of the gazebo. She saw the top of the little girl's head. Grady was visible from the waist up. What she couldn't see was whether or not the *Nomad* had returned, so she headed toward the wooden stairs. She was halfway there when Nick appeared at the top.

NICK FELT ANDIE'S EYES on him even before he shifted his gaze to meet hers. In jeans and a T-shirt, she looked closer to Sarah's age than his. And there was something in her stance, perhaps in the lift of her chin or in the way she held her hands clenched tightly at her sides, that told him she was mustering up all her strength to deal with her situation. Beneath the tough exterior she was determined to show him, something told him that she was just as uncertain about herself as Sarah was.

Courage layered over fear, strength over vulnerability. That's what he saw in Andie Field, and the contrasts appealed to him almost as much as her long legs. But he couldn't afford to be attracted to Andie Field, especially since his priority was getting rid of her.

Sailing always helped him think clearly, and sometime during the morning's battle with the wind and water, he'd completely eliminated Andie as a suspect in the attempt to kidnap his niece. For some reason Mendoza still hadn't gotten back to him, but Nick had no doubt she'd come up squeaky clean. As he drew closer to her, he suddenly realized just what she reminded him of as she stood there, her feet planted apart, ready to do battle. A guardian angel. She cared about Sarah. Too much perhaps. And she wasn't going to be happy with his decision. But she'd survive, and she'd make sure Sarah did, too.

"We have to talk," Andie said.

The sound of Sarah's laugh floated to them on the breeze.

"Where we won't be interrupted," Andie added.

With a brief nod Nick gestured toward a path that cut through the woods at a right angle to the house. They walked in silence, Nick leading the way down a steep slope eased by flagstone steps. Andie focused on the man in front of her. Even from the back, Nick Heagerty was intimidating. She let her gaze move from the broad shoulders to the narrow waist and hips. But it was more than physical strength. There was an inner kind of power that seemed to emanate from him. She'd felt it at the train station just before he'd taken her gun.

This was a man who would be very much at ease at the helm of the *Nomad*, a man who would give orders and expect them to be obeyed without question. Since she'd left the Boston police force, she hadn't taken orders from anyone. And she had a lot of questions for Nick Heagerty.

Suddenly they stepped out of the trees into a sun-splashed parking lot that bordered one of the low-slung buildings Grady had identified as the winery. As Andie walked across it and waited for Nick to use his key, she reviewed her strategy. She'd had all night to plan it, but she didn't kid herself that the man in front of her would be easy to convince.

One thing she was sure of: he cared for his niece. She could only pray that would be enough.

The first room that Nick ushered her into was huge. Sun poured through a picture window, glinting off the glass-fronted cabinets filled with wine bottles and brass plaques. One wall was covered with framed photographs. Andie recognized Rose in her wedding dress. The man standing next to her was a fairer, stockier version of Nick with hair the same shade as Sarah's. He appeared in other pictures, one in a football uniform, one in a cap and gown. After a second look, Andie spotted Marguerite, younger and softer-looking, standing next to a man who must be Nick's uncle.

"Ms. Field?"

Before she turned, Andie searched the wall one more time. But she hadn't been mistaken. There were no pictures of Nick.

The office Nick led her into was the size of a storage room, though it did have a window with a view of the back parking lot. She counted five pieces of furniture, a desk, three chairs and a long, low cabinet beneath the window. Each piece had the slick quality of something mass produced. She thought of her own office. It wasn't much larger, and though she prided herself on being neat and organized, her place was cluttered compared to Nick's. Five years he'd been here, and the room was still as stark and impersonal as if it were waiting for a new tenant.

Except for a painting of a storm-tossed sea. Curious, she moved closer to study it while Nick pressed the button on his message machine. She let her gaze follow the sweep of the brush strokes. The play of light across the grayish green of the waves and the sky suggested the same energy that she sensed in Nick. Energy that he kept tightly leashed. But like the lightning in the painting— Her train of thought was interrupted when Lieutenant Mendoza's voice filled the room. "I'll be there at nine-thirty."

Nick grinned as he sat on the edge of the desk. "He never wastes words." Then he glanced at his watch. "A half hour. That should give us time." He met Andie's eyes. "I've given a lot of thought to what's best for Sarah, and I want you to take her away as soon as possible."

It didn't surprise him when she set her jaw and moved toward him until only a chair separated them. He'd known she'd disagree with his decision. What was totally unexpected was the quick thrill of anticipation he felt at the thought of crossing swords with Andie Field.

"This isn't a shipment of wine we're talking about. This is your niece. I'm here to make sure you do what's best for her."

"Then take her away," Nick insisted. "She's just suffered a terrible loss. If she stays until she becomes attached to this place, to me, she'll have even more losses to deal with when she eventually leaves. And she *will* have to leave. Rose sent you here on a fool's errand."

"Perhaps." Her hands tightened on the back of the chair. "But I promised Rose and Sarah that we'd give this 'fool's errand' a two week trial. I intend to keep that promise."

Nick studied her for a moment. Her anger was a tangible thing in the room, and her face had the look of a warrior's. He'd thought of her as his niece's guardian angel, but now she reminded him more of an archangel, ready to wage war. A formidable opponent, Ms. Andie Field. Under other circumstances, he might have enjoyed rising to the challenge, but in this instance they both wanted what was best for a nine-year-old little girl. Taking another tack, he asked, "What if I told you that I'll be leaving Heagerty Vineyards right after our annual wine festival on Labor Day weekend?"

Andie's eyes widened. "You mean Marguerite's right. You're going to run away again?"

Nick's smile didn't reach his eyes. "Aunt Maggie has always had me figured out to a T. The runaway, the ne'er-do-well."

"Oh, cut it out!" Andie moved around the chair to stand right in front of him. "That facade of yours might fool some people. It might have fooled me if I didn't know you were a navy SEAL. That doesn't quite fit the image of the black sheep! And this place, what you've accomplished here—it isn't the work of a ne'er-do-well. Does your aunt know that you've made the family business solvent for the first time in ten years?"

Nick stared at her. The archangel look was back on her

face. Was she ready to do battle for *him?* The thought should have amused him, but he was oddly moved. "People believe what they want to believe. In your line of work, you must have noticed that."

"You could prove her wrong."

Nick couldn't prevent a grin. This time he was truly amused. "You don't know Aunt Maggie. It would be a waste of time. Besides—" he reached to tuck a loose strand of hair behind her ear "—I'd rather conserve my energy for more pleasurable activities."

Andie stayed right where she was, determined to ignore the heat that shot along her nerve endings where his finger had barely brushed her skin. "Inertia doesn't take any energy at all. All you have to do is stay here and keep what's yours. How can you possibly turn your back on all of this? It's your heritage."

"That's where you're wrong. I only inherited this place by default. Who could possibly have predicted that my father and brother would be killed in the same boating accident? Aunt Maggie will be very happy to quote you the odds against that happening. She was all set to use them in court when she contested the will. But I made her an offer she couldn't refuse. All she had to do was give me a free hand around here, and in return, I agreed to leave just as soon as her son Jeffrey was ready to run the place. I intend to keep my promise, too."

Andie frowned. "Why does her son have any more of a claim on the place than you do?"

Nick shrugged. "Aunt Maggie would argue that Jeff has Manetti blood, and part of the deal that her father made when he sold his vineyard to my grandfather was that she would marry Uncle Mike, and then the whole place would eventually belong to a Manetti again. John Manetti didn't believe that a woman could run a vineyard, and he thought he was doing the right thing to protect his family when he sold it. But nothing was ever written down. And when Uncle Mike died before he took over the vineyard, my grandfather decided to change his will and leave the place to his other son rather than his grandson. Not that Aunt Maggie gave up, mind you. She made sure that Jeff went to Cornell and studied winemaking so that he'd be ready to take over one day."

"And you're going to let him," Andie said.

"Seems like the fair thing to do. Besides, I'm not comfortable staying where I'm not wanted. Are you?"

One thing Andie had learned to spot early on during her years on the police force was a brick wall. She tried another approach. "Okay. So Marquerite was right that you're running away again. She also said that the death of the little girl was an accident. Was she right about that, too?"

"She talked about it?" Nick asked.

"Briefly. What kind of an accident?"

"Cars," Nick said before he thought to stop himself. He'd forgotten for a moment that she'd been a cop. And a good one, too—he'd have put odds on it. Even now, she was waiting, listening, giving him the opportunity to fill in the silence, just as if she had him in an interrogation room. Perhaps a few hard facts would convince her to take Sarah and run.

"I was in high school and it was the night of the state championship basketball game. We won, and afterward the team had a little celebration on the football field behind the school. I had a beer before I started home. A car ran a stoplight, and I swerved to avoid it. When I woke up in the hospital, they told me my car had turned over in a ditch." He ran a finger over the scar beneath his eye. "Aside from a bump on the head and a few stitches, I was fine. But I learned that a three-year-old girl in another car had been killed. Supposedly it happened because they'd had to swerve to avoid me."

Andie frowned. "It was an accident. You weren't to blame."

"I'd been drinking."

"One beer?"

"I shouldn't have been driving."

"But you weren't charged with anything," Andie observed pointedly.

"Before charges were even mentioned, some money exchanged hands. It wouldn't do at all for Heagerty Vineyards to get any bad publicity."

"Okay." Andie raised a hand as she began to pace again. "Your family bribed the cops. But you said 'a car ran a stoplight.' Not *your* car. So it wasn't your fault."

Not once during the hours that he'd lain in the hospital repeating his account of the accident over and over had anyone told him that he wasn't to blame. Everyone had believed that he was. "It turned out that I was the only one who recalled seeing the car that ran the stoplight." He shrugged. "Arguing the point wouldn't have brought back the little girl."

Andie didn't know exactly when she'd moved toward Nick. But she was suddenly aware of how close they were. He was still sitting on the edge of the desk, so they were eye to eye. This close his eyes seemed less gray, more green, like the color of the storm-tossed sea in the painting. And she could see, whether she wanted to or not, the flicker of desire in their depths. Andie thought of the lightning flashes in the painting, hot, exciting. And very dangerous. Her hands clenched into fists at her sides again, but it wasn't anger she was feeling this time.

She was *trouble*, Nick reminded himself. They were only inches apart and he felt the unexpected tug, the heat, and a churning that settled in his very center. Attraction he could handle. But it was more than that. And it was more than that he admired her for being such a good advocate for his niece. He knew that what he was feeling for Andie Field, what he'd been feeling almost from the first, was much more basic and elemental. Whatever it was that simmered between them would eventually erupt with all the power of a storm at sea.

She felt something, too. He could see it in her eyes and in the way her pulse was beating at her throat. For the first time he noticed the thin gold chain she wore. It dipped below the neckline of her T-shirt. Curious, he lifted it, a figure carved in antique gold. He couldn't quite make it out. Wings?

"An angel?" he asked.

"Yes." Andie was surprised at how weak her voice sounded. She could still feel the heat where his fingers had brushed along her skin. Worse still, she was almost sure she wanted to feel it again. "It's my lucky charm."

"Does it work?"

She wasn't aware of when he'd moved closer. But she could feel his breath on her lips. Warm. He hadn't released the chain. She should move away. Now. But running away from trouble never solved anything. It was always better to face it head-on. At least that's what she told herself. She couldn't possibly be staying put because she wanted the taste, the feel, of his lips on hers. Then she felt the chain go taut and the links press against the back of her neck.

"Don't..." She was sure she'd said the word. In her mind she had, but the only sound she heard was a strangled gasp of pleasure. He wasn't even kissing her. There was just the barest brush of his lips against hers. No one could possibly mistake it for a kiss. So why did she feel weak? Why had her legs suddenly turned to liquid? She didn't try to move for fear she couldn't.

Nick didn't move, either. He could have, he told himself. But if he did, he'd pull her closer, deepen the kiss, taste the passion. He could feel it simmering, struggling to break free. And that sound she'd made, that shuddering sigh of surrender.... If he touched her, he wasn't at all sure he could stop.

Even now as her breath trailed over his lips and whispered into his mouth, he could picture quite clearly what it would be like to make love with her, quickly, right here in his office. It would be wild.

Insane.

And the worst mistake he could make. What was he thinking of? Certainly not his niece.

Tucking the good luck angel back in her shirt, he stepped away. Her eyes were still open, but they'd clouded. The moment he saw them clear, he said, "Maybe you'd better change your mind about staying for two weeks. If not for Sarah's sake, then for your own. Or we'll have to deal with what's happening between us."

Andie stared at him. She'd no idea how long they'd stood there, not kissing exactly. Now she watched his lips curve into a smile, easy, relaxed. If she were only sure that her arms would move, she would have taken great pleasure in punching him. One good left jab to his chin.

But at least the anger sprinting through her helped. There were times she cursed her temper. This wasn't one of them. It brought strength back to her legs and clarity to her mind. "We'll deal with it then. Because I intend to keep Sarah here for two weeks." She placed her hands on her hips. "Promises aside, how could you think I would take her away until we find out who tried to snatch her yesterday?"

"She's got a point."

They jumped apart as they turned to face Lieutenant Mendoza. Neither of them had heard him open the door. Neither was sure how long he'd been standing there.

"I don't recommend moving her anywhere until we figure out who tried to kidnap her. I just talked to her on my way in. According to Grady, she seems to be settling in quite nicely. And she's safe here. Why mess with success?" Settling himself in the nearest chair, Mendoza pulled a well-used notebook out of his pocket and flipped it open. "You want the report on Ms. Field first? It's nothing she can't hear."

At Nick's nod, he continued. "Boston police says she was a good cop. Brave, too. Saved her partner's life in a nasty shoot-out in an alley a year ago. A young male drug dealer, fourteen, got killed in the crossfire. Justifiable homicide was the ruling. They were sorry to accept her resignation."

Though her hands had balled into fists, Andie said nothing. Ten years of her life summed up in a few short sentences. She concentrated on relaxing as she sat on the arm of a chair.

Mendoza flipped to another page. "No one at the state fairgrounds saw anyone tampering with the tire." He shot an approving glance at Andie. "Fingerprints on the gun and the envelope check out to a local thug, Rochester area, name of Gilbert Barstow. Five foot seven, one hundred thirty pounds, he served five years in Attica for armed robbery a few years back. His rap sheet's the length of my arm. Rochester police are cooperating. They're circulating pictures on the street in case someone's seen him recently."

"If this Gilbert Barstow lives nearby, that could mean the kidnapper's local, too," Nick said.

"Not necessarily. Old Gil could have made a lot of contacts at Attica. So far, I've got nothing back on the Boston relatives."

"Sarah's uncle Conrad has money problems." When she had the attention of the two men, Andie continued. "He's gone through the trust fund his father left him, paying off gambling debts. Control of Sarah's money would allow him to continue in his present life-style. Rose was worried that he'd file a custody suit. It may be one of the reasons she kept her plans for Sarah a secret until the will was read." Andie turned to Mendoza. "What have you found on Marguerite and Cousin Jeffrey?"

"What's their motive?" Nick asked. "They certainly don't need Sarah's money."

Andie shifted her gaze from the lieutenant to Nick. "They're both banking on you to stick to your agreement and leave Heagerty Vineyards. Then all of a sudden you get custody of your niece. They might be frightened you'll change your mind."

"She's got a point." Mendoza leaned back in his chair. "I checked on them anyway. At the time of the kidnapping, Jeffrey was delivering his speech at an international wine conference in the Napa Valley, assisted by Mrs. Heagerty's personal assistant, Sandra Martin. And your Aunt Marguerite was home all day."

"Either one of them could have hired this Gilbert Barstow," Andie said.

"You can eliminate Jeff," Nick said. "The truth is he's been trying to convince me to stay. Without his mother's knowledge, of course. I think it's just cold feet. He'll feel much more confident about running the place once I'm gone. As for Aunt Maggie, I can't see her hiring an ex-con from Attica."

Rising, Andie began to pace. "All right. Leave them out for the moment. Could the attempt to kidnap Sarah be connected in some way to the problems you've been having at the winery?"

Nick stared at her. "What do you know about that?"

"Grady mentioned that someone doctored a bottle of wine in your wine-tasting store."

Mendoza was smiling when he met Nick's gaze. "Boston was right. She's good. I know you wanted to keep a tight lid on it, but my advice is to tell her everything. She'll probably dig it up anyway."

Nick turned to Andie. "Two weeks ago someone slipped ipecac into a bottle of Chardonnay in the wine-tasting room. It's a drug used to elicit vomiting when poisoning is suspected. Two bikers got very sick. They thought it was food they'd eaten for lunch. But Sally Ann, who runs the wine store, was suspicious enough to have the bottle tested. Since then we've changed the locks on the storeroom, and Sally Ann personally supervises the transfer of cases."

"Grady said *problems*," Andie said. "Plural."

Mendoza stifled a chuckle, but Nick didn't smile. "Last June we were pressing strawberries for one of our fruit wines. We make them three or four times a year, just for fun, and we invite groups from schools and tourists to watch the winemaking process. It's a great public relations event. Right after the press, the juice goes into a tank where it's refrigerated to a uniform temperature before it's removed to one of the vats for fermentation. Someone broke the temperature gauge on the tank, and we might have lost the whole harvest if I hadn't noticed right away and borrowed a tank from one of our neighbors. If we'd lost the wine, it wouldn't have meant much financially. But if something like that happened during the grape harvest, I wouldn't have been able to borrow equipment. We could have lost up to a year's worth of Chardonnay."

"Do you think it was intended as a threat?" Andie asked.

"I considered that possibility, and I didn't take it lightly. That's when I called the lieutenant here, and he put me in touch with a friend of his, Jake Nolan, who's a security expert. He redesigned and updated our security system."

"I'd like to take a look at it if you don't mind."

Mendoza laughed out loud this time. "I'll be glad to take you on a grand tour before I leave. If Nick doesn't mind."

"Be my guest. But I'm not sure I see a clear connection between the attempt on Sarah and the problems here at the winery. Kidnapping is a far cry from vandalism."

"If someone has it in for you, wants to make you look bad, then kidnapping Sarah right from under your nose might have some appeal. Or it could be more general. Someone wants to hurt Heagerty Vineyards. Sarah *is* a Heagerty," Andie said.

There was silence as the two men weighed her suggestion.

"As a theory, it has possibilities we can't ignore." Rising, Mendoza stuffed his notebook into his pocket. "Whoever it is has an inside connection. They knew about the arrangements for Sarah's arrival. I'll recheck disgruntled employees and rival wineries."

"And in the meantime, what do we do?" Nick asked.

At the door, Mendoza turned back. "I'd tell you to sit tight and wait. But it'd be a waste of my breath. Besides, with a little girl in danger, I'll take all the help I can get. Which reminds me, I told her I'd say goodbye before I left." He glanced at his watch, then back at Andie. "I'll meet you in the security room for that tour in about five minutes, Ms. Field." He shifted his gaze to Nick. "You know, it might not be a bad idea if the two of you joined forces. That old cliché is usually true. 'Two heads are better than one.'"

For a moment after Mendoza shut the door to the office behind him, neither Andie nor Nick said a word. Then Nick broke the silence. "He's right."

"You think we ought to work together? As partners?"

*Partners.* The word hung between them in the room.

"Seems logical if we want quick results," Nick said. "For Sarah's sake, the sooner we find who's behind this, the better."

And the sooner you think you'll be rid of us, Andie thought. But it was a logical plan. And she might be able to make it work to her advantage, too. Working with Nick should give her plenty of opportunities to change his mind. "All right," she said as she walked toward him. "If we're going to work as partners, we ought to lay down some ground rules."

"If you need them," he agreed.

Not for one moment did she trust his meek, amiable tone. In spite of his grin he was taking her measure just as surely as she was taking his. "First, we'll be on equal footing. I don't take orders."

"I'll try not to give any," Nick said.

"And since our main concern is Sarah's safety, anything of a personal nature between us is out of the question."

"*Personal* meaning..."

Andie's eyes narrowed as she moved closer. "You know very well what I mean. Just before Lieutenant Mendoza interrupted us, you told me we'd have to deal with what was 'happening between us' if I stayed here for two weeks. You were trying to intimidate me." She poked a finger into his chest. "And don't deny it."

"I won't deny what I felt. What about you?"

She didn't deny it because she couldn't. When he looked at her the way he was looking at her now, she could almost feel some of her brain cells shut down. What she couldn't feel was any sensation in her legs below her knees.

"If what you'd like to negotiate is a hands-off policy," Nick continued, "I'll agree to it temporarily."

"Temporarily?"

Nick smiled as he tucked a strand of hair behind her ear. "Until we're satisfied Sarah is out of danger."

"Fine." She agreed only because she had to know if her legs would work. Andie drew in a breath, pivoted on her heel and began to walk. Five steps took her to the wall, and she felt a surge of relief as she turned back. "No secrets. Anything we find out we share."

"Agreed. Anything else?"

"Not that I can think of." While she was on a roll, she headed for the door.

Her hand was on the knob when Nick said, "Andie?"

"Hmm?"

"Haven't you forgotten something? We should shake hands on our agreement."

Turning, she gave him her best smile. "You're the one who's forgetful. You just agreed to a hands-off policy."

Nick threw back his head and laughed. The sound was rich and full. Infectious. Andie had to resist the urge to join him, but she was smiling as she stepped into the hall-way.

"Andie, one more thing."

She glanced back at him.

"For the security room, turn left. It's the third door on your right."

She managed not to slam the door behind her. She hadn't forgotten her appointment with Mendoza. She *hadn't*.

THE SECURITY ROOM was very impressive. Lieutenant Mendoza introduced her to the guard who was monitoring ten television screens displaying pictures of various areas of the estate.

"Your friend did a good job," Andie said.

"Jake left the force because he wanted to do something to help people *before* they became victims of crime. I still miss him," Mendoza said.

Before they left, he used a remote control device to change the angles on two of the cameras near the back of the house. Andie noticed that one of the screens then had a direct view of Sarah's bedroom window and the sloping roof beneath it.

Chalk one up for Mendoza, she thought. As she followed him to his car, he gave her a brief rundown on the light and sound alarms that completed the rest of the system.

The lieutenant was in a hurry. Understandable, considering that the sun was beating down unmercifully and his office was a forty-five minute drive. The air was stirred only when a car whipped past on the highway. Andie felt her T-shirt clinging, and she didn't envy Mendoza his suit. She waited until he opened the door to let the heat out before she asked, "Why did you drive all the way out here? You could have given Nick that report on the phone."

"I got his machine, and I don't trust cellulars."

"I think you wanted to check out the angles on those cameras personally," Andie said.

"So?"

"You're conscientious. That's important to me. Sarah's my responsibility."

He nodded at her. "Mine, too, now. No extra charge."

As he climbed behind the wheel, Andie said, "Before you go, I want to ask you a question about Nick."

He looked at her. "Professional or personal?"

"Personal. I've eliminated him as a suspect."

"Mind if I ask why?"

"Because if he'd wanted to kidnap Sarah, it would be a done deed."

Mendoza grinned at her. "Exactly."

"And if his motive were more convoluted, if he wanted to scare us off, I don't think he'd use Sarah that way."

"No. What's your question?"

"Do you remember the state basketball championship game twenty years ago?"

"I'll never forget it. My team played against Nick's, and we lost."

"What do you know about the car accident that happened later that night?"

Mendoza's eyes narrowed. "Never heard a word about it."

"A little girl was killed. Nick was blamed, but no charges were filed. Nick says money exchanged hands. His family wanted it hushed up. I'd like to get a look at any police reports that were filed."

Mendoza studied her for a moment. "You think there's a connection to the kidnapping attempt?"

"No. This is personal, but it has to do with Sarah. Will you help me?"

"I'll see what I can find out." He started the car, then winced at the blast of heat from the air-conditioning system.

"Nick won't be happy," Andie said.

"No." He looked at her. "A word of advice about Nick Heagerty. On the basketball court, I could never predict what he would do next. He doesn't always play by the rules."

Andie thought suddenly of those few moments when his lips had been touching hers. She was *not* going to call it a kiss. It had been more of a promise. A warning.

A truck raced by on the highway. The blast of heat hit her as she watched Mendoza pull out onto the road.

She thought of the ground rules she'd just established with Nick. She'd do well to remember that he might not play by them.

# 3

*PARTNERS.* Nick shook his head as he reached into the closet for a shirt. What in the world had he been thinking? With the exception of Grady, he'd never had a partner in his life. The whole idea of depending on someone, when the only person you could really depend on was yourself.... Stepping in front of the mirror, he met his own eyes squarely. He had no one to blame but himself. He'd been the one to suggest they take Mendoza's advice and work together. He grabbed his slacks off the bed and pulled them on. About the only use he had for his suite of rooms at Heagerty House was to change into his dinner clothes. His "Aunt Maggie duds" as Grady called them. He stepped into his shoes.

If a man had to have a partner, she might as well be bright. Andie's intelligence would be very useful. Not only would it come in handy while they were working together to catch whoever was threatening Sarah, but in the end, he would use it to convince her that Sarah would be better off with someone else.

Glancing back to the mirror, he shoved the knot in his tie into place. He was the last person on earth that Rose should have entrusted her little girl to. His gaze moved to the scar under his right eye. Even now he could picture in his mind that other little girl. He'd gone to the funeral mass and stood at the back of the church. He would have gone to the graveyard, too, but the family was going to bury her in Florida near their new home. Though the casket had been closed, there'd been a picture nestled on top in a spray of flowers.

He'd seen it quite clearly as they'd carried her out of the church. The photographer had caught her laughing, full of life, her arms reaching out to someone she loved.

Over time, the details of her face had blurred a little in his memory. But then each year her features would have been changed by the passage of time. Time that his one act of carelessness had robbed her of.

Nick pushed away his thoughts and, grabbing his jacket, strode toward the door. If Andie Field wanted to play by rules, he'd give her one. Logic over emotions. It was the one rule he believed in.

In the hallway, he stopped short. Below him on the landing, Sarah and Andie were kneeling with their faces pressed against the spokes of the banister, looking like two kids on Christmas Eve hoping to catch Santa in the act.

Only it wasn't a holiday scene they were viewing, he thought as he recognized his cousin Jeff's voice.

"I don't see why I have to sit on the board of the Rochester Philharmonic."

"It's a family tradition." Marguerite's voice held as much tension as her son's. "Your father, your grandfather—"

"Only on the Heagerty side," Jeff interrupted. "I'm John Manetti's grandson, too. And all I want to do is make good wine."

It was an old argument, Nick thought as he watched Andie rise in one fluid movement. Intellectual and sensitive, Jeff had inherited his grandfather's talent for winemaking but none of his mother's love for the social life that went with running Heagerty Vineyards. If Marguerite would only ease the pressure, her son might feel a lot more confident about running the winery on his own. But it was not going to be his problem much longer.

In fact, the problem that deserved one hundred percent of his attention was beginning her descent into the lion's den.

She was wearing loose-fitting, lemon-colored slacks and a

matching jacket. The slacks only emphasized the length of her legs, and the jacket did little to camouflage her femininity. Tonight she wore her hair held back from her face on one side with a gold clip. The other side swung forward as she leaned over to say something to Sarah. As they walked into the parlor, Nick watched the little girl slip her hand into Andie's.

He found himself envying the warmth and the comfort the little girl would find in Andie's touch. But when he took Andie's hand in his, it wouldn't be comfort alone that he'd be seeking. And the warmth would quickly change to heat. He could imagine just how those hands would feel. The palms wouldn't be too soft or too smooth. And when they moved over his skin, they'd make him burn...

With a frown, Nick headed for the stairs. Foremost in his mind should be how to get rid of Ms. Field. Not what it might be like to get her into his bed.

ANDIE SQUEEZED Sarah's hand as they stepped into the parlor. To boost the little girl's confidence—or perhaps her own. But no one even glanced up at them as they moved down the length of the room. Marguerite was totally engrossed in her lecture to the young man sitting in the adjacent wing-back chair.

The crown prince, Andie decided as she studied him. Jeffrey Heagerty was a younger, leaner version of his grandfather, but with none of the confidence that the man in the portrait over the mantel projected. Seated on the edge of the chair with his hands pressed flat on his knees, Marguerite's son looked ready to bolt.

On the other hand, the woman seated on a stool at Marguerite's feet seemed perfectly at ease. She was young and striking with olive-colored skin and dark hair. She was also totally detached from the drama taking place in front of her.

"Mother, I won't have time for the kind of social schedule you're proposing. Can't Nick take on some—"

"Not on your life!"

Turning, Andie found Nick at her side. Though he was smiling, his tone was cool as he continued. "Aunt Maggie, you're slipping. Our guests haven't been offered a drink yet."

"Nick, did you hear?" Jeff sprang out of his chair and hurried toward his cousin. "Three gold ribbons!"

"I didn't expect any less. We'll go for a sail after dinner and you can fill me in on the details. Right now I want you to meet your cousin Sarah and Rose's good friend, Andie Field."

"Ms. Field," Jeff nodded. Then leaning over, he took Sarah's hands in his. "Welcome, little cousin. I can't offer you wine, but there's some grape juice in the drink cart."

The moment Jeff led Sarah away, Nick pressed his hand against Andie's back and propelled her forward to the young woman who had now risen from her position at Marguerite's feet. "This is Sandra Martin, Aunt Maggie's personal assistant."

Andie found her hand gripped firmly and then released. "May I offer you a glass of Heagerty Chardonnay?"

Andie barely had time to nod before Marguerite signaled Nick to come closer. She spoke in a low voice. "While you're sailing, please remind Jeffrey of his obligations."

"And waste my breath? Jeff is quite aware of his obligations to the winery. He just sees them differently than you do. He loves the winemaking. Look at him with Sarah."

Andie turned with Marguerite to watch Jeff fill Sarah's glass with juice. "This comes from the same grape that we use to make our Chardonnay," he said.

"Except the kind the adults drink is put in a big vat and then in oak barrels," Sarah said.

"Someone's already taken you on a tour then?"

Sarah nodded. "Grady."

"Well, that's not the whole story of winemaking. C'mon, I'll show you." Taking Sarah's hand, Jeff led her to the wall of shelves that flanked one side of the fireplace. "Here it is. My grandad gave me this book when I was your age. It tells the story of the grape before it gets to the pressing machine."

Nick was chuckling as he patted his Aunt Marguerite on the shoulder. "Give it up, Aunt Maggie. He'll never be a civic bigwig. But he's a hell of a winemaker. It's in his blood."

Andie had taken a glass of Chardonnay from Sandra Martin and was on her way to join Jeff and Sarah when Nick's cellular phone rang. She glanced back at him then, wondering if it was Mendoza.

"You're sure?" Nick asked. "Have the guard take him to my office. Then you come up to the house."

With a glance at Jeff and Sarah, Nick leaned down to whisper something to his aunt before he took Andie's arm and led her out of the room.

"Was that Mendoza?" Andie asked as she hurried to keep up.

Nick closed the front door before he answered. "It was Grady. The security guard at the gate had a little run-in with Conrad Forrester. He's demanding to see his niece. Claims he wants to personally make sure she's all right after the attempt to kidnap her."

Andie stopped short. "We shouldn't leave her alone."

"Relax, I told Grady to go up to the house and keep an eye on her."

"How did Conrad find out about the kidnapping?" Andie asked.

"Good question. Mendoza was going to make sure that nothing was leaked to the press."

Andie's mind was racing as they walked down the drive. The sky was still gray in the lingering twilight, and overhead a gull let out a lonely cry as it banked and soared out over the lake. At the door to the winery, Andie stopped Nick with a hand on his arm. "Thanks for not inviting him up to the house."

He turned to her. "No problem, partner. We may not agree on everything, but until we're sure he's not the kidnapper, I don't want him anywhere near Sarah."

Gratitude was the most comfortable word to describe what she was feeling as she walked ahead of him into the building.

"Where's Sarah? I demand to see my niece!"

Nick saw little family resemblance between Rose or his niece and the ruddy-faced, decidedly robust man bearing down on them.

"Sarah is eating dinner," Andie replied in a calm voice.

"I'm surprised she can eat at all after what she's been through." Conrad aimed a narrow-eyed glare at Andie. "I'm holding you responsible for this. Sarah would still be safe in her grandmother's care if it weren't for your meddling."

"She's safe in my care now, Forrester." Nick stepped in front of Andie and was pleased when Conrad Forrester took a quick, involuntary step back. "How did you learn about the kidnapping attempt?"

Conrad's eyes narrowed. "That's none of your business."

"That's where you're wrong. As Sarah's legal guardian, everything that concerns her safety is my business."

"Mr. Heagerty?" The question came from the security guard who had followed Conrad down the hall.

"I can handle this," Nick said. He certainly wanted to. His hands were already clenched into fists, and Conrad Forrester's chin made a very tempting target. He just might have given in to temptation...if Andie hadn't stepped between them and opened the door to the reception room.

She glanced back over her shoulder. "Why don't we discuss this in private? Nick, I think Conrad might enjoy a glass of that very nice Chardonnay I was tasting. He's had a long drive."

Conrad moved first, tugging on his tightly knotted tie, as he followed Andie through the reception area and into Nick's office. But Nick had a tough time hiding a grin as he closed the door and pulled a chilled bottle of wine out of a small refrigerator in the cabinet behind his desk. Perhaps having Andie as a partner was going to have even more advantages than he'd thought. They couldn't have fallen more easily into the "good cop, bad cop" routine if they'd worked together for years. Sticking to his role, he handed the bottle to Andie to uncork and pour while he stood sentinel at the door and kept an unsmiling look on Sarah's other uncle.

Andie waited for Conrad to take a swallow of his wine and mop his brow before she repeated Nick's question. "How *did* you learn about the attempt to kidnap Sarah?"

Setting his glass down, he pointed an accusing finger at her. "Don't think that you can soften me up with wine. I intend to take my niece with me when I leave."

"You're upset, Conrad." Andie sat in a nearby chair and folded her hands in her lap. "That's perfectly understandable. We're all very concerned about Sarah's safety. That's why we want to know how you found out about the attempted kidnapping."

Conrad swallowed half his wine. "I have my sources."

Andie looked at Nick. "We'd better notify Mendoza."

Nick walked to his desk and began to punch numbers into the phone while Andie continued. "It was Lieutenant Mendoza's idea to keep it from the press. He'll be curious about your source."

Conrad wiped his brow again. "Look, there's no need to involve the police. I called here this morning because I was very concerned about Sarah, and Mrs. Heagerty told me everything, including the fact that Sarah's having nightmares. And it's all your fault! You're the one who encouraged my sister in her mad scheme to uproot that poor child and send her here."

Andie's voice was level when she spoke. "Why don't we leave Rose out of this discussion?"

"All right." Conrad shot a nervous glance at Nick. "All right. I don't want to speak ill of the dead." Reaching for his glass, he drained it in two gulps. When he continued, his voice was calmer and grew more confident as he spoke. "Rose's death has been hard on all of us. But it's time to think rationally now. I want to be reasonable." He looked at Nick. "You're a bachelor. I have a wife and two daughters. My youngest is only two years older than Sarah. She would fit right in with us and be a part of a real family." He leaned forward. "It's got to be obvious that I'm the best choice to raise Sarah."

For a moment there was silence in the room. Nick could feel Andie's eyes on him. "It wasn't obvious to Rose," he said.

Conrad stood. "You're going to be difficult then?"

"*Difficult* isn't the right word, Conrad. We're all trying to do what's best for Sarah." Andie rose to refill his glass. "Why don't we try to see this from Rose's point of view?"

Nick found himself relaxing as Andie began to enumerate the advantages that life at Heagerty Vineyards would have for Sarah. She was as patient and methodical as she'd been earlier when she'd questioned Mendoza about his investigation. Her style was very different from his own. With someone as pompous as Conrad Forrester, he would have favored intimidation. The man reminded him a little of a whale. But each time he erupted from his chair to spout off, Andie was able to calm him down. Seemingly without effort. The cool, aloof persona she'd slipped on for dealing with Rose's brother contrasted sharply with the ready-for-war archangel who had faced him just hours ago in this office.

Suddenly the whale shot up from his chair again. "If you

really care for her, you'll let her come home with me right now."

"The police have advised us that it's not safe to move Sarah at the present time," Andie said.

"I demand to speak with her!"

"No." Andie and Nick spoke the word in chorus.

"I'm her uncle. You can't stop me from seeing her."

When Conrad moved toward the door, Nick stepped into his path. "Just try it."

Eyes glittering with rage, Conrad whirled back to Andie. "This is outrageous! We'll see what a judge has to say about this."

"You're welcome to come back another time, Conrad, perhaps when you're more composed," Andie said. "I know that you wouldn't want to upset Sarah."

Nick stepped away from the door and opened it. A security guard moved into the room. "This gentleman will escort you to your car."

Blustering but defeated, Conrad followed the guard out of the room. The moment he was out of sight, Andie was up and pacing. "He'll file a custody suit just as soon as he gets back to Boston. Near the end, Rose was so worried about that." She turned to face Nick. "The last thing that Sarah needs right now is to be dragged into court."

"Relax." Nick filled two glasses with wine. "The court system operates very slowly. Sarah could be in college before she has to appear before a judge."

Andie took the glass of wine he handed her and suppressed the urge to toss it at him. How could he make light of the very real possibility that Conrad might actually get custody of Sarah? Patience, she reminded herself as she drew in a steadying breath. Time was going to work on her side. How could he be with Sarah every day and not grow to love her? Arguing with him at every turn was not going to get her to her goal any faster. But as she watched the amusement grow in his eyes, she would have bet that he knew exactly what she was thinking. And he was laughing at her to boot! "What's so funny?" she asked.

"Nothing," Nick assured her, raising one hand. "I just can't help admiring the way you do that."

She frowned at him. "What?"

"Pull your temper in. I know from experience that it's not the easiest trick to learn."

Andie's brows rose. "Oh?" Very slowly she raised her glass as though to toss its contents in his face. He didn't flinch. Finally, she shot him a smile and touched her glass to his. "May the family court system in Boston grind to a screeching halt."

Nick threw back his head and laughed. To her surprise, Andie found herself relaxing for the first time since their encounter with Conrad Forrester. She took a sip of her wine, and then another. "This is good."

"It's funny, but the wine sells better if it tastes good."

She was laughing as her eyes met his over the rim of her glass. And for a moment she could have sworn he was touching her. Even though he wasn't. He couldn't have without moving. But that didn't seem to change the fact that she could recall each sensation she'd experienced earlier when they'd been standing much closer. And she felt a tug, even stronger than the one she'd felt when he'd pulled on the gold chain.... She lifted her hand to touch it, to make sure it was still lying along her throat.

As Nick watched her finger the chain, he took a sip of his wine, hoping it would ease the sudden burning sensation he felt. He'd almost kissed her earlier today. He wanted to kiss her now. And the wine wasn't helping. Instead, the flavor made him wonder even more about her taste. Like the Chardonnay, she'd be tart, perhaps with a hint of lemon, but not nearly so cool. With a frown, Nick set his glass down and refilled it. His fingers were tight on the bottle. He willed them to relax and forced his thoughts back to Rose's brother. "Conrad wasn't impressed."

"Hmm?" Andie said.

Nick raised his glass. "With the wine."

"He's a simpleton!"

"Well, that's one thing we can agree on. It makes me wonder if he could have masterminded that kidnapping attempt."

"It didn't have to be *his* plan," Andie proposed. "Who knows what kind of characters he's come across with the kind of gambling debts he's run up?"

"Still, kidnapping is a drastic way to get money."

"But it might appeal to Conrad," Andie argued. "He's never had to work a day in his life. All his money's come the quick and easy way."

Nick's brows lifted. "So did Rose's."

"But she didn't seem to focus her life on it. And in the end..." Her shoulders rose and fell. "It didn't get her what she truly wanted."

Nick watched her move to the desk and reach for the wine bottle. When her hand trembled, just slightly, he closed his fingers around hers to steady her glass as she poured. He didn't miss the quick gleam of unshed tears in her eyes before she averted them. She was grieving. Not surprising. When would she have had the time when she was spending so much of it caring for Rose's daughter? Touching his glass against hers, he said, "To Rose. She was a beautiful woman."

Andie sipped her wine. Why did it always catch her unaware when he was kind? Setting her glass down, she said, "We'd better get back to Sarah."

"She's fine. Grady's with her. You worry too much about her. She's a very strong little girl."

Andie's chin lifted. "Strong or not, she needs a family. One that wants her."

"In my experience, families like that are hard to come by."

Nick met her eyes squarely. "Or were you one of the lucky ones?"

"No, not exactly." She picked up her glass and took another sip of her wine. "I never knew my father. And my mother...well, she was always looking for something. A new job, a new home, a new boyfriend. I lost count of how many times we packed up and moved into a new town in search of Utopia."

Nick studied her for a moment over the rim of his wineglass. "So you understand the lure of the nomad's life."

Andie stared at him for a moment. "No. I hated it. I wanted more than anything to stay in one place and have a real home."

"And that's what you want for Sarah."

"Yes."

"Sarah won't find that with me. The life of a nomad suits me just fine."

Andie opened her mouth, then shut it. She wasn't going to win this argument tonight. He looked so...so implacable. Time was her ally, she reminded herself. "We'd better get back to the house."

"I don't suppose I could interest you in playing hooky?"

"Hooky?" Andie asked.

"You know, like when you used to skip school, or church, or call in sick while you were on the force?" Nick studied her for a moment, then shook his head. "I forgot. You like to follow the rules. You never played hooky, did you?"

"Of course, I did."

"Come for a sail then."

She hesitated just a moment, but it was time enough for Nick to see the change in her eyes. Regret?

"I just don't feel right, leaving Sarah alone."

Nick's brows rose. "Grady's with her. She's perfectly safe."

"But it's only her second night here—"

"Then I'll give you a rain check, partner." With a grin, he put his arm around her and drew her with him out the door. "But you're going to regret it once we're trapped at that table listening to Aunt Maggie."

IT WAS VERY LATE when something woke her. Andie sat up and listened.

"Andie..." Sarah's voice was close and tight with fear.

Reaching out, Andie linked her fingers with the little girl's. "What is it, sweetie? A nightmare?"

"Someone's outside my window."

"Stay here." Andie leapt up and pushed Sarah onto the bed. Quickly, she grabbed shoes and jeans, pulling them on as she continued. "Dial four-two-zero on the phone and tell the security guard what you saw." She paused to run her hand over Sarah's hair. "Don't leave this room 'til I get back."

Sarah's window was open five inches, but all Andie could see outside was blackness. As she pushed up the sash, there was a break in the clouds and a slender figure in a dark, hooded sweatshirt was suddenly silhouetted by the pale moonlight. She saw him crouch at the edge of the sloping roof, cling for a moment and then jump.

Andie grabbed the flashlight from Sarah's nightstand and stuffed it into her waistband. Then she swung her legs over the window ledge and dropped onto her hands and knees. A cat burglar she wasn't. Besides, it was only stunt people in movies who actually ran over rooftops. The scrape of shingles against her hands gave her some comfort. Friction would slow her down if she started to slide down the steep slope. As her fingers closed over the gutter, she emptied her mind and focused on details. Bracing all her weight on her forearms, she lowered her legs over the edge. The moment gravity began its inexorable pull, she breathed a quick prayer, relaxed her muscles, and dropped.

The swift, sudden impact jarred her to the core. But even as the shock waves rippled along her nerve endings, Andie concentrated on listening. An owl hooted once, then again from a nearby tree. Gravel crunched, then scattered. The sound carried clear in the warm night air. She sprinted toward the driveway. By the time she reached it, her lungs were already on fire. Just before clouds once more blanketed the moon, she saw a shadow separate itself from the trees that lined the drive.

Pulling her flashlight out, Andie raced into the woods. The shortcut Nick had shown her this morning would save time. If she didn't fall. Aiming the light low, she tore down the flagstone steps. Over her own ragged breathing she heard shouts. An alarm pierced the stillness of the night with its wail. She stumbled once, using a tree to stop her fall, then scrambled away with bark still stinging her palms.

When she broke through the trees into the parking lot, the floodlights blinded her for an instant. Then she saw a slender figure streaking around the loading dock to the back of the building. She raced after it. Behind her she heard cries, a stampede of feet racing up the driveway.

*Wrong way!* She hadn't the breath to shout it. She could only pray as she kept chanting the words in her head that the thought would carry. At the back of the winery, a fence ran close to the building, and ahead of her, perhaps fifty yards, her hooded prey suddenly pitched forward to the ground. Andie increased her pace. She was ten feet away when he sprang to his feet on the other side of the fence and sprinted into the trees.

The moment she reached the spot where he'd fallen, she dropped to her knees, rolled onto her back, and wiggled herself beneath the chain-link fence. Scrambling to her feet, she swept the ground with her flashlight and found the edge of a path. An old one, overgrown with weeds, but she could feel beneath her feet the depressions once made by tires.

Her progress was slowed now by the tall grass, and as her breathing steadied, Andie listened for other sounds. The alarms were fainter now, muffled by the trees. And she could hear the breeze moving pine needles and scattering dry leaves. When the path suddenly forked, she stopped. She couldn't hear anyone running. She aimed her light over both paths, then veered to the right where the branch of a small sapling had snapped.

She'd covered less than ten yards when she became aware that the darkness seemed denser, the air cooler. Pausing for a moment, she moved the flashlight in a half circle. The trees seemed to be crowding closer on each side. What if she'd chosen the wrong path? In front of her, she saw weeds pushed over, to her left, the white wood of a freshly broken branch. But it was still quiet. Too quiet. Was someone waiting up ahead? Turning her light off, she hurried forward.

The path ended abruptly in a small clearing. Overhead, only a wisp of cloud covered the moon, and the pale light poured down. The shape of a cabin was unmistakable. It looked deserted. Eerie. She crept toward it slowly. In spite of the care she took, a board on the first step groaned, announcing her arrival.

She jumped to the side of the door, then reached to twist the knob. One hard push sent it squealing on its hinges. The sound of wood slamming against wood assured her that no one was waiting behind it. Still, she counted off ten seconds before she entered and swept her light around. It was a one-room log cabin with two windows, a wood-burning stove tucked into a corner, two stools and an old table, paper bags on the floor. Empty.

Andie was halfway across the room before she realized she was gripping the flashlight with two hands as if it were her gun. She willed herself to relax and managed to draw in one steadying breath before she heard the sound of twigs snapping. Turning off her light, she slipped quickly behind the open door.

Holding her breath, she waited. Moonlight fell in pale, patchy rectangles across the floor. All she could hear was a breeze rustling pine needles, the hoot of an owl…and the creak of that first step. Tightening her grip on her flashlight, she waited, listening.

It wasn't a sound this time. Just a sudden lessening of light as a shadowy figure filled the doorway. She shoved the door hard and felt it connect with something solid. Then it sprang back at her, slamming her into the wall.

The impact was still singing through her and she was blinking away stars when both her wrists were gripped and yanked up behind her back. Even as her flashlight fell with a clatter, she kicked her assailant in the shin. Then she stomped on his foot, hard. The second she heard the harsh groan, she threw all her weight forward to topple them both to the floor. The hold on her wrists tightened. She was about to use her knee when her opponent suddenly scissored his legs, trapping hers, and she found herself flat on her back beneath a crushing weight.

"Andie?" Her hands were immediately released. "Are you all right? What the hell's going on?"

She recognized Nick's voice even before she made out his features in the patchy moonlight.

"Someone tried to get in Sarah's window," she said.

"Sarah told the guard that much when she called the security room." He didn't tell her that he'd arrived in time to see her race across the roof. Nor did he tell her the fear that had gripped him when he'd seen her lever herself off the edge and drop to the ground. "Who was it?"

"He was slender, five foot seven, wearing a hooded sweatshirt."

"Your friend, the skinny chauffeur?"

"I'd be willing to bet on it. How did you know to come here?"

"One of the cameras in the security room caught your wild dash across the parking lot. Burrowing under the fence delayed me a bit."

"It didn't slow Skinny down." Andie realized suddenly that she was whispering. Not intentionally, but because Nick's weight was crushing her. She put some effort into finding her voice. "Would you get—"

"Shh!" Nick clamped a hand over her mouth. When she started to wiggle, he used his weight to still her. "Listen."

His voice was only a breath in her ear. She tried to ignore the ripple of awareness it sent through her. Just as she tried to ignore the solid wall of his chest, the hard length of his thigh. But even as she put all her effort into listening, she was aware of the tremor in her own body. Or was it his? Then she heard it. The muffled sound of an engine. A boat?

She pulled his hand from her mouth. "He's getting away!"

"Relax." Levering his weight up a little, Nick tucked a strand of hair behind her ear. "He'll be halfway across the lake by the time we get to the water. The cliff isn't so steep here, but it's still a tricky descent."

"You're pretty familiar with this place."

"It was part of the Manetti estate. But John didn't sell it to my grandfather. He used it for fishing. Sometimes he'd ask me to go with him."

"Fascinating." She pressed both her hands firmly against his shoulders. "But could we postpone any stories of your childhood until you get off of me?"

Nick chuckled. But he didn't move.

Andie's eyes narrowed. "You're not going to be laughing for long if you don't move."

"In a minute." He rubbed the curl he was holding between his thumb and his finger. It was impossibly soft. "I do my best thinking in a horizontal position."

"You can lie on the floor of this cabin all night and ponder the mysteries of the universe. Just let me up first."

He hadn't lied to her. He did do his best thinking in a horizontal position. The problem was what he was thinking about. No, not thinking so much as wondering. The way her body held firm and unyielding beneath his had him imagining what it would feel like softened in surrender. The paleness of her skin in the moonlight made him think of porcelain, delicate and cool to the touch. How long would it take him to make it heat?

And the way her lips parted suddenly with an annoyed huff of breath had him anticipating how those lips would feel pressed against his. Hot? Moist? As hungry as his own? He'd thought about kissing her often enough during the past two days. And nights. Perhaps it was time to satisfy his curiosity. One thing experience had taught him—reality rarely lived up to expectations. If he kissed her, perhaps he might rid himself of the desire he felt for her, once and for all.

His mouth was only a breath away from hers when she moved her hands to his ribs and gave him three, quick pinches.

His laugh erupted easy and rich. And in defense, as well as surrender, he levered himself up and settled her beside him on the floor. "I thought you always played by the rules, Field."

"I've been known to bend them."

"I'll keep that in mind."

She was on her knees when he grabbed her wrist.

"So help me, Heagerty—" She paused to follow the direction of his finger. The paper bags. She'd seen them earlier in that quick sweep she'd made with her flashlight. When Nick lifted one, she saw the fast-food logo on the side. Then he turned it over and wrappers dropped to the floor.

"Our skinny friend likes cheeseburgers and French fries." She lifted a cigarette butt. "It's still warm." Her eyes met

Nick's. "Maybe his chubby girlfriend was waiting here for him."

Nick spread out a hankie. "Matches, too. Mendoza can check for prints." For a few minutes they worked in silence, transferring the small pile of debris to the square of white cloth. Nick tied the edges together carefully while Andie turned on her flashlight and swept the room one more time.

"Who besides you knows about this place?" Andie asked.

"Aunt Maggie. It would belong to her now."

"And Jeff?"

"I can't believe that either of them had anything to do with trying to kidnap Sarah."

It was on the tip of her tongue to ask him why he continued to defend two people who were trying to drive him away from his home, but there was something in his voice, in his eyes, that had her reaching for his hand instead. "I had an old sergeant who used to say that objectivity is the key to success in an investigation."

Understanding. He'd seen it before in her eyes when he'd told her about the accident. Once again, it sent a flood of conflicting emotions running through him. Hope? Fear? He'd taught himself not to want understanding, not to need it. But that didn't keep him from linking his fingers with Andie's. Nor did it keep him from realizing that he was losing his objectivity where Andie Field was concerned. With some effort he dragged his gaze away from her and looked around the room. "All right. Objectively speaking, Aunt Maggie wouldn't be caught dead in a place like this. And Jeff probably doesn't even know it exists. He was only two or three when his grandfather died."

"I suppose Conrad could have discovered this place before he showed up at the gate," Andie said. "But it's hard to picture him walking through the woods, or even climbing up from the beach. If we go with the theory that our friends Skinny and Chubby were hired to kidnap Sarah, they could have stumbled across this place while they were getting the lay of the land, so to speak. And that brings us back to square one. Unless Mendoza gets some incriminating prints from the trash we've collected, everyone is still on the list."

"You're good, do you know that?" Nick asked.

"I'm just thinking like a cop." Andie tried to tell herself his compliment meant nothing to her, despite the warm feeling of pleasure that spread through her.

"You always start to frown when you're thinking professionally." He traced a finger along a tiny line on her forehead.

It wasn't just pleasure she was feeling this time. She wasn't sure she could find a word to adequately describe the sensation that his touch had sent singing along her nerve endings. There was a voice at the back of her mind telling her to get up, walk away. It was dangerous to stay. But he was still holding her hand, and she was almost sure he wouldn't give it up easily. Besides, hadn't he warned her they'd have to learn to deal with what was happening between them? As a cop she'd discovered early on that it was always better to know exactly what you were up against. Then you could plan a defense.

When he moved closer, she didn't back away, but met his mouth with her own. As his lips moved over hers, teasing, testing, her hand tightened in his. They touched nowhere else, but desire spiraled quickly. Each sensation was something to be savored. His mouth was firm. She'd expected that. But it was giving, too, and she was shocked at how much she wanted to take.

Kissing him was as breathtaking as her first chase in a police car. She recalled the thrill, the exhilaration as she'd closed the distance. There was no stopping, no turning back. She heard a quick gasp of pleasure. Was it her own? Then she moved closer to take more of what she wanted.

There was so much heat. She could almost feel the flames

licking at her skin, burning along her nerve endings. For one reckless moment she understood why moths were compelled to fly into the fire.

The cabin was cold and dark. The pale moonlight, the breeze that rattled the windowpanes only added to the chill. But all Nick knew was that her lips were hot and moist and every bit as hungry as he'd imagined. Her flavor had the sharpness he'd anticipated, dreamed about. Beneath it was a sweetness that he'd known would be there. What he hadn't counted on was that he was already craving more. With her taste filling him, her scent wrapping around him, it was easy to forget that the last thing he needed in his life right now was a woman, especially one with an agenda so opposed to his own.

When he ran his hands up her arms to her shoulders, he should have pushed her away. But he didn't. It was only a kiss. It shouldn't be clouding his brain. It shouldn't be draining away his will, his strength. Control was something he never lost. But he knew if he touched her now, the way he wanted to, there would be no turning back.

Nick pulled slowly away. He wasn't aware of when his hands had moved to frame her face, but he couldn't seem to pull them away. He wasn't steady. That was something he would think about later. The thought slipped into his mind that he would never be able to forget the softness of her skin, the angle of her cheekbones, the silky texture of her hair. And her eyes. In the pale moonlight, he saw himself in them. Trapped.

He pulled back further to free his mind of the image.

Andie stared at him, groping for words. In a minute they would come. She was sure of it. Perhaps when he stopped touching her.

It had only been a kiss. But it hadn't been like any other kiss she'd shared before. Not one of them had changed her life.

Ridiculous. There. *Ridiculous* was a good word. She tried for another. *Absurd.* In a moment she'd have more. Enough to explain what she'd just felt. What she was still feeling.

What she needed was distance. Now. Very cautiously she pulled away. His hands brushed her shoulders as he dropped them to his sides.

"I wonder what it will be like the next time," Nick said.

Andie didn't tell him there wouldn't be a next time. Nor did she bother trying to convince herself of that. Lies just wasted time. All she could do was make sure it was a long time before Nick Heagerty kissed her again. Certainly not until Sarah was safe. *Sarah!* It shocked her to realize that she hadn't thought of the little girl once since she had tumbled with Nick to the floor of the cabin.

"We have to get back," she said.

Nick nodded, but he was careful not to offer her a hand when she stood. She was at the door by the time he'd gathered the bundled hankie and the fast-food bag. "Andie."

She turned back. "I'm not going to lie. I enjoyed that."

"Me, too."

He was smiling now, she noted, but he wasn't entirely relaxed. "And I've no doubt the next time would be..." She paused, searching for the right word.

"A very pleasurable and satisfying diversion."

"That's the whole point. Until we find out who's trying to kidnap Sarah, we don't have time for diversions, and I think we ought to stick to our rules."

"Agreed." Rising, he walked toward her, then dragged a finger along her jaw until it rested under her chin. "But once Sarah is safe, we'll find the time. That's a promise."

She didn't back away. Instead, brows raised, she looked around the room. "And hopefully a better place?"

He let out a chuckle before he threw a friendly arm around her shoulder and led the way out of the cabin.

# 4

IT WAS WELL after midnight when Nick turned the knob on Sarah's door and found it locked. Hurrying down the hall, he tried Andie's. It was locked, too.

Chalk one up for Andie Field, he thought. In her shoes, he wouldn't have trusted anyone in Heagerty House, including himself. He'd spent the past two hours working with Mendoza and Jake Nolan who'd designed the security system, to make sure that it couldn't be penetrated again. By morning, the staffing personnel would be doubled. Instead of easing his tension, the strategy session had only increased his frustration and tightened the knot of fear in his stomach. He'd moved his gear off the boat and into his suite of rooms, but he wasn't going to sleep until he saw with his own eyes that Sarah was safe.

Nick fished a thin wire out of his back pocket and slipped it into the lock. Thirty seconds later he was inside. Moonlight poured through the windows, splashing in wide ribbons across Andie's room. It was empty. Fear sprinted through him as he strode through the connecting bath to Sarah's room.

Andie was curled up on the bed next to his niece. For a moment Nick simply looked at them. They slept on their sides, facing each other. Their hands were joined as if they had reached out sometime during the night and found what they were looking for. There was trust there, he thought, and a loyalty that deserved that trust.

Something moved through him then. Envy? Surely not.

He'd long ago schooled himself to live without either loyalty or trust. Both offered paths to betrayal.

Deliberately, he fastened his gaze on Andie. Asleep, she looked as defenseless as Sarah. And just as vulnerable. Awake, she'd fight hard to conceal it. Nick moved closer. There was something about her...something that drew him and tempted him to rethink decisions he'd made long ago. What was it?

She certainly wasn't a beauty. Her nose was a bit too short, and her chin jutted out just a little too far, especially when she was springing to someone's defense. Part of what appealed to him so strongly was that ready-to-do-battle look in her eyes. It promised passion, hot and ripe. And that drew him, too. He moved his gaze down the length of her strong, slender body. He could recall exactly what it had felt like molded to his on the floor of the cabin. And those legs. The jeans she wore emphasized their length. A man only had to look at them to wonder how they might feel wrapped around him.

Very slowly, Nick let his gaze return to Andie's face. He wanted her. There was no denying it. But it wasn't merely desire that pulled at him. Desire was simple, and its fulfillment was easy. But nothing about a relationship with Andie Field would be either simple or easy. Already she was stirring up emotions in him, needs that he thought he'd buried long ago. No, what he felt for her was more than physical.

She stirred slightly, tightening her hold on Sarah's hand. Nick watched quietly until her grip relaxed and she settled once again. There wasn't anything she wouldn't do to protect Sarah and keep her promise to Rose. He remembered the way she'd dropped off the roof. Loyalty that fierce.... No, it was dangerous to even think about wanting it. Needing it. Nick began to back out of the room. The smart thing to do was to keep his distance from Andie Field. For Sarah's sake as well as his own. He could agree with Andie one hundred percent on that. They couldn't afford any diversion that might distract them from any threat to the little girl's safety. Plus any involvement between Andie and himself was bound to affect Sarah in other ways. The last thing he wanted to do was to hurt her more than he had to.

Andie stirred again. This time, she sat up in a quick, fluid movement. He said nothing, but he knew the instant she recognized him by the way the tension left her shoulders. Signaling her to follow, he turned and moved into her bedroom.

As he flipped the light switch and waited for her to join him, a book on her nightstand caught his eye. It was open and lying facedown. Curious, he picked it up for a closer look. Jane Austen? Smiling, he shook his head. A woman who toted a gun as comfortably as most women carried their makeup, and she read Jane Austen. Fascinating. He set the book down and turned to face her.

"What have you found out?" Her voice was hushed.

"Nothing." Admitting it brought all his frustration flooding back.

"Nothing?" Barefoot, hands on hips, she began to pace. "It's been over two hours. What have you and Grady and the good lieutenant been doing all this time?"

"Mendoza's got everything we took from the cabin. He'll deliver it personally to the labs and push for results. We've doubled the number of people on security, guards will be patrolling the grounds, and the cabin's under twenty-four-hour surveillance. Jake Nolan's *very* upset that someone breached his security system."

"*He's* very upset!" She moved to the window. "Someone was right out there on that roof. Ever since I got back here, I keep thinking, *what if...*"

She didn't complete the thought. Neither did he, even though the same words had been playing a drumbeat in his head all during his two hour meeting. He joined her at the window. "We'd have stopped them."

She turned to him then, placing a hand on his arm. "I'm sorry. I know you're doing everything you can. It's just...."

He covered her hand with his. "Hey, we're partners. We're going to keep her safe. If they get through the security system, they'll still have us to deal with." Simply saying the words out loud helped him to believe them. "How is Sarah?" he asked.

"Tough." Her lips curved slightly as she said the word. "Kids are. They can handle more than you think."

"She already has."

For a moment neither of them spoke. Though he couldn't have said why, talking to her, touching her, had accomplished what none of the carefully laid-out security precautions had. Suddenly his tension was flowing out as easily as water from a dam. And replacing it, radiating from where their hands were still joined on his arm, was a warmth, sweet and strong. He didn't understand it, wasn't even sure that he wanted to. What he wanted, more than anything else, was to take her in his arms and simply hold her.

"Andie..." he whispered.

A sound from the hall interrupted him.

Andie was the first to react, signaling Nick to the door. She moved to one side, he to the other. With her eyes on him, she reached for the doorknob, and at his nod, yanked it open. He moved like lightning then, and there was a startled gasp as he jerked the shadowy figure in the hall into the room.

"Aunt Maggie, what brings you here?" Nick asked.

"I..." Clasping her hands together, Marguerite glanced from Nick to Andie. "I couldn't sleep..." Flustered, she took a step back. "I didn't mean to—"

"Relax," Nick cut in with a grin. "You haven't interrupted a romantic tryst. I came to check on Sarah."

Marguerite nodded stiffly. "I was worried about her, too."

"There's no need," Nick said. "I've doubled the security staff. There'll be guards patrolling the grounds twenty-four hours a day. And until we find out who's trying to kidnap her, I'll be sleeping here in my suite instead of on the boat."

Marguerite's chin lifted. "Surely you don't suspect anyone in this house of being involved."

"What I think is that I'm going to make sure any future attempts fail."

Marguerite met his gaze steadily for a moment. "I want her kept safe." Then she walked out of the room.

Nick waited until she'd disappeared into the shadows before he closed the door and turned to Andie. "What do you think?"

"She seemed genuinely concerned."

"But..." Nick prompted.

"I can't help but wonder if she has another reason for checking to see how 'safe' Sarah is." Her eyes narrowed suddenly. "How did you get in? I locked both doors."

With a frown, Nick glanced at the door. "It took me less than thirty seconds with a wire. I'll have Grady put dead bolts on first thing in the morning."

Andie shook her head. "No. The last thing Sarah needs is to feel she's being locked up like a prisoner. You can't do that to a child. That's exactly what her life would have been like if she'd had to stay in that mausoleum of her grandmother's. Besides," she continued as she began to pace, "if someone in this house *is* responsible for what's going on, the last thing they want is to confirm our suspicion of that. That's why Skinny had to use the roof instead of the front door. Next time..." Her voice trailed off as she turned back to Nick.

"Next time we'll catch him," he finished.

As long as she was looking at him, she could almost believe it. She had to believe it. For the first time she noticed he was tired. Exhaustion shadowed his eyes. She moved toward him. "You'd better get some sleep. Sarah and I will be fine."

"I could stay here," he said.

She stopped short. "I thought we settled that."

The grin he shot her was both wicked and appealing. "Well, you did mention something about a better place." Then before she could reply, he raised his hands, palms out. "But I swear the offer was strictly legit. I was thinking sentinel duty, not diversions. However, I could be persuaded..."

"In your dreams, Heagerty," she said as she moved past him to open the door.

Chuckling softly, he ran one finger along the line of her jaw before he left. "You've got that right, Field."

RESTLESS, Andie paced the length of her room, rereading the note Nick had sent up with a breakfast tray. Sometime during the night there'd been a breech of security at the state fairground's exposition building, and he and Grady had left at dawn to check on the wine they'd stored there. The rest of the very brief message cautioned her to sit tight with Sarah.

Crumpling the note, Andie jammed it into her pocket. Sit tight? While someone was still out there hatching another plot to kidnap Sarah? Drawing a deep breath, she stopped in front of the window seat and watched a small, motorized fishing boat make its way down the center of the lake. The sun shot sparks of light off the ripples left in its wake. She had to keep calm. Years of experience had taught her that good detective work required patience and a clear head. Along with careful preparation. Moving to her nightstand, she fished a small key from beneath it and unlocked the drawer. With Nick and Grady gone she really had no choice but to keep her gun within reach. Especially after what had happened last night. Pulling out the small leather pouch, she fastened it around her waist.

She could hardly fault Nick and Grady for checking out problems at the fairgrounds. There was an outside chance that it was connected to the attempts to snatch Sarah. The problem was that she would have given almost anything to be with them. Sitting tight just wasn't her style.

"Do we have to stay inside all day?"

She turned to watch Sarah pause in the doorway of the bathroom connecting their two rooms. The little girl was dressed in navy blue shorts and a matching vest trimmed with gold braid.

*All dressed up with nowhere to go* was the thought that drifted through Andie's mind as she beckoned her into the room. "Not if I can help it," she said.

Sarah glanced at Andie's jeans. "Could we go shopping?"

Andie thought fast. Not a mall. The crowds would be too risky. There had to be a village close by.... "We need a car."

"Oh."

Smiling, Andie ran a finger down the faint line that had formed on Sarah's forehead. "Isn't it lucky that I'm a detective? And the person I suspect most of being in charge of the cars is your great-aunt Maggie. C'mon."

But Marguerite was nowhere to be found. And all they discovered in the garage were oil stains on the floor.

"Looks like we're temporarily without wheels," Andie said.

"It's that symphony thing they were talking about last night. Jeff didn't want to go, but I guess he did." Sarah fell into step beside Andie as they walked along the drive toward the water. "Are we the only ones here now?"

"Of course not. You can bet your aunt Maggie's chef is in the kitchen. I think he sleeps there. There are people at the winery, too, and your uncle has hired more guards." She scanned the grounds quickly, hoping to see one. But she didn't.

For the first time she noticed how quiet it was. The air was still, the silence unbroken except for the lonely call of a gull as it banked overhead then flew out over the water. The low drone of a motor had her glancing at the lake. The fishing boat she'd seen earlier was making its way back, this time following the line of the shore.

In spite of what she'd just told Sarah, it felt as if they were alone on the estate. If something happened, if someone came up the wooden stairs from the beach.... Unbidden, the question slipped into her mind. *If she cried out for help, who would hear?*

The sudden crunch and scatter of gravel from behind had her whirling and reaching for her gun. She had the pouch unzipped before the message got to her brain that the tall, slender man in the straw hat must be a gardener. The wheelbarrow was a big clue, she thought in disgust as she rezipped her pouch. She watched as the man parked his wheelbarrow and began to trim a nearby hedge.

It was only as her own tension drained that she realized Sarah was pressed close against her side. She slipped her arm around the little girl and gave her a quick hug.

"That scared me," Sarah said.

"Me, too."

"Really?"

"Yep." Andie extended her free hand and shook it. "My fingers are still all tingly."

"Mommy told me over and over that I shouldn't be scared."

"Of course she did, sweetie." Andie laid her hand on Sarah's cheek. "She didn't want you to be frightened about your future. She wanted you to know that even though she had to leave, someone would be here to look out for you. And to love you. But sometimes it's perfectly all right to be scared." She paused to glance over at the straw-hatted gardener. "And you shouldn't feel ashamed. Even if it turns out to be someone who just wants to trim a hedge. That way you're careful."

"Do you think Uncle Nick's ever scared?" Sarah asked.

"Sure. But right now he's doing something about it.

There's a chance that the problems at the fairgrounds might have some connection to what's been happening to you." Andie quickly explained about the incidents of vandalism at the winery. "So that's why he's checking it out. And that's what we should be doing, too. We should be trying to figure out what's going on here instead of jumping out of our skins like ninnies just because a wheelbarrow sneaks up on us."

Taking Sarah's hand in hers, she led the way down the drive. "How would you like to help me do a little investigating?"

"Really?" Sarah asked.

"Really. I work better with a partner. Let's go talk to the lady who runs the wine store."

"Sally Ann's cool," Sarah said.

"Oh?"

Sarah took a little skip. "I met her when Grady took me on the tour. You'll like her."

Andie squeezed Sarah's hand. "I knew I picked a good partner."

*Cool* was one way to describe Sally Ann Tanner, Andie supposed. Though she was tall, six feet at least, it wasn't her height that made the biggest impression. Nor was it the gypsy-style clothes she wore. It was Sally Ann's hair that fascinated Andie. Sarah, too, she surmised from the way the little girl was gazing at it. It was bright red, cropped short, then gelled into sharp-looking spikes that stuck out like a porcupine's quills.

But when the young woman beamed a warm smile at Sarah and poured her a glass of grape juice, Andie decided Sarah was right. She did indeed like Sally Ann very much.

"I blended it myself," Sally Ann explained as she filled a second glass for Andie. "I wanted to open the store in the morning, and since very few people drink wine before noon, I figured I had to give them another reason for stopping by."

Andie looked around the room. At least half the space was

taken up with glass cases displaying finely crafted jewelry and pottery. Two women were looking through a pile of handwoven rugs on a nearby table. "It looks like you've succeeded."

"I figured that if I could get people in here, eventually we'd sell more wine. And we have."

"But if someone became seriously ill drinking the wine, it could change all that," Andie said.

Sally Ann shot a quick look at Sarah.

"We know about the incident with the ipecac," Andie explained. "Nick and I think there might be some connection between that and what's been happening to Sarah."

Sally Ann covered Sarah's hand with hers. "Everyone who works here knows what happened last night, sweetie. And it won't happen again. We're all going to be looking out for you." Then she turned to Andie. "What can I do to help?"

"Do you know of anyone who might hold a grudge against Nick? Someone's who's quit or been fired?"

"No. He's a great boss. When I came here four years ago, I was a single mom, and I needed a job. He hired me, told me I would make a salary plus commission on any sales, and gave me a free hand. He's like that with everyone."

"Do you know anything about his past, before he went away?"

Sally Ann shook her head. "That was before my time."

"What about when he came back five years ago? Was there anyone who seemed unhappy about his sudden return?" Andie asked.

Sally Ann thought for a minute. "To tell you the truth, most of the people around here seemed to have forgotten that there even *was* a second Heagerty son until he showed up."

Andie thought of the wall of pictures in Nick's outer office. His family seemed to have forgotten him, too.

"You know, there's one person who might be able to tell

you about Nick's past. Mrs. Mabrey, the librarian in Toller-ville. She's been here forever, and she knows everyone."

"How do we get there?" Andie asked.

"Tollerville's a straight shot down this side of the lake, about fifteen miles."

As Andie rose from the table, Sarah grabbed her hand. "We don't have a car. Remember?"

"Not a problem." Sally Ann grabbed a fishnet bag and pulled out a ring of keys. "You can take mine. You can't miss the library. It's a huge white building with pillars and pots of geraniums on the porch."

"THAT'S QUITE A BUMP you've got." Nick pressed the security guard back into his chair when he tried to get up. In the light thrown by the single bulb overhead, Reynaldo Juarez looked pale and even younger than the nineteen years he admitted to. The electricity in the exhibition hall had been off since the break-in, and the air was humid and stale. Reynaldo was shivering in spite of the blanket he had wrapped around him.

"Better stay put in that chair until Lieutenant Mendoza gets back," Nick added. "He'll see that a doctor checks you out."

The young man twisted his hands and gave Nick a nervous glance. "I'll be fine. I didn't black out for very long."

"And you called the lieutenant as soon as you came around. You did the right thing."

"I just stepped out for a minute," Reynaldo hurried on to say. "To have a cigarette with one of the guards."

As Nick listened to the young man retell his story, he found his mind wandering. Back to Andie and Sarah. He'd checked their room before he'd left. They'd been sound asleep in Sarah's bed, and they'd been turned toward each other, holding hands again. They'd looked so vulnerable. He hadn't been able to rid his mind of the image.

"I don't even remember being hit," Reynaldo said. "But when I came around, I was in here, and everything was just the way you see it. The wine hadn't been touched."

The break-in was what needed his attention now, Nick thought as he glanced over to where Grady was meticulously going over each and every case of wine. He'd better keep his mind on it. The metal storage bins they'd used didn't appear to have been tampered with, and there'd been no scratches on the padlocks. Just to make sure, Grady was checking the tape he'd personally put on each case.

Stuffing his hands into his pockets, Nick walked over to join him. The sooner they figured out what had happened, the sooner he could get back to the vineyard. There was absolutely no reason for the edginess he was feeling. But then there'd been no reason for his sudden urge to turn back halfway through the long drive to the fairgrounds. Andie and Sarah were safe. Jake Nolan had arrived to brief the new security men before he and Grady had left, and he'd promised to stay until they'd returned.

Still he couldn't rid his mind of the picture of Sarah and Andie, alone and sleeping....

"No one's been in these boxes," Grady said.

"So why did they break in?" Nick asked.

"Good question." Mendoza stepped into the small circle of light. "It was definitely an inside job. They knew exactly which wires to cut to shut off the electricity and the alarm system." He walked over to join Nick and Grady at the storage bins. "Then they knocked out two security men to get in the building. But after all that, they didn't even try to pick a lock."

Grady rubbed his chin. "They had to know we'd find evidence of the tampering, and we'd replace the wine. Maybe they figured, why bother?"

"But someone on the inside would have known about the

padlocks and the bins. So why did they bother at all? It doesn't make sense," Mendoza argued.

"Unless the whole thing was a diversion. To get us away from the vineyard." Nick was punching numbers into his cellular phone even as he strode quickly out of the exhibition hall. "See that Reynaldo gets to a doctor," he called over his shoulder to Mendoza.

He was still listening to an unanswered ring as Grady drove them through the fairground gates. "No answer at the main house," he said as he punched in more numbers.

"Sally Ann, have you seen my niece? What?" Swearing, Nick turned to Grady. "They've left the estate."

SALLY ANN WAS RIGHT, Andie thought as she drove down the main street of Tollerville. The library, with its white pillars and geranium-filled pots, was a cinch to spot. But so was the dark blue car that had been following them since shortly after they'd pulled out of the winery gates. She glanced into her rearview mirror, then at the library parking lot coming up quickly on her left. Without slowing or signaling her intentions, she made a sharp turn and swung onto the graveled drive. Braking to a stop, she twisted in her seat. As the man in the blue car drove by, she got a quick glimpse of a well-muscled arm and shoulder, strongly defined features, and dark hair pulled back into a short ponytail. Definitely not her old friend Skinny. Still, there was something familiar about him....

"He's following us, isn't he?" Sarah asked.

"We'll know in a minute," Andie said as she got out and hurried around to open Sarah's door. When the driver pulled into a parking place further up the street, she gripped Sarah's hand and hurried her across the lawn and up the steps to the library. Once inside, there'd be some measure of safety. And more options than she could hope to find on a deserted stretch of highway.

Opening the screen door, she urged Sarah across the threshold before she glanced back. When she saw the man tuck a package under his arm and start across the street toward the post office, she let out the breath she was holding.

The large, sunny room she followed Sarah into didn't remind her of any library she'd ever been in. Oh, it was quiet enough, except for the sound of a child's giggle. Andie's attention was drawn immediately to a brightly painted alcove where a young policeman sat hunched over a miniature table reading to a group of wiggling toddlers.

A large orange cat rose from its nap on a windowsill to approach them with a confident stride. Looking well-fed and very much at home, it nudged its way beneath Sarah's hand and produced a satisfied purr as she began to stroke it.

"Esmerelda, don't be rude!"

In spite of her prim, navy blue suit and sensible shoes, the tiny woman hurrying toward them looked more like a fairy godmother than a librarian. Silvery-white hair framed her face in feathery curls, and the blue eyes peering at them over reading glasses were sharp and filled with warmth.

"You must be Rose Heagerty's daughter," she said, extending her hand to Sarah. "I'm Mrs. Mabrey. You won't remember, but we met a long time ago. Your mom used to bring you here often."

Sarah's gaze moved around the room. "I think I remember...the smell...."

Mrs. Mabrey nodded. "Old books. It's the best smell in the world. Your mother loved it. She loved to read, too. Do you?"

At Sarah's nod, Mrs. Mabrey whirled and briskly led the way into an adjoining room. Running her fingers along a shelf of books, she plucked one off and handed it to Sarah. "This is the story of a young lady, a few years older than you, who had to move to a new city when her parents got a divorce. You might like it." She studied Sarah over the rims of her glasses. "What's your favorite book?"

"Grandmother gave me *Jane Eyre* for Christmas."

"You'll love it. I read it for the first time when I was thirteen. But at your age you might like Nancy Drew better." She pointed to a table. "They're full of murder and mayhem." Leaning close to the little girl, she spoke in a confidential tone. "Your mother told me once that she'd read every single one. But she had to do it at night with a flashlight because your grandmother didn't approve of them."

Wide-eyed, Sarah went to investigate, and Mrs. Mabrey turned her attention to Andie. "What can I do for you, Ms. Field?"

Andie grinned at her. "Sally Ann Tanner told me you knew everything."

Mrs. Mabrey waved a hand. "She exaggerates. If I were truly omniscient, I'd know who's trying to kidnap Sarah." At Andie's surprised expression, she elaborated. "Word travels fast in small towns. There's not much to do but gossip." She glanced over at the little girl. "This is one of those times when I'd rather be a detective than a librarian."

"Maybe you can," Andie said. "I want to know anything you can tell me about Nick Heagerty's past."

Mrs. Mabrey frowned. "You don't think Nicholas—"

"No," Andie hastened to assure her, and then explained the problems at the vineyard. "If someone is out to hurt Nick and they're just using Sarah to get to him, I need to find out everything I can about him, any enemies he might have, and I want to know everything about the accident he had on the night of the state basketball championship twenty years ago."

"You *are* a good detective if you've gotten wind of that. It certainly was hushed up around here." Whirling, she was halfway across the room before she turned back. "Wait here. I'll be back in a flash."

And she would, Andie thought. The woman moved like lightning. She glanced around the room. It was quieter than the main reading room, cozier, too. Instead of tables, there were comfortable-looking sofas and several large, over-stuffed cushions scattered around the floor. Sarah sat cross-legged on one of them. She glanced up as Andie approached.

"Nancy Drew is a detective, just like you," she said.

"Well, not *exactly* like me. She drives a nicer car."

Sarah's eyes widened. "You read these books?"

"Yep." Lifting a strand of Sarah's hair, Andie gave it a tug. "That's one of the few things I had in common with your mother. Besides liking you."

Mrs. Mabrey breezed into the room, waving Andie over to a table where she opened a large, leather-bound album. "I've been keeping scrapbooks for years on the local wineries." After flipping through pages, she paused at some newspaper clippings. There was a photograph of Nick holding a trophy.

Leaning closer, Andie found herself studying the picture as carefully as she'd studied the one she'd clipped to his file. Though he was much younger, she recognized the dare in his eyes, the recklessness in his grin. If she'd met him when she was a girl, she would have found him irresistible. His hair was mussed, too, as if he'd just raced down the court. Just looking at it was enough to bring back the sensation of running her fingers through that hair. The softness, the springy texture. She shifted her gaze to his mouth. Curved in a smile, it offered an invitation. And there was that memory, always lingering at the back of her mind, of just what those lips could offer when they were pressed against hers.

"He was quite a heartthrob in those days," Mrs. Mabrey said. "Of course, young girls are always attracted to a rebel."

Andie ruthlessly reined in her wandering thoughts. Good

heavens, she wasn't sixteen and at the mercy of her hormones. "In what way was he a rebel?" she asked.

"Sarah's father, Patrick, was the firstborn, the favored son." Mrs. Mabrey pointed to a photo on the opposite page. It was one Andie had seen hanging on the wall at the winery. "He always did exactly what was expected of him, and he did it well. For a younger son, that's a hard act to follow. And Nick had a strong independent streak. When he was about ten, his father told him he shouldn't be hanging out here in the library. It made him look like a sissy. Patrick Heagerty Senior was big on public image. After that, Nick used to sneak in here after hours. He'd climb in an upstairs window, check out what he wanted, and leave me a note. By the time he got to high school, his rebellion was more open.

"His father and brother had both been all-state in football, but Nick went out for the basketball team. It caused a lot of talk. His father never forgave him, never even went to one of his games." She turned the page and pointed to a picture. "On the night of the state basketball championship, the other members of the Heagerty family attended a symphony and then threw a fund-raising party at the vineyard."

Andie studied the newspaper photo. It was in a society column. She'd seen the original hanging on the wall outside Nick's office. "Is there any mention of the accident?"

Mrs. Mabrey shook her head as she turned more pages. "The family managed to keep it out of the papers. It wasn't even mentioned in the obituary for the little Martinez girl, as I recall." She paused to run her finger down a small column. "See. It gives the date, but no cause of death. Although—" she turned back to the society column "—there's a sentence here in Loretta Glass's column. See. 'An evening marked with triumph and tragedy...' I've often wondered if she was referring to the accident. Do you really think there could be a connection to what's happening now?"

"A little girl died, and nobody wants to talk about it.

Sometimes wounds don't heal when you try to bury them too deep." Andie glanced at Sarah. "Where can I find the Martinez family?"

"They moved away right after the accident. I heard that they opened a restaurant in Florida somewhere. Father Murphy was their parish priest. He might know more, though I've heard that his mind wanders a little. But mine does, too." Closing the scrapbook, she tucked it under her arm and headed toward the door. "Come along, you two. We'll go upstairs to my office while I look up an address. Sarah, you just pick out any two of those Nancy Drew books. Then you can come back for more next week, and I'll get to see you again."

The instant Andie stepped into the main room of the library she spotted the man out of the corner of her eye. A newspaper covered half his face, but the hair and the build were unmistakable. They belonged to the driver of the blue car.

Coincidence? She considered the possibility for the length of time it took her to follow Mrs. Mabrey up the stairs and into her office. No, she couldn't afford to take the chance. A quick glance confirmed that there were only two exits from the room, the door they'd just walked through and another behind Mrs. Mabrey's desk. A solitary window took up most of the space on an interior wall and looked down on the main reading room of the library. Through it, Andie could see that Mr. Blue Car hadn't moved. And the police officer was no longer in the alcove.

Mrs. Mabrey was busy at her computer when Andie said, "There's a man who may be following us. He's sitting at a table near the door reading a newspaper. Could you see if you know him?"

Without a word, Mrs. Mabrey went to the window. A moment later she hurried back to Andie and spoke in a low voice. "I've never seen him before." Plucking a backpack off a hook, she stuffed the album and Sarah's books into it. Then she scribbled something from the computer screen onto a piece of paper. "Father Murphy is still living in the rectory on County Route 66," she said. When she glanced up at Andie, there was a mischievous gleam in her eye. "If you go out the front door, he'll follow you. If you exit the back way, I can keep him busy while you escape. If all else fails, I'll plant a book on him, and when he tries to leave, the alarm will go off."

"Lead the way," Andie said.

Mrs. Mabrey opened the door to a bathroom and pointed to a window over the toilet. "He'll never even know you've left." She turned to Sarah. "It'll be a squeeze, but your uncle Nick used it regularly when he was just about your age." She glanced at Andie. "You'll be on the back porch roof. There's a trellis you can climb down."

Andie climbed onto the toilet seat and raised the sash. She gave the narrow opening a dubious look. Nick had only been ten.

"Nancy Drew could do it," Sarah said with great confidence.

Outnumbered, Andie stuck first her leg and then her hip through the opening. If Nick and Nancy could do it.... Taking a deep breath, she placed her other foot on the toilet tank for leverage, then ducked low and pushed and wiggled and pulled until she finally made it onto her hands and knees on a steeply sloping roof. She glanced briefly in the direction of the gutter before she turned back to take the backpack from Mrs. Mabrey. She slipped it on, one arm at a time. When she saw Sarah's leg, she inched herself down a few shingles. In a matter of seconds the little girl was at her side.

Mrs. Mabrey poked her head through the window. "You'll find the trellis directly below you. It's sturdy."

"Stick close," she cautioned Sarah. "We'll do this very slowly." Out of the corner of her eye she could see the lake

through the trees. The breeze had picked up, and halfway
down, a good push of air hit them.

"Steady. Keep low," she said to Sarah. Inch by inch, she
moved closer to the edge of the roof. Her fingers were less
than two feet from the gutter when one of the shingles suddenly slid from beneath her knee. The weight of the backpack shifted, pulling at her, and for one moment she teetered
before she pressed her palms flat against the roof and leaned
toward Sarah. Even as she regained her balance, she heard
the sound of the falling shingle slapping against the side-
walk below.

Taking a deep breath, Andie pushed the image of it out of
her mind as she began to inch her way toward the gutter. The
moment her fingers curled around it, she peeked over the
edge. The trellis was just where Mrs. Mabrey had said it
would be, and it looked sturdier than she'd expected. Swing-
ing one leg over the edge, she found a toehold. When her second foot was in place, she turned to face Sarah. "Watch what
I do. Then wait until I'm all the way down before you follow."

Three steps down, another gust of wind hit and Andie felt
the trellis sway. She flattened herself against it and waited.
The moment it steadied, she made her way quickly to the
ground.

Gripping the sides of the trellis with both hands, she threw
all her weight against it. Then she looked up. "All right,
Sarah." She held her breath as she saw the little girl swing
her legs over the edge of the roof. "One step at a—" Before
she could even finish the warning, Sarah was beside her on
the ground. Then Andie heard footsteps on the gravel
drive.

Shoving Sarah behind her, she drew her gun and leveled it
at the man as he rounded the corner of the house. For a moment she stood there, feet braced, her weapon aimed at the
man's chest. He was tall and dark-haired, and it was only as

he came to a full stop that she recognized him. Heart pounding in her throat, she willed her finger to relax on the trigger.

"Uncle Nick!" Sarah raced from behind her to hurl herself into her uncle's arms.

# 5

NICK GRABBED SARAH and held her tight as the emotions rolled through him. He wasn't even sure he could identify them. He'd faced death before, so he'd recognized it in that split second when he'd stared into the barrel of Andie's gun. Yet it hadn't been simply fear that he'd felt. At least not the kind that had been churning inside him since he'd learned that Andie and Sarah had left the vineyard.

Nor was it merely relief that he was feeling now. Or anger. Though he *was* angry. Furious, in fact. Ever since Mrs. Mabrey had told him how they were making their great escape out the bathroom window. He knew the slope of that roof intimately. He aimed a glare at Andie over Sarah's head. "What were you thinking of? I told you to sit tight at the vineyard."

Andie's brows lifted as she walked toward him. "I'm not used to taking orders from a partner."

"We were being detectives like Nancy Drew," Sarah said.

He ran his hand down Sarah's hair. "Who's Nancy Drew?"

"A fictional female detective," Andie explained. "You're probably more familiar with Frank and Joe Hardy or Sam Spade."

"This isn't fiction. And not even Sam Spade would have been this—" he shifted his gaze to Sarah and then back to Andie "—reckless."

"You're not mad at us are you, Uncle Nick?" Sarah asked.

"No. No, I'm not, sweetie." And it was true, Nick realized

as he tightened his hold on his niece. His fury was with himself. He never should have left them alone.

"You got here just in time to save us, Uncle Nick. I was sure you would," Sarah said as she snuggled closer to him and pressed her lips to his neck. Nick went perfectly still. He was sure his heart had stopped. He didn't even move when the loud alarm sounded.

"Mrs. Mabrey," Andie said, racing past him and leading the way to the front of the house. "She promised she'd stop the man who was following us. There he is." Andie pointed to the tall man with the ponytail standing between the librarian and Grady on the front porch.

"Andie, I'd like you to meet Jake Nolan," Nick said. "After the breach of security last night, he decided to become personally involved."

"Mr. Nolan." As Andie extended her hand, she studied the man closely. Her eyes narrowed suddenly. "You wouldn't happen to be moonlighting as a gardener at the vineyard, would you?"

"Yes, ma'am." He smiled. "I left my straw hat with my wheelbarrow."

Andie turned to Nick. "We had a rule, *partner. No secrets.* If you'd kept me fully informed—"

"Later," he said with a quick glance at Sarah. "Right now, I'd like to get the two of you back to Heagerty House. Mrs. Mabrey, thank you for taking such good care of my niece."

"My pleasure. And it's good to see you, Nicholas. Don't be a stranger. And don't be too hard on these young ladies. They didn't do anything that you wouldn't have done."

No one spoke until Mrs. Mabrey disappeared into the library. Then Nick turned to Andie. "After you, partner."

ANDIE GLANCED at her watch as she stepped out of the kitchen. Midnight. The witching hour. Sarah had finally drifted off halfway through her first Nancy Drew book. When Grady, who had been reading it to her, offered to stay, it was all the encouragement Andie needed. She knew she wasn't going to sleep one minute until she tracked Nick down.

But she didn't intend to face him empty-handed. Her first stop had been the kitchen where she'd talked Pierre into making a sandwich. It hadn't taken much persuasion once she'd described how thrilled Sarah had been with the *pomme frites* at dinner. Potatoes fried the authentic French way had tasted like heaven.

As she hurriedly made her way down the dark hallway to the front of the house, she tightened her grip on the paper bag she was carrying. Nick might see the sandwich as a bribe. Andie didn't much care as along as it worked.

Somehow the "later" they'd promised each other at the library had never materialized. Nick had done a quick disappearing act the moment they'd returned. As the day wore on, it became increasingly clear to her that she and Grady had been assigned bodyguard duty. Grady had hunted up fishing poles and taught Sarah how to bait a hook and cast a line from the shore of the lake. The little girl had been delighted. Andie had been frustrated.

The interminable length of the day had given her plenty of time to replay in her mind that one moment when she'd had her weapon aimed at Nick's heart. Her own heart seemed to stop for a second each time she thought about it. Then she'd get it pumping again by imagining what he was doing all day without her.

In her mind she could picture quite clearly, Nick and Lieutenant Mendoza and Jake Nolan, their heads close together, plotting strategy and making decisions!

Her steps quickened as she hurried across the foyer. It had to stop. If she was going to be able to protect Sarah, she had to know what was going on. She pulled the door open.

"Andie."

She jumped a foot when she saw Nick standing there with a bottle of wine in his hand.

"I was looking for you," she said.

"You've found me. What's in the bag?"

"You missed dinner. I asked Pierre to make a sandwich."

Nick's brows rose. "You actually talked him into making something as mundane as a sandwich? I'm impressed." He lifted the bottle of wine. "Looks like we have all the makings of a picnic. Your place or mine?"

Andie struggled to prevent a smile as she led the way up the stairs and down the hall to her room. "We might as well let Grady get some sleep."

The moment they stepped through the door, Grady put down his book, and after nodding at both of them, left. For a second, just after she heard the door click shut, Andie felt nervous. Ridiculous.

She had a plan. All she had to do was stick to it. Lifting the sandwich out of the bag, she divided it onto two napkins.

"What's up?" Nick asked as he uncorked the bottle and filled two glasses. "I can't believe you went to all this trouble just to feed me."

She took a quick swallow of the wine he handed her. "First, I want to apologize."

"Me, too."

She stared at him.

"You first."

"Okay." But it wasn't as easy as she'd thought it would be. Not when he was smiling at her as if they were sharing some private joke. She struggled to focus. "I don't much like that I had a gun pointed at your heart earlier today."

"Forget it. You were protecting Sarah."

"But I wouldn't have even had to pull it out if I hadn't taken Sarah off the estate." She swallowed more wine. "You were right. I was reckless." Her glance fell on the book

Grady had left on the chair. "I was a cop long enough to know that I'm no Nancy Drew."

"Or Sam Spade?"

This time she couldn't prevent her warm response to the humor in his eyes. No, it was more than that. She saw understanding, too. As an ex-navy SEAL, he would know the responsibility that went with carrying a gun and having to use it. She suddenly felt her tension ease. "No, I'm certainly no Sam Spade, and I'll take that as a compliment." Smiling, she sat on the arm of a chair and began to swing her foot. "Now, it's your turn."

For a second Nick didn't say a word. It wasn't the first time he'd seen her smile. So why hadn't he noticed before how it seemed to transform her whole face? Or was he only imagining that her lips had softened, that the amber flecks in her eyes had brightened? For the second time that day he could have sworn that he felt his heart stop.

"Well?" she prompted. "You did say you were going to apologize."

"I should have filled you in about the changes Jake and I made to increase security. Then you could have taken Jake along with you instead of climbing off a roof to escape from him."

"That's a very nice apology. But you know what they say about the proof being in the pudding. How about letting me in on what you've been up to all day?"

Nick's expression sobered. "I spent most of it waiting to hear from Mendoza. One of his men found a manager at a fast-food restaurant near the thruway who remembers a chubby woman in a nurse's uniform with a skinny boyfriend. The place has been staked out all day, but so far the daring duo hasn't shown up."

"Did they find any prints on the trash from the cabin?"

"One set matches with Skinny's. Mendoza notified the Rochester police. They're still keeping an eye on his old neighborhood." Nick took a drink of his wine. "The truth is that we're no further along than we were yesterday."

Andie studied him over the rim of her glass. She knew exactly how he felt because she'd been feeling the same way all day. Frustrated and helpless. "Thanks for filling me in."

Nick's brows rose. "No secrets, right, partner?"

Andie took a deep breath. "Right. The thing is I haven't told you everything, either. Exactly." She set her glass on the table and clasped her hands together. "I asked Mendoza to check into any accident reports that were filed on the night of your state basketball championship twenty years ago."

"You asked him to do *what*?"

Of course she hadn't expected him to like it. But she certainly hadn't prepared herself for the swift flash of fury that seemed to leap from his eyes. She swallowed to ease the sudden dryness in her throat.

"What happened that night has been over and done with for twenty years," Nick said. "What gives you the right to poke around in it?"

His eyes were still hot, his voice arctic, but Andie's gaze never shifted. "Sarah gives me that right. I want to know who's after her. Not that I suspect you. I don't." She paused to search for the right words, the ones that would make him understand. "If there's any chance at all that you made an enemy back then, someone who wants revenge, and who's ruthless enough to use a nine-year-old girl to get it, I'll do anything to prevent it. That's why we went to the library today."

"Sarah knows I killed a little girl?"

"No. And you don't know that, either." She paused for a moment looking at him intently, then continued. "I haven't mentioned the accident to her. She was too busy discovering her first Nancy Drew book when Mrs. Mabrey showed me the album." Moving to the bed, she knelt to pull the album out from underneath, then opened it to the page that held the notice of the little girl's death. "Mrs. Mabrey is amazing. She keeps one of these on every family in the area. But you can see for yourself that there was no mention in the paper about the accident, not even in the obituary. Don't you find that odd?"

Nick didn't move any closer to the album. He didn't even glance down at it. "My father wanted it hushed up, and he always knew how to get what he wanted. He packed me off to prep school, he gave money to the Martinez family so that they'd move, and he made sure that there was no written record. He erased it."

*He didn't erase it for you.* The words formed in her mind, but she didn't say them out loud. Instead she went to him and took his hands. "I don't want to stir up painful memories. But I made the *no secrets* rule, so I thought I'd better abide by it."

"You have," Nick said.

"You're not going to ask me to stop?"

"Would you if I did?"

When she shook her head, Nick shrugged. "It's your time. You've got a perfect right to waste it."

Andie let out the breath she'd been holding. "Well, if I'd known it was going to be that easy, I wouldn't have gone to all the trouble of getting that sandwich."

"It's too late to take it back. You're already sharing my wine." Releasing her hands, he continued, "In the interest of keeping you fully informed, you should know that taking Sarah off the grounds may have been the smart thing to do. Mendoza and I believe that the break-in at the state fair exposition building was staged to lure Grady and me away from here."

"Did something happen while we were gone?"

Nick shook his head. "I questioned all the security people. The only thing they saw out of the ordinary was a fishing boat that seemed to be too close to the shore."

"I saw it, too, just before Sarah and I left."

"I called everyone on this side of the lake. No one could identify the fisherman. It's obvious that Skinny and his friend have been getting inside information all along. They may have scratched whatever they were planning today when they were informed that you and Sarah had taken off."

"Your aunt Marguerite and Jeff were gone, too."

"They could have an accomplice."

Andie set her glass down and began to pace. "So there's a spy on the estate feeding information to Skinny and friend about every measure we're taking to protect Sarah... someone who would know everyone's schedule each day." She paused at the window and glanced out at the sloping roof. "Someone who would know which bedroom Sarah was in. But they couldn't have known Mendoza would choose that particular morning to change the angle of the security cameras." Turning, she faced Nick. "To keep Sarah safe, we've got to make sure that no one knows what we're doing. I've been thinking..."

She still was, Nick thought as he watched her pace again. He could almost hear the wheels turning. He'd known her for less than a week, and already there was so much he'd learned about her. If she had to, she'd scale a roof in pursuit of a suspect. She might not like carrying a gun, but she'd use it. He'd seen the determination in her eyes when she'd aimed it at him. But he'd seen fear, too. The contrasts in her fascinated him. But it was the rock-solid dependability that drew him. That and the way she held a little girl's hand in her sleep.

"Well?"

"Hmm?"

"Haven't you been listening?" Andie asked. "I've been trying to think of a way to protect Sarah without making her a prisoner on this estate. We'll have to work together, of course. That's the advantage that the Hardy boys always had over Nancy Drew. They had their own built-in backup." She beamed a smile at him. "We'll just take her somewhere new each day. We can announce it at the breakfast table. No one will know where we're going until the last moment."

"What if we're followed?" Nick asked.

"I'm planning on it. You have enough security people to keep us under surveillance. You and I take care of Sarah while they watch for Skinny and Chubby to make their move. The daring duo won't be able to make any plans in advance. That way we'll have a better chance of nabbing them."

Nick studied her thoughtfully. "I don't like the idea of taking Sarah off the estate."

"Better a moving target than a sitting duck." She continued to pace, thinking aloud as she walked. "The longer we keep Sarah here, the sooner this inside person can figure out a weakness in the security system you've set up. They've already managed to get to her bedroom window. Today, they were probably trying to get up here from the beach. What's to keep them from eventually walking right in her bedroom door? If we keep Sarah moving, this insider might make a mistake. And I know we can keep her safe."

"I wish it were that simple," Nick said.

"It *can* be. It *will* be if we truly work together as partners." She walked toward him, hand extended. "No more planning sessions with Mendoza and Jake Nolan where you leave me out in the cold. No more secrets. And we both stick close to Sarah. Two guardian angels are better than one. Deal?"

"You're forgetting one thing," Nick said, taking her hand.

He was wrong. She hadn't forgotten. The moment that his palm pressed against hers, Andie remembered exactly how it had felt to have his hands moving over her, his mouth pressing against hers. She recalled, too, just how much she'd wanted that kiss to go on.

She didn't say a word. Something had lodged in her

throat. Not fear. Just nerves. She could handle that. It was the funny, tingling sensation radiating from her stomach out to her fingertips that worried her more. She recognized it as anticipation.

"I've been thinking a lot, too," Nick said. "Last night I decided that it would be best for all of us if I kept my distance. But I was wrong." With his free hand he lifted the small charm she wore around her neck. He noticed the gleam of real gold beneath the tarnish. "Who gave you this?"

"My ex-partner."

His fingers tightened on the charm. He hadn't known before that jealously could burn, nor that it had the bitter, metallic taste of copper. "Why did he give it to you?" he asked.

"That's none of your—"

"No secrets between partners, remember?"

Lifting her chin, Andie felt the press of the chain against the back of her neck. "His grandmother gave it to him when he first became a cop. She told him one day it would save his life. The night I shot that kid in the alley, he insisted that I take it. He believed that I'd saved his life, not the angel, and he said it was his way of returning the favor."

Slowly, Nick released the charm so that it rested once more against her throat, but he held on to her hand. "I guess that's all right then."

"What's that supposed to mean?" She jabbed a finger into his chest. "Just who do you—"

"I'm your *new* partner. And I'm going to be a lot more than that. If we're going to follow your plan and work as closely as two guardian angels, just how do you suggest we deal with what's happening between us?"

"We're adults. We can handle it."

Nick's laugh erupted, deep and rich. "No argument there. Part of the pleasure comes from imagining just how good the handling will be."

Andie gave him a hard look. "Get this straight. I don't

sleep around, I don't have casual affairs and I'm not afraid of you."

As he looked at her, his expression sobered. He didn't release her hand, not yet. And she didn't pull away. As much as she might want to, she wouldn't run. He knew that about her, too, and courage was a quality he'd always admired. "No secrets between partners, remember? I want to be very clear up front that I want you. We can postpone what's going to happen between us until we're sure Sarah's safe. But then..."

"*Until* then, we're going to lay down some ground rules."

"I'm not big on following rules," Nick warned.

"We'll keep them simple. Number one, no unnecessary touching."

Together, as if in response to a signal, they drew their hands apart. Then in an unconscious gesture that had Nick grinning, Andie immediately wiped her hand on her jeans.

Nick reached for his wine, took a sip. "In the interest of clarity, perhaps we should define *unnecessary*."

Andie's brow lifted. "You're a bright man. Let's just say that if I'm drowning, you can rescue me." The quick gleam in his eye had her hurrying on. "And you can stuff the comments on mouth-to-mouth resuscitation. Most of the time we're together, Sarah will be with us. Other times we'll just have to avoid any romantic situations."

"No more meetings in dark, deserted cabins," Nick said.

"Or midnight picnics," she said, glancing at the small meal spread out on the table.

"I guess I'll have to take it back to my room."

"I wouldn't," she warned as he reached for her half of the sandwich. "Since touching is out, I might have to use my gun." Then with a smile, she settled herself in a chair. "Besides we agreed to share before we laid the ground rules."

His laugh erupted once again as he sat down across from

her. "You know, you just might convince me that there's some value to following rules after all."

"We just agreed—"

"Relax. We agreed on the essentials. We both want to protect Sarah. And getting involved in a relationship would distract us. So we'll wait."

Andie studied him. Not for a minute did she trust the bland, innocent expression on his face. But she couldn't exactly disagree with what he'd said. She turned her attention to her sandwich. Lifting the top, she inspected the contents.

"Where's your sense of adventure?" Nick asked.

"Pierre was muttering in French while he made this. I don't like surprises." She took a tentative bite.

"As a cop, did you always do things by the book?"

"Absolutely. It was the only way for a woman to survive on the Boston police force. This sandwich is good, by the way."

"You never were tempted to improvise, substitute Plan B?"

"Plan A usually worked."

"Why did you become a P.I.?"

Andie shrugged as she brushed crumbs off her fingers. "I wanted to be my own boss."

"See? Deep down, you don't like rules, either."

When she glanced up, it was understanding she saw in his eyes, and she knew that it was more dangerous than the desire she'd seen earlier. She shifted her gaze to his sandwich. "Are you going to eat that?"

Nick raised his hands in surrender. "Not if you're going to threaten me with a gun again."

Laughing, she tucked her feet under her and leaned back in her chair to watch him eat. "If you hate rules so much, how did you manage in the navy?"

"I loved the sea. Have you ever sailed?"

She shook her head.

"I could teach you."

Andie stared at him then. There was no mistaking the sincerity of his offer. And she could imagine exactly how it would be, sailing with him. She could almost feel the sway of the boat and the wind whipping against them. And she could picture quite clearly his naked torso, gleaming in the sunlight, his hands strong on the tiller. Very tempting, she thought. "I don't think so," she said.

He was smiling as he rose. "Rules again. And you wonder why I don't like them."

She followed him to the door, intending to lock it, but she was totally unprepared when he turned and brushed his lips lightly over hers. It wasn't really a kiss. And nothing like the one they'd shared in the cabin. The one she couldn't seem to get out of her head. This time his mouth was teasing and soft. Tempting.

Much later, she would remember that she didn't do one thing to stop him. She didn't reach for him, didn't touch him at all. She just stood there...drowning. When she opened her eyes, he had stepped away. She wasn't sure how she was still standing without his support.

"The best thing about rules is breaking them," he said as he pulled the door shut.

# 6

NICK BRAKED as he eased the convertible around a sharp curve. The rap song blaring from the radio competed with the ominous roll of thunder overhead.

As the car came out of the turn, he glanced at his two companions. Andie and Sarah seemed oblivious to the dark clouds rolling in over the lake. They were leaning back against the seat, totally caught up in the rhythm of the song, whatever snatches of it they could hear before the wind whipped it away.

Sarah had chosen their destination, but he'd selected the car, Jeff's red convertible. And he wasn't sorry. The little girl's solemn expression had vanished the moment he'd lowered the top. And he could still feel the warmth that had spread through him when she'd smiled at him.

He wasn't as happy with where Sarah wanted to go. A shopping mall. Her choice had surprised him. His first impulse had been to object. He might have if Jake Nolan hadn't insisted on assigning three more of his people to follow them whenever they left the estate.

His family's reaction when Sarah had announced their plans had been more than enough to reassure Nick that no one had anticipated them. Jeff had immediately objected. A California wine merchant was flying in to tour the winery, and he expected Nick to meet with him. What was he supposed to tell him?

Initially Marguerite had been annoyed since Jeff would have to miss an important board meeting. But she'd rallied quickly and switched to her lecturing mode, reminding Jeff that he was perfectly capable of running Heagerty Vineyards by himself.

Only Sandra Martin's response had surprised Nick. She'd been angry. Not that she'd said anything. She rarely did. Nor had there been any overt reaction on her face. But the roll she'd chosen so carefully from the sideboard had ended up untasted and shredded on her plate. Could she be that upset that she would have to attend a board meeting in Jeff's place?

What had Andie made of it? he wondered. They hadn't had any time to discuss it. When he glanced over, he saw Andie and Sarah busily shoving a new tape into the tape deck. He couldn't recall seeing either of them this relaxed before. The speed and the wind were working their magic. On him, too. He could feel the tension easing from him as he changed gears and accelerated in anticipation of the coming hill. If they loved fast rides in convertibles, they were going to love sailing.

The thought hit him with sudden clarity that he was thinking of the future. A future that included Andie and Sarah.

*Give it up, Heagerty,* he said to himself as his hands tightened on the wheel. Down-shifting, he pressed his foot on the gas pedal as the road began to climb again. Hadn't he learned his lesson long ago? Today was all there was.

The first large drop splashed against the windshield as the car reached the top of the hill. In the valley to his left the sun glinted off the peaked skylights of the shopping mall. To his right, black clouds swirled closer. Lightning arced jaggedly toward the opposite shoreline. He was about to pull off the road to put the top up when his eyes met Andie's briefly, just long enough to see the laugh and the dare. Returning his gaze to the road, he pressed his foot down hard on the accelerator.

* * *

"WE BEAT THE STORM" Sarah shouted above a crack of thunder as they pulled into a parking space. Together, they worked to secure the convertible top, but drops were already falling. Several hit them as they raced toward the mall entrance.

Breathless and laughing, they pushed through the glass doors, then turned to watch as a sheet of water whipped across the parking lot, drenching everything in its path.

Andie turned to him then. "Great driving!"

"Awesome," Sarah added.

Nick glanced down at his niece. Her long blond hair was tangled, but her cheeks were flushed and her eyes glowed with an excitement he hadn't seen there before. He ran a finger down her nose. "Your mother wouldn't agree. If she were here, she'd probably have me horsewhipped."

"Nonsense," Andie said. "She would have loved it." As she spoke, she pulled Sarah's hair back from her face and began to fashion it quickly into a braid. "Remind me to tell you about the time your mom and I rented a tandem bike, you know the kind that two people can ride. I made the mistake of letting your mother steer, and I still have a scar on my knee."

"Really?" Sarah asked.

"I'll show you later, kiddo." Fishing a piece of ribbon out of her pouch, she tied the braid, then turned Sarah around to study her. "Okay, you'll pass."

Nick watched her as she combed her fingers through her own hair. It was mussed much as it had been the first time he'd seen her when she'd pointed a gun at him in front of the train station. He'd wanted to touch it even then. He wanted to touch it now, to smooth it back from her face. He knew exactly how it would feel against his skin, smooth and slick like silk.

"We're ready."

It was Andie who had spoken, but as he checked his wan-

dering thoughts, he noted that they both were looking at him
with the same expectant expression on their face. He felt as if
he were letting them down when he said, "Sorry, ladies. I got
you here, but that's the extent of my expertise."

"Not a problem," Andie assured him as she pushed
through a second set of glass doors. "I grew up in shopping
malls."

The long hallway was filled with people, some strolling
leisurely along, others moving at a fast, determined clip. A
small group had clustered around a clown juggling balls on
a platform. Nick tightened his grip on Sarah's hand and
stuck close to Andie.

Sounds lapped at them from all sides. Laughter and ap-
plause for the clown, a brief blast of a song from a portable
radio, and the sharp, insistent cry of a child.

He very nearly walked right into Andie when she stopped
in front of a kiosk to study a brightly illuminated map of the
mall. Above it was an alphabetical list of stores, each coded
to match a location on the map. One name caught his attention just as Andie pulled his arm to draw him into a huddle.

"We have to have a plan," she announced.

"Shopping requires a plan?" Nick asked.

"Shopping is serious business. Sarah wants brand-name
jeans, so our best bet is the two anchor stores." She pointed
up at the map. "They always build the big department stores
at the ends of the mall. That way shoppers have to walk by
all the small stores to get from one to the other. The hope is
that we'll be distracted and lured in to buy something we
don't really need. Those small stores are our enemy. So
here's the plan. Rule number one, absolutely no stopping until we get the blue jeans. Agreed?"

"Agreed," Sarah said solemnly. Since Andie seemed to expect it, Nick nodded his head. And then she was leading the
way again.

As he watched the quick, efficient way she walked, the

skill with which she avoided an aggressive-looking woman with a clipboard, it occurred to him that she was treating the shopping trip with much the same care and attention to detail that he might have given to one of the missions he'd led when he was in the navy. Oh, the atmosphere was different. Instead of being in a hot, humid jungle at night, they were in a crowded mall in the middle of the day. And they had skylights overhead to protect them from the steady, insistent rain.

He pushed the memories away, preferring to devote his full attention to the woman in front of him as she cleared a path for them around a cluster of Boy Scouts, then signaled for a quick left at the fountain. He couldn't help but wonder if she would make love with the same precisely thought-out strategy that she seemed to devise for everything else she did. It would be very tempting to break that kind of concentration. How long would it take him? he wondered. How long could he wait to find out?

A stranger, jostling against him, brought him back to the present with a start. As he tightened his grip on Sarah, he glanced quickly around. No one seemed out of place. He couldn't even spot one of Jake's men.

Andie turned, a question in her eyes. Annoyed with himself, he shook his head and signaled her to go on. There would be time enough to indulge his fantasies later. He glanced down at his niece, then back at Andie. He was going to make the time.

Then he suddenly grinned as Andie adroitly led them to the other side of the mall to avoid a toy store.

A shopping plan. It amused him at the same time that it presented a challenge: could he get her distracted before they reached the department store?

It was the sharp, persistent barking that drew Nick's attention. The puppy was in the glass window of the pet shop. The moment Sarah stopped to look, the little pooch stumbled over paws much too large for the rest of him, then skidded and bumped his nose smack into the glass in his eagerness to greet them. Behind him, his siblings continued to nap in a snug little pile, oblivious to the din their brother was creating.

"Remember our rules..." Andie began. Her words faded the moment she saw the puppy.

"The best thing about rules is the fun of breaking them," Nick said.

The moment Sarah placed her palm against the glass, the dog began to lick it frantically.

"It's not like it's something Sarah doesn't need," Nick ventured. "She could definitely use a good watchdog." He glanced at the tag around the puppy's neck. "And Brutus has *watchdog* written all over him."

Right on cue, Brutus stopped licking the window and barked.

Sarah glanced up at her uncle. "Can I really have him?"

"You bet, sweetie," he said. The sudden dryness in his throat surprised him.

"Can I keep him in my room?" Sarah asked.

"That's up to Andie," he replied.

"Your aunt Maggie will have a fit," Andie said.

"I'll handle Aunt Maggie," Nick promised.

"Okay," Andie said. "Since Sarah definitely needs a watchdog, we can *bend* the rules, and he can stay in our room." She sent Nick a narrow-eyed look. "Just this once."

TWO HOURS LATER Andie sank into a cushioned seat on a small bench near the department store where they were finally going to buy Sarah's jeans. There was a salesgirl with a short, short skirt and frizzy blond hair who was going to signal them as soon as a dressing room was free.

In the meantime Nick and Sarah had taken the puppy outside for the fourth time since they'd bought him. It was part of the house-breaking instructions that the pet store owner had given them. Brutus had to get used to relieving himself outside. So far, the puppy hadn't learned a thing except to bark at everyone.

The familiar sound had her glancing up. Brutus was tugging on his leash and dragging a laughing Sarah and Nick with him.

Andie couldn't prevent a smile. Nick Heagerty had found at least half a dozen ways to *bend* the rules on their way to buy the jeans. Each one had delighted his niece even more. And Andie had to admit she was amused by them. He'd even teased her, calling it Plan B. *B* for *bending*, that is.

The food court had provided a bonanza of opportunities for him. First he'd suggested a carousel ride and then pizza. Then Sarah had become his willing partner in discovering new delaying tactics. When Nick had insisted that they have their picture taken with the puppy, Andie couldn't have said who'd spoiled the greater number of shots by making faces.

Brutus let out a bark, then did an abrupt about-face and tangled Sarah's legs in his leash. Nick carefully freed her and ran a hand down her hair. Andie felt a sudden tightness in her throat. They looked so right together. So happy. For a moment she found herself wishing that the day could go on forever. Even more, she found herself wishing, longing.... No, she ruthlessly reined in the thought before she could complete it. She had a plan, a strategy. She was going to convince Nick that Rose was right, that he was the perfect choice to be Sarah's guardian. And she couldn't afford any diversions. Today was a good start, but she didn't fool herself for a moment that Nick was won over yet.

When they finally reached her, they collapsed on the bench, except for Brutus who jumped onto her lap and began to lick her face. "Any luck this time?" she managed once the puppy had subsided and snuggled into a little ball on her lap.

"He's a good watchdog. I think we'll have to settle for that," Nick said. "Keep a tight grip on his leash or he'll get away again."

"Again?" Andie asked.

Clapping a hand over her mouth, Sarah giggled.

"It's a long story," Nick explained.

"I have a dressing room free now." The short-skirted, frizzy-haired salesgirl held a hand out to Sarah as she shot Brutus a regretful look. "I can't allow the dog in the store, but I'll bring her back out here to model the jeans for you."

"You'll stay with her?" Andie asked.

"I'll stick like glue," the girl promised.

"I'm exhausted," Nick said as he leaned back against the bench.

"You've come to the wrong person for sympathy," she said. "If we'd followed my rules, Plan A, we'd be back at the vineyard right now."

"But we wouldn't have had much fun," Nick observed casually. "And admit it. You had fun."

"I did." She was smiling when she turned her head to find him close beside her. This close, his eyes seemed even darker, like the sea when it was churned up by a storm. His mouth was close, too. So close, she could feel his breath along her skin when he exhaled. It would be wise to move away. She was going to, in just a minute.

And then his lips curved in a smile. "You'll have fun when we make love, too. I want you to know that."

And she did. Hadn't she already imagined what it would be like? Dreamed of it?

It was Nick who finally pulled away. "Think about it."

His eyes were lighter now. In amusement or satisfaction, she wasn't sure. Taking in a deep breath, she hoped that her voice would be steady. "What I'm thinking is that Rose was right to choose you as Sarah's guardian."

She saw the amusement fade from his eyes before he turned away. "I haven't changed my mind about that."

But he was looking at Sarah, Andie noted. The salesgirl was just leading her into a dressing room.

"You're fond of her," Andie said. "And you're so good with her. I haven't heard her giggle...well, for months, certainly not during the whole time Rose was ill."

"Having fun with her is one thing. Raising her is a different story. I'm not the right person to do that."

There was a bleakness in his tone that had her hands clenching into fists. She thought of the album Mrs. Mabrey had given her, filled with photographs of his high school career. Photos that were missing from the pictorial family history that graced the wall in the winery office. She thought of how alone he'd been for so many years. "Yes, you are. And I won't give up until I convince you of that."

Nick looked at her then. The warrior look was back on her face. The one he'd seen so often when she argued on Sarah's behalf. But it wasn't just Sarah she was defending now. It was him. He wasn't sure he could define the emotion that moved through him. But he knew that he wanted her more than he'd wanted any woman.

Reaching out, he ran his fingers along her cheek and threaded them through her hair. The texture was just as he'd imagined earlier, slippery, cool silk. "I was wrong. Not about the fact that we're going to make love. Because we are. We're going to have fun, too. But it will mean more than that. Much more."

The blunt words were enough to have her heart hammering hard against her chest. More than enough to have desire coiling hot in her stomach. People strolled by. A baby cried. She wasn't aware of anything, anyone but Nick. Lord, but his eyes were beautiful. The color of the sea, mysterious, inviting. And in their depths, she could see the storm she sensed before, and the promise of passion. She might have been able to pull back from the passion. But the need was there, too. And she found it irresistible. Without any conscious thought, she leaned forward, and her lips were just brushing his when the puppy began to bark. Quick, sharp, staccato barks. Then she felt the jerk of the leash as Brutus pulled free.

Nick rose first. "Damn! Not again."

Scanning the crowd, Andie spotted Brutus immediately. "There. By the bookstore." It was then that she saw the man. He was wearing a cap and pushing his way through the crowd, but there was no mistaking his build. Skinny. She ran after Nick. Grabbing his arm, she pointed. "The chauffeur."

"Stay with Sarah," he said as he raced away.

She'd run three steps before his words sank in. Sarah. Whirling, she ran toward the store. Once inside, she scanned the place. She couldn't even see the salesgirl. A sliver of panic raced up her spine.

The store was so crowded. She pressed her fingers against her throat to ease the knot of fear that had lodged there. How long had it been since she'd seen Sarah? Five minutes? Ten? How much time had slipped by while she'd been looking at Nick, thinking of him? She shouldn't have taken her eyes off the little girl, not even for a minute.

She started with the dressing rooms first. Methodically, Andie knocked on each door, called Sarah's name, and then pulled the doors open. Sarah wasn't in any of them.

Ignoring the knot of fear twisting in her stomach, she slowly made her way between the racks of clothes, checking each one. If Sarah had bent over or sat down for a minute to rest.... Andie breathed a quick prayer that it was so, but when she reached the back of the store, she still hadn't found her.

She hadn't found the salesgirl, either. There was some comfort in that. Crossing to the cashier, she cut in front of a customer and described Sarah and the salesgirl to her. The young woman suggested the dressing rooms.

"I've already tried them," Andie said.

The cashier shrugged. "Maybe she's on a break."

"She promised to keep Sarah with her," Andie said. "Where would she go?"

The cashier shrugged and turned back to her customer.

Gripping her hands tightly together, Andie fought down a wave of panic as she hurried toward the store entrance. But there was no sign of Sarah out in the mall, either. Where? She forced herself to think. *Where?* Whirling, she made her way quickly to the back of the store. There had to be a stockroom. Pushing back the curtain, Andie shouted Sarah's name.

The room was long and narrow and divided by shelves. She checked down each aisle. No one. Skinny had been alone, hadn't he? Closing her eyes for a moment, she recalled the image. There'd been a crowd around him. He'd pushed someone aside in his hurry. She hadn't seen anyone else. Not the chubby nurse. Certainly not Sarah. And she wouldn't have gone quietly.

It was then that she saw the back door. It was slightly ajar with light pouring in. What if Skinny had just created a diversion while his chubby sidekick had dragged Sarah out the back way? Racing to the door, Andie jerked it open.

WITH BRUTUS TUCKED under his arm, Nick threaded his way through the crowd. His other quarry had escaped. He'd gotten within an arm's reach of Skinny when the sometime chauffeur had grabbed a wheelchair and shoved it toward him. It had been all he could do to keep the young boy from tumbling out of it.

By the time he'd resumed the chase, Skinny had disappeared into the crowd. Then Brutus, barking loudly, had skidded joyfully into his leg. "Good boy," he said as the pup licked his chin. But the question nagging at the back of his mind as he hurried back to the store was, Where was the chubby nurse?

The bubble of fear only subsided when he saw Sarah sitting next to Andie on the cushioned bench near the store. There was another woman who rose with them as he approached.

Andie made the introductions. "This is Ms. Markham. Jake Nolan assigned her to keep an eye on Sarah. She was kind enough to step outside with Sarah and the salesgirl when the girl took her break."

"Thank you, Ms. Markham." Then Nick turned his attention to a solemn-faced Sarah. "Nice jeans," he said, and was rewarded with a smile. Finally he spoke to Andie. "Well, partner, do you by any chance have a strategy for getting us out of here?"

"No more *B* plans," she warned.

"Agreed." Nick took Sarah's hand in his and followed Andie meekly to the nearest exit.

IT WAS A LITTLE after ten when Andie knocked on the side door of the winery. Brutus had fallen asleep, and Grady was teaching Sarah to play Monopoly. She was about to knock a second time when Nick pulled the door open.

"I was just about to come and get you. Mendoza's due in half an hour. He's bringing Jake Nolan with him," Nick said.

"We need to talk privately first." Andie walked past him and led the way to his office.

"If you're upset about what happened at the mall—"

She whirled to face him. "Of course, I'm upset. I didn't have my mind on Sarah. For five, maybe ten minutes, I was thinking of no one but you."

More than anything he wanted to go to her. To hold her, to erase the worry in her eyes. To make her think of no one except him again. But because she was right, because he'd been struggling with his own feelings of guilt all afternoon, he didn't move. "Jake's people had it covered," he said.

"Yeah." Andie began to pace. "This time we were lucky.

But the whole time I was searching that store for Sarah I couldn't help thinking that Skinny might've been creating a diversion. And that while he had our attention, his chubby sidekick had managed to snatch Sarah." Once more, she whirled to face him. "It was my idea to take her away from here." She raised her hands and dropped them. "I thought that together we could protect her. But we couldn't."

"We not only could, but we did. And Mendoza and Jake will be able to tell us when they get here exactly what calls were made from the house this morning. That will tell us if Skinny was tipped off or if he followed us the way Ms. Markham did."

Andie studied him for a moment. The dark shadows under his eyes testified to his exhaustion. More than anything she wanted to go to him, to touch him, to comfort him. She stayed where she was. "I know that you don't want any of your family to be involved."

"If you're trying to protect my feelings, I assure you—"

Shaking her head, Andie raised a hand. "It's not that. I discovered when we got back today that the album is missing."

At Nick's blank stare, she hurried on. "The one Mrs. Mabrey gave me. I showed it to you, remember? I had it under my bed, and it's gone."

"Why would anyone want it?" Nick asked.

"Good question. I've had all afternoon to think about it, and I'm more and more convinced there has to be a connection between that night twenty years ago and what's going on now."

"Sarah didn't have anything to do with that little girl's death," Nick said.

"No, but she's a little girl too, and she's entrusted to your care. What if someone wants an eye for an eye?"

"She's got a point," Mendoza said from the doorway. Jake had already settled himself in one of the chairs.

"Don't you guys ever knock?" Nick asked.

Jake grinned. "We would have if we'd interrupted anything...interesting."

Ignoring the comment, Nick said, "I owe you for assigning Ms. Markham."

"We both do," Andie added.

Jake waved a hand, his grin fading. "She's a good operative. But you can save the thanks for when we catch whoever's behind this. One of my other people spotted Skinny's getaway car. A chubby woman was driving. He wasn't close enough to his own car to give chase, but he got a plate number."

Flipping through his notebook, Mendoza settled himself in the other chair. "So do the state and local police within a one hundred mile radius. Plus, there was a call made from Heagerty House at nine this morning to a pay phone about a mile up the highway. Unfortunately, there's no way to tell who made the call or who received it. That's another reason we didn't knock. We didn't even park in the lot. This place has too many damn ears."

For a moment there was silence in the room. Then Nick spoke. "Andie's having second thoughts about taking Sarah off the estate again."

Jake leaned back in his chair. "It's up to you. It wouldn't hurt to give the police some time to track down the car. In the meantime, I can reassign Ms. Markham and the other extra people I've hired to beef up the security here."

"I don't mind admitting that I'd breathe a little easier if Sarah stayed close to home for a few days," Mendoza said. "It would give us time to check into Ms. Field's theory that the kidnapping attempts are related somehow to that accident twenty years ago." Pausing, he drew some papers out of his pocket and spread them out on Nick's desk. "I finally managed to get copies of the accident reports along with sketches that the police made when they arrived on the scene. Nothing in them contradicts the presence of a third car."

"Are you saying..." Nick began.

"All I'm saying is that you could have been right about the third car. And the police could have been asked to leave it out. Or perhaps they left it out because someone else gave them a different description while you were unconscious."

"Who?" Nick asked. "And why?"

"Excellent questions," Andie said as she began to pace. "You believe that your father used his money and influence to hush the whole accident up. That he paid the Martinez family to suddenly relocate to Florida. Maybe the money also bought their silence."

Nick shook his head. "That doesn't make any sense. It was their daughter who died. Wouldn't they want the truth?"

"Grief does things to people," Andie said. "Sometimes it's a motivation for revenge."

"Okay. I agree that we ought to check into it," Nick said.

"We can start with Father Murphy. Mrs. Mabrey says he was the pastor where the Marinez family went to church," Andie said.

"Fine." Tucking his notebook into his pocket, Mendoza walked toward the door. "I'll get in touch with some contacts down in Florida. See what you can find out on this end."

"I'll reassign my people," Jake said.

For a moment after the two men left, there was silence in the room. Then Nick said, "It might be better if we worked separately on this. Why don't I check out Father Murphy while you stay here—"

"Not on your life!" Andie crossed the room until she stood toe to toe with him. "We're partners, remember?" She poked a finger into his chest. "There's no way I'm going to let you go hotdogging off on your own while I play Monopoly with Grady and Sarah."

"You're the one who wasn't happy with what happened at the mall," Nick stated flatly.

"And you're the one that said we'd get quicker results if we worked together on this. Plus, nothing would have happened at the mall if we'd stuck to our ground rules." She poked him again for emphasis. "I don't want Sarah in danger one minute longer than she has to be. Besides, she'll be perfectly safe with Grady and the marvelous Ms. Markham."

Nick's eyebrows rose. "Do I detect a note of jealousy?"

Andie frowned. "You don't detect squat."

Quite suddenly, Nick wanted to laugh. For the first time since they'd left the mall, he felt his tension ease. And the only reason for it was the woman standing in front of him. Her hands were fisted on her hips, the archangel look was back on her face. She looked marvelous. And though it might have been wiser to steer a separate course, Nick knew he was quite simply happy to have his partner back.

Sitting on the edge of his desk, he said, "I suppose you have a strategy for handling Father Murphy?"

Andie lifted her chin. "We're sticking to our ground rules?"

When he nodded, she sat in a chair. "As a matter of fact, I do have a plan...."

# 7

Nick drove past the white, steepled church and parked the convertible at the side of the road in the shade of a tall hedge. "I still say our best bet is to break in and take a look at the records. I know it's risky but it's the only way we'll get any information about the Martinez family."

Andie shot him a cool look. They'd been debating—no, make that arguing—about strategy ever since they'd decided to visit Father Murphy. "I'm not sneaking into a rectory."

"You'll see. The straightforward approach will be a waste of time. Priests don't like to give out information. The most you'll get out of him is some mumbo-jumbo about the seal of confession."

Andie climbed out of the car, then looked back. "You're not coming, I take it?"

"I won't be any good as Plan B if I blow my cover this early in the game."

Without another word, she turned and started back down the road. Almost immediately, the hedge gave way to a stretch of lawn. With its red shutters and wide front porch, Father Murphy's home looked more like a small cottage than a rectory. An old graveyard with a stone fence lay between it and the steepled church. Andie caught a glimpse of a flower garden in the backyard just before she turned up the flagstone path.

As partners, she and Nick couldn't have been more different. She preferred planning, order, meticulous calculation. He liked to rely on his instincts, improvise on the spur of the moment. No wonder he preferred to wander the seas alone. He *was* a nomad! Breaking into a rectory! Ridiculous! A few simple questions would get them the information they needed.

She climbed up the steps and knocked on the front door. From inside she could hear the insistent whine of a vacuum cleaner and above it the bright music of a TV game show. But it wasn't a priest who opened the door. Instead, Andie found herself looking down at a small boy who was sucking on his thumb.

She crouched down until she was eye to eye with the toddler. "Is your mom here?"

The little boy looked at her, wide-eyed and silent.

"I bet you're not supposed to talk to strangers. That's—"

"Danny!" A young woman in her early twenties raced down the hall, scooped the little boy up into her arms, and glared at Andie. "Whatever it is you're selling, we don't want it."

Andie managed to get her foot across the threshold just as the woman tried to shut the door. "I'm not selling anything. I want to talk to Father Murphy."

"He's retired. And Father Jensen is out."

"I just want to ask Father Murphy a few questions."

"What about? He never gets any visitors."

Andie smiled. "Then hopefully this will be a pleasant surprise for him. May I come in?"

"He's taking a nap right now."

"I can wait."

"Look, lady. I'm working for my aunt today. She had a doctor's appointment, and if I don't get through cleaning the office, she'll have a fit. You want to see Father Murphy, you call her this afternoon and make an appointment. She'd be the one to answer your questions anyway. The old priest has trouble remembering his name. Okay?"

"Fine," Andie said. The moment she pulled her foot free of the door, it was closed in her face.

She fully expected Nick to be waiting in the car, eager to gloat. But he was gone. Tapping her foot, she was considering the wisdom of going back to the cottage when he suddenly slipped through a gap in the tall hedge.

"Ready for Plan B?" he asked.

Andie's eyes narrowed. "What do you have in mind?"

"I'll distract the pretty little housekeeper while you slip into the office. I left the window in the back open for you. There's a filing cabinet marked Church Records. I left that open, too. If you'd kept her busy for thirty more seconds, I'd have had the file. As it was, I barely made it back out the window."

"I can't believe you did that. If you'd filled me in on your plan, I would have tried to keep her longer. Although I didn't exactly make a good first impression. She thought I was a child snatcher."

Nick shot her a grin. "Want to bet I have more luck?"

Andie didn't dignify the question with a reply. Instead, she turned and climbed through the gap in the hedge. Keeping her eye on the cottage, she made her way quickly along the stone fence that surrounded the graveyard. When she saw Nick climb the steps and knock, she made a dash to the back of the cottage.

The window was open, just as he'd promised. It took her only seconds to lever herself up and wiggle through it. With her eyes on the door to the office, she listened hard. Though she couldn't make out the words above the noise of the TV, she could hear the rumble of Nick's voice. Letting out the breath she was holding, she crossed to the file cabinet and pulled open the drawer. Grabbing the folder marked Martinez, she opened it on the desk.

There were two baptismal certificates. Juanita and another child six years older. She tried to decipher the spidery handwriting. Santino or Santina? Beneath them, she found letters addressed to Father Murphy with a Sarasota, Florida, return address. Andie hesitated only a moment before she stuffed them into the waistband of her jeans and pulled her T-shirt out to cover them. Leaving the baptismal records in the file, she closed it and placed it back in the cabinet. When she turned, the housekeeper's little boy was standing in the doorway.

Smiling, she waved as she backed slowly toward the window. When she felt the sill at the backs of her knees, she threw one leg over the ledge, ducked her head and dropped to her hands and knees on the ground.

"May I help you, young lady?"

It was the black shoes she saw first, and her heart plummeted. Very slowly she moved her gaze up the long, black robe. The elderly man had wispy, white hair, pale blue eyes, and he was as thin and frail as his voice.

Getting quickly to her feet, Andie wiped her hands on her jeans. "I'm looking for Father Murphy."

"Father Murphy," he repeated. For a moment he looked puzzled. Then his expression cleared and he nodded. "I'm Father Murphy. Would you like to sit for a while in the garden?"

Andie took his arm and led him across the lawn to a cushioned chair near the flower beds. Once he was settled, he pointed to the different rows of blooms, naming each one. When he looked at her, his eyes were quite lucid. "Did I get them right? Some days I can't remember them all."

Andie smiled as she sat on the grass near his feet. "I can only vouch for the roses. They're lovely."

The elderly man studied her for a moment. "Do I know you?"

"No. I'm staying over at Heagerty Vineyards, and I came to ask you about the Martinez family. They used to be members of your parish, but they moved away about twenty years ago."

He frowned for a moment. "Martinez?" Then suddenly he smiled. "Lucia. She used to stop by after church to admire my garden. She came by a few days ago. Last week, I think it was. Such a lovely young woman. Two beautiful children."

"The woman I'm thinking about would be older, in her late forties. One of her children died twenty years ago."

"Lovely young woman," Father Murphy murmured as he leaned back in the chair and closed his eyes.

"What do you think you're doing?"

Andie turned to see the housekeeper running across the lawn. She had her son clutched tightly in her arms. "I told you to call and make an appointment with my aunt."

Though the woman kept her voice low, Andie could hear the anger vibrating in it. "He's an old man, and he needs his rest."

Rising, Andie raised her hands, palms out. "I'm going."

She found Nick waiting in the car this time.

"Sorry," he said. "The phone rang, and she insisted on answering it. Then I heard her tearing out the back door."

Andie raised an eyebrow. "So you took off?"

He shot her a grin. "I knew my partner would know how to handle the situation. What did you get?"

"A face-to-face interview with Father Murphy."

He gave a low whistle. "I'm impressed."

"Don't be. His memory's sporadic at best. He claims that Mrs. Martinez visited him last week, and she was a beautiful young woman."

"She'd be close to fifty, right?"

Andie nodded, then remembered the letters. She pulled them out. "I got these from the file."

"You actually *stole* something from a rectory?"

She smiled sweetly at him. "Plan B. You'd had about five minutes with the housekeeper. I figured your charm was wearing thin. Besides, you're so good at breaking and entering, I knew you could easily return these when we're finished."

Nick laughed as he shifted in the seat to face her. "Admit it, Field." He ran a hand down the length of her arm. "Life is a lot more fun if you break a few rules."

For a moment she couldn't speak. There was something so appealing about the laughter curving his lips and the challenge in his eyes. For just a moment she allowed herself to wonder what it might be like to meet that challenge.

Nick leaned forward and brushed his lips against hers. "There you go. Just keep thinking about it. It won't be long."

When he pulled back, it was more than laughter she saw in his eyes. There was a hint of need. And in spite of everything, she wanted to fill that need. Drawing in a deep breath, she dropped her glance to the letters she still held in her hand and quickly divided them up. "Business first."

"The postmark's Sarasota," Nick observed as he slipped folded pages out of the first envelope. "That narrows it some."

For a time they read in silence. A car sped past, stirring up dust and pushing a hot blast of air against the car. Neither of them glanced up. Andie finished first. "In every one of these, Lucia Martinez talks about Juanita as if she were still alive. And she doesn't even mention the older child."

"She'd lost a child. For years, I used to try and imagine what that must be like."

The pain in his voice made her glance up. His hands had fisted, crumpling the letters. She covered his hands with hers. "You don't think there's any chance that Juanita survived?"

"No," Nick replied in a flat tone. "I went to the funeral. Later my father showed me the death certificate along with the check he'd written to the little girl's parents. He wanted to make sure I knew what I'd done and how much it was going to cost him to protect the Heagerty name."

Without thinking, Andie laid her hand on his cheek.

"If I just hadn't—" Nick began.

"It was an accident. You've got to stop blaming yourself."

"What do you know about it?" There was anger, hot and ripe, in the look he gave her. It took only seconds to fuel her own.

"Plenty. Do you think you're the only person who's ever caused a child's death? For months after I shot that boy in the alley, a day didn't go by that I didn't replay every single moment in my mind, trying to find some way that I could have done it differently. If I'd just aimed lower, or maybe higher. Or a little further to the left."

"And your partner might have been dead."

"I know that." She took a deep breath and let it out. Temper. She couldn't afford to let it get in the way of what she wanted to say. When she spoke again, her voice was calm and she met his eyes steadily. "I know that I saved my partner's life that night. But I can't bring the boy back to life. And I had to learn to accept that. Once I did, I realized I had two choices. I could wallow in regrets, or I could let it go and get on with my life."

Nick's eyes narrowed. "I've gotten on with my life."

"By running away! You're still letting something that happened twenty years ago influence every decision you make!"

Control wasn't something he lost easily. But the hell of it was she was right! It was the last rational thought he had as he reached for her. But the moment his lips touched hers, the anger streamed away, and all he could feel was her. The quick heating of her skin beneath his hands, the softness of her lips as they yielded, and the honeyed warmth of her mouth as he deepened the kiss. And her taste, sweet, tart, and addictive.

He wanted more. Craved more. Desperate, he took his

mouth on a journey to her throat where her blood pulsed against his lips. A quick nip of his teeth drew a low murmur from her. It took a minute for the sound to penetrate. His name.

He was trembling as he took her mouth again. And when it yielded, soft with invitation, he knew he was lost. Nothing, no one had ever made him feel this way. Even as he plunged deeper, greedy for every nuance of her flavor, fear sliced through him. He should push her away now, while there was time, and run. But even as the thought formed in his mind, he was dragging her closer and jerking her shirt out of her jeans.

His hands were rough, desperate, as they moved over her. But she pressed closer, eager, until they found her breasts. He'd never touched her quite like this before. Beneath the urgency and the demand, there was something more. More than the heat, more than the desire that radiated from him, she could feel his emotions. So free. She had no defense against them as they poured into her.

Even as she ran her hands up his arms to grip his shoulders and urge him closer, she felt a part of herself give way. And then she was tumbling in a free fall, deeper and deeper. Everywhere he touched her, there were tiny explosions that tempted and promised. No one had ever made her feel this way. It was delightful. It was terrifying. And she didn't want it to stop. It would be easy, so easy to forget the rules she had laid down, and the reason for them. It would be so easy to believe that there was only this moment and this man.

A truck raced by on the highway. Gravel spewed and pinged against the fenders. Dust swirled up in spirals. The car was still vibrating when Nick found the strength to drag his mouth away from hers. With an oath, he buried his face against her and struggled for control. His breathing was fast and ragged, as if he'd run to the top of a very steep cliff. And he'd very nearly jumped off with no thought of anything or anyone but her. No one had ever made him feel this way.

He wanted to push her away. The moment he trusted himself to move, he would. But when she laid her cheek against his and murmured his name, he simply held her.

"What are we going to do?" she asked.

"Several things come to mind," he said.

"I'm serious." But Nick could feel her lips curve against his neck before she continued. "We can't..."

"We not only can, but we will," Nick affirmed. "But I promised we'd stick to your rules for a while longer. And I'm not sure that the front seat of a car fits your rule about a 'better place.'"

Andie pulled back then so that she could see him. There he sat, his hair still rumpled by her hands, grinning. It was at that moment, with the sun streaming down on them, that she suddenly realized what she hadn't quite grasped seconds ago in his arms.

She was in love with him. Not just for the way he could make her feel when he touched her. She was in love with the man who had bought his niece a puppy so she would feel safe at night. With the man who had been isolated and driven away by his own family. With the man who, in spite of everything that had happened to him, could still see the funny side of life.

A man who was willing to abide by her "rules" even when *she* was ready to toss them aside.

She wanted to shout it out loud.

She wanted to get out of the car and run.

But she could do neither because there was Sarah to think of.

"You're right," she finally said with a brief glance around the front seat. "I've always found a car too cramped." Then praying that her hand would be steady, she began to gather up the letters that had fallen crumpled and forgotten on the floor of the car.

When his hand covered hers, she jolted. Nick smiled, pleased by her reaction. And he was very much aware that his own pulse hadn't quite steadied.

"We've got to concentrate on finding who's after Sarah," Andie said.

"Agreed." He leaned over to pick up the remaining letters. "Did you notice they were all written within the first two years after the accident?"

"Odd," Andie murmured as she sorted through the letters, checking the postmarks. "Why would she stop writing so abruptly? Unless..." Suddenly she glanced up at Nick. "In the last ones I read, she was almost incoherent. You don't think—"

He pulled his cellular phone out. "Mendoza can check the death records and mental hospitals in the Sarasota area. You make the call while I drive."

He was turning the key in the ignition when she took his hand. "I want to make a stop on the way back to the vineyard."

"Where?" Nick asked.

"The intersection where you had the accident."

He turned to look at her. "Why?"

She met his eyes steadily. "If I'm right, and there's a connection between what happened that night and what's happening to Sarah, then it all started there."

He said nothing for a moment because his first impulse was to say no. The last time he'd been to that intersection had been on the night of the accident. Not once in the five years since he'd returned to Heagerty Vineyards had he driven through it. Coincidence? Nick recalled the accusation she'd hurled at him earlier, that he was running away. "It's not exactly a fresh crime scene," he said. "What do you expect to find there?"

Opening the glove compartment, Andie exchanged the small pile of letters for a folded manila envelope. "I'm not sure. I brought the copies of the accident report with the sketches the two cops made of the accident that night. I thought if I walked through it, I might be able to get a clearer idea of what happened. I could do it by myself, but you were there."

"Okay." When he saw the surprise in her eyes, he continued. "You accused me of running away. Maybe it's time I stopped."

Except for making the call to Lieutenant Mendoza's office, they said nothing during the drive. The sun was hot, the air cool as it whipped by. The road twisted along the shoreline, offering a glimpse of sparkling water every now and then. It was a perfect day for a sail, or a ride in a convertible. But Nick's hands were tense on the wheel. He concentrated on relaxing them as he glanced over at Andie. She sat, staring straight ahead. Even in profile, he could see she had that warrior look on her face.

He didn't smile, but as he turned the car down the road to the intersection where the accident had occurred, some of his own tension eased. As they drove away from the lake, the land became hilly, the breeze warmer.

Nick heard the bark of a dog as he drove past a farm, but he focused on the road. This is the way he'd come that night, he suddenly realized. The turn he'd just taken was the same one he'd used over and over to get home from the high school. Ahead, he could just see the yellow light blinking, and he automatically took his foot off the gas pedal. Ten feet from the intersection, he pulled to the side of the road.

Andie looked at him then. "Ready?"

"What's your plan?"

"I thought we could walk through it. It's something I like to do at a crime scene. I know it sounds corny, like a scene out of an Agatha Christie novel, but it makes it easier for me to picture what really happened. All you have to do is be your car. I'll be the Martinez car." Opening the envelope, she handed him a copy of the accident report. "Give me a few minutes to get to the other side of the light."

When he nodded, she climbed out of the car. On one side of the road, corn grew in neat diagonal rows. On the other, a deep wide ditch separated the highway from a field overgrown with tall grass. Wildflowers bloomed where they pleased, blue and yellow. Fat bees buzzed around them.

It didn't surprise her that the scene looked so ordinary. Most crime scenes did. She'd often thought the mundane appearance of a crime scene emphasized the futility of what had occurred there.

As she reached the intersection, a truck slowed to a stop. She waited for it to pass before she walked in a wide circle, checking the visibility from all four directions. Only one approach presented a problem. The road from the north climbed a steep hill just before it leveled off at the light. Shading her eyes, she turned to study it. What she could see before it curved out of sight reminded her of a rippled ribbon. Anyone driving from this direction wouldn't see the red light blinking until they were almost upon it.

She glanced down at the rough sketch of the accident, then turning around, she moved to the lane in the road where the Martinez car had been drawn. When she'd paced twenty yards away from the intersection, she turned and began to approach the blinking caution light.

Leaning against the side of the convertible, Nick watched Andie work. Thorough. That's what she was, he thought as he watched her shove grass aside and move into the ditch where the police sketch had placed the Martinez car. He might tease her about strategy and force her to bend her precious "rules," but there was a relentlessness to her methods he admired. He watched her climb out of the ditch, swat a bee away, then pace back down the lane the Martinez car had driven along that night.

That night. He didn't want to think about it even now.

Overhead, a crow cawed loudly as it circled the cornfield. Nick made himself look around. The scene seemed peaceful enough. The only warning of danger was the traffic light blinking; yellow in one direction, red in the other. As he looked at it, he began to think. Pushing himself away from the car, he paced down the road away from the light, the way he'd seen Andie do. Turning, he forced his thoughts back twenty years.

It had been a dark night. Humid. He could recall how thick the air had been. Heavy and misted with the threat of rain, it offered only the slightest relief as it pushed through the open windows of his car. The only sound had been the radio. A Beatles song with a slow, steady rhythm. He'd been using it, he recalled, to keep his foot easy on the accelerator. Slow was better because of the high he was on, not so much from the beer he'd drunk, but from their basketball victory. He remembered braking slightly as he'd approached the intersection.

Ordinarily he wouldn't have had even one beer. Not while he had the car. He wouldn't have been driving at all if his father had come to the game. The symphony concert and the benefit party that Marguerite and Michael were hosting at the vineyard had provided just enough of an excuse for his family to miss it.

Ahead he could just make out the glow of the yellow light blinking on and off. Slowly he walked forward. The lights of the oncoming car had appeared quite suddenly, twenty yards away, then ten. He was only two car length's from the intersection when another set of headlights appeared to his left, and then the ones in front of him had disappeared, blocked by the other car speeding through the intersection.

Nick felt a cold stab of fear, a hot bubble of panic. He could recall how his hands, slick with sweat, had slipped on the steering wheel before he got a good grip and turned it hard. He could hear the scream of tires on asphalt, smell the burning rubber. Then his car teetered for one precarious moment before he was thrown across the seat and the pain exploded in his head.

"Nick!"

He blinked twice before he realized that it was Andie standing in front of him. She was holding his hands. He gripped hers hard. "There was a third car," he said.

"I know. And it caused the accident. You weren't to blame." Withdrawing her hands, she pulled the police sketch from her pocket and pointed to the drawing. "Look. Coming from your direction, there are no skid marks in the left lane. It's the Martinez car that skidded into the oncoming lane of traffic before it turned over into the ditch. He pulled the wheel left, and you pulled to the right. And you did it to avoid the car running the red light. The police should have seen it."

She turned to look at the ditch. Choked with grass and wildflowers, it gave no sign of the tragedy that had occurred there so many years before. "If Mendoza can just locate Mr. Martinez—" She came to a sudden stop and whirled to face him. "Your Aunt Maggie might know something about what went on that night. She was very nervous the day she told me about it."

"Aunt Maggie." Nick nodded as he met her eyes squarely.

# 8

NICK DROVE FAST on the way back to the vineyard. It took skill and concentration, so he didn't have to think. And he didn't want to think about the possibility that Marguerite might have known something about the accident all these years, something she'd kept hidden. During his stay in the hospital, she had been the only person who'd visited him. The only one who'd listened to his story. Had it all been an act? No, it was better if he didn't even consider that possibility. Otherwise the knot of ice in his stomach that he recognized as rage just might break free. Anger would get him nowhere with Aunt Maggie.

When the guard waved him through the gate, he drove past the turn to the garage and parked the car instead on a verge of grass near the stairs to the beach. What he needed, wanted more than anything, was a long sail. Meeting the challenge of high winds would help him regain his perspective.

Three quick strides brought him to the edge of the cliff. The water was mirror smooth. The *Nomad* sat so still in the water, it looked like a painting. The quick, staccato barks of a dog brought his attention to the sandy beach just as Sarah's delighted giggle floated up from below. She was struggling with a fishing pole, bent almost in half, and hanging from its hook was a fish.

"It's huge," Andie said as she reached his side. Even as she spoke, the pole bent further, snapping the line, and the fish began to flop over and over again on the sand.

Brutus raced toward it, yapping sharply, then paused to sniff. When the fish flipped over, the puppy raced away, barking furiously, then skidded, digging his paws into the sand, and rushed back to attack again. Just in time, Grady grabbed the broken line and hoisted the fish out of harm's way. Sarah made a grab for Brutus, missed and fell onto the sand.

Andie laughed. "It's better than a keystone cops movie."

"Don't let Grady hear you say that." Nick was chuckling as he led the way down the steep wooden stairs to the beach.

The moment Sarah spotted them, she gave up chasing Brutus and raced toward them across the sand. Her new jeans were soaked, her feet bare, and when she held out her arms, Nick scooped her up and settled her on his hip as if he'd been doing it for years. She smelled like fish and sunshine, and when she pressed her cheek against his, he felt his heart turn over. What was left of the cold knot in his stomach melted.

"Did you see?" She was laughing, breathless.

"It's almost as big as you are," Nick said.

"How did you pull it in?" Andie asked.

Sarah shrugged. "Grady told me what to do. It was easy."

"She's a natural born fisherman," Grady added, lifting the fish higher to keep it out of Brutus's frantic reach.

Sarah turned to Nick. "Grady said he'd cook whatever I caught. Can he?"

Nick thought briefly of the conversation he'd yet to have with Marguerite, and the strained, formal dinner that would inevitably follow. "Absolutely. We'll have a picnic on the boat, and if the wind picks up, we'll go for a sail."

After hugging Nick tightly, Sarah scrambled back down to the sand, then began to walk back to the water. With one hand, she beckoned Grady to join her. "C'mon, we've got to clean it."

Nick laughed out loud as he turned to Grady. "I always

thought that the one thing you needed was a good woman ordering you around.''

''Same goes, my friend.'' Grady was grinning from ear to ear as he followed Sarah across the sand to a large, flat rock that extended out into the water.

Andie said nothing. She wasn't sure she could. Her throat was tight, her heart full. She simply watched Sarah climb up to kneel on the rock. When Brutus joined her, she scooped the puppy onto her lap. The moment she did, the dog calmed. When Grady opened his tackle box, Sarah leaned over to inspect the contents.

*Where in the world was the prim and proper little girl she'd ridden with on the train?* That was the question Andie wanted to ask Nick. But she couldn't. How right Rose had been to send her little girl here. To this man. Turning, she looked at Nick. Did he know how his face softened whenever he was around Sarah? Was he even aware of how comfortably he'd held her only moments ago? There were so many things she wanted to say to him and couldn't. It was too soon to give voice to any of her thoughts.

And she might never have to. Very soon Nick would understand for himself how right it was for him to keep Sarah and raise her. And when he did, her job would be over. She could go back to Boston and begin to build up her business.

She thought of it now. How excited she'd been about the small office she'd leased. The pride she'd taken in the even smaller list of clients she'd built up. Each one had been understanding and loyal when she'd temporarily turned them over to her ex-partner from the Boston police force. She fingered the angel charm as she thought of him. He'd retired at the same time that she'd resigned, and she'd offered him temporary work whenever he wanted it.

It all seemed ages ago. How long had she been away? A matter of days, but it felt like weeks. On the train ride from

Boston, she'd been eager to go back. Now the thought made her feel empty, lonely.

Because, like Sarah, she was no longer exactly the same person she'd been only days before.

"Let's find Aunt Maggie," Nick said.

She turned to find him looking at her, his expression sober. She wouldn't have to leave until they solved the mystery of who was threatening Sarah. It was the one thing she could do for both of them before she left. Andie held on to the thought all the way up the narrow flight of wooden stairs.

THEY HEARD raised voices the minute they entered the foyer. Sandra Martin hurried toward them down the hall.

"Mr. Heagerty, I was just coming to look for you. Jeffrey is so angry...." She let her own words trail off as Jeffrey's voice drowned them out.

"I don't understand you. You claim you have my interests at heart. I've told you that I need time!"

"You've had time. Five years." Marguerite's voice was calm, controlled. "Now you must face up to your responsibilities and run Heagerty Vineyards as your father and grandfather would have wanted you to."

"How do you know what they'd want? Are they speaking to you from the grave?"

"Jeffrey! I won't take that tone from you!"

"Never mind!" There was the sound of footsteps on hardwood floors. "It's useless for me to talk to you. You don't understand. You never have!" Jeffrey stormed into the hallway, paused for only a moment when he saw Nick, then strode toward him, waving a folded newspaper. "I had nothing to do with this."

"What is it?" Nick asked.

"The society column. Mother had lunch with her friend, Lonnie Harris, yesterday. Now it's common knowledge that you're going to sign the papers turning the winery over to me at our annual festival on Labor Day. Maybe you can talk some sense into her.'' Tossing the paper on a table, Jeff pushed past them.

The sound of the front door slamming was still vibrating in the air as Nick and Andie walked down the length of the drawing room to where Marguerite sat in the wing-back chair.

Sandra Martin spoke from the archway to the hall. ''Shall I go after him?''

Marguerite pressed a hand to her temple. ''Yes, per-haps—''

Her reply was interrupted by the sound of a car engine roaring to life. Seconds later the red convertible could be seen through the window, spewing gravel as it raced down the driveway.

Marguerite rose hurriedly from her chair, holding her hands out to Nick. ''Stop him. Please.''

''Relax, Aunt Maggie. A few miles and he'll calm down. That's why he bought the car,'' Nick said as he settled himself in the wing-back chair across from hers. ''It's an escape valve.''

Marguerite turned to Sandra Martin. ''Go after him.''

When the young woman hesitated, Nick said, ''She'll never catch him. But if you really want to stop him, you can give the state police a ring and tell them to be on the lookout for a red convertible. Of course, there'd be the public scandal to take care of once the police arrested him.''

''Mrs. Heagerty—'' Sandra began.

Marguerite waved a hand. ''Never mind. Let him go.''

''Should I remove the tea things?'' Sandra asked.

''Later,'' Nick said as he reached for the pot and poured himself a cup. He waited for the young woman to leave the room before he met Marguerite's frown with a smile and shook his head. ''Aunt Maggie, Aunt Maggie, don't you know that if you play with fire, there's always the chance of getting burned?"

Marguerite's chin lifted even as she lowered herself into her chair. "I didn't—"

"Yes, you did. You purposely had lunch with Lonnie Harris at the *Rochester Democrat and Chronicle* so that she would print that little item about the wine festival. And you fully intended to light a fire under both Jeff and me."

Marguerite's eyes narrowed. "You gave your word."

"And I intend to keep it. I said I would turn the winery over to Jeff just as soon as he was ready to run it."

"He is," Marguerite said.

"I agree."

When Marguerite's mouth simply dropped open, Nick's smile widened. "Your problem isn't with me. It's with Jeff. *He* doesn't believe that he's ready yet. And the more you push him, the more he's going to rebel. Didn't you learn anything from observing what happened to me twenty years ago?"

Admiration was what Andie felt as she sat down on the low ottoman a few feet away. He'd walked into an explosive situation, diffused it, and then shifted his aunt's attention to the topic he'd come to discuss.

"I encouraged you to make peace with your father," Marguerite responded as her frown deepened.

Nick sipped his tea and nodded. "Yes, you did. All those days that I lay there in the hospital, you were the only person who came to see me. I've never forgotten that. And I ended up taking your advice. I didn't argue when my father told me that he was sending me away to school. You got me to believe that if I accepted his plan, and for once in my life didn't try to bolt in the opposite direction, I could somehow earn his forgiveness."

Andie listened as Nick went on, describing the days he'd spent in the hospital, believing that he'd been responsible for the death of a little girl. No wonder he had a soft spot for Marguerite, she thought as she studied the woman. She'd been his only visitor other than the police. But Marguerite was not happy with the turn that the conversation had taken. Her knuckles had turned white, her shoulders and jaw had tensed.

When Nick paused to pour himself more tea, Marguerite spoke. "You could help matters considerably if you would give Jeff the same advice right now. He pays attention to you."

"Perhaps. But I'm not sure the advice is sound. It didn't work for me."

Marguerite's face blanched. "What do you—"

"My father never forgave me. He never answered one of the letters I sent after I went away to school."

"He would have," Marguerite argued. "He needed time."

"And I didn't give him enough. I ran away from school and disgraced myself forever in his eyes." He set his cup on the glass-topped table. "There's a lesson there. You might learn from my mistakes and stop pressuring Jeff. All he's asking for is time."

Every inch the matriarch, Marguerite rose. "I don't need your advice about what's best for my son. He'll never accept his responsibilities to me and to this vineyard unless you leave."

Leaning back in the chair, Nick stretched out his legs and crossed them at the ankles. "I fully intend to leave. But not until this business with Sarah is settled to my satisfaction."

"Send her back to her grandmother."

"Do you have any reason to believe that Sarah would be any safer in Boston than here?" Andie asked.

Marguerite aimed a cold look at Andie. "Common sense tells me that she'd be safer with her grandmother. And I resent your constant implications that someone in this household might have something to do with the kidnapping attempts."

"It's not merely Ms. Field who suspects that. The police also believe that someone here is involved," Nick said. "The same person, perhaps, who stole the album from Ms. Field's room."

"What album?" Marguerite asked.

"Mrs. Mabrey, the librarian in Tollerville, gave me a pictorial history of the Heagerty family," Andie explained.

"What does this album have to do with anything?" Marguerite addressed the question to Nick.

"Now that's the question I keep coming back to. It seems that the album contained newspaper clippings of everything that occurred the night that Juanita Martinez died. Ms. Field has a theory that the accident is connected somehow to the danger that Sarah is in." With one hand he stopped his aunt's reply. "I thought it was a stretch, too, until I revisited the scene of the accident today."

Marguerite sank slowly into her chair. "I should think you'd want to forget all about that night."

"That's what you encouraged me to do, wasn't it? Forget about it. Put it in the past. Go away to school until my father's anger had cooled, and then return as the prodigal son, welcomed with open arms. There's only one small problem. The story didn't end that way. And now I find that my niece's life may be in danger because things were covered up that night."

"Covered up?" Marguerite gripped the arms of her chair. "That's ridiculous!"

"That was my first reaction, too. But when we went back to that intersection today, we had the sketches the police drew of the accident. I told you the first time you came to see me that I'd seen a third car. It ran the blinking red light, and I ended up in the ditch trying to avoid it. You believed me, too. I could see it in your eyes."

For a moment Marguerite said nothing. Then she turned to Andie. "It happened such a long time ago. Why are you digging it all up again?"

"Did you ever talk to Mr. and Mrs. Martinez about the third car?" Nick asked.

"I assumed the police did—"

Nick rose from the chair. "Forget the police. What about you? What about my father? Did you ever tell him about the third car?"

Marguerite's hand went to her breast. "You... I..." She paused for a moment. Pressing her lips firmly together, she rose from the chair and drew herself up to her full height. "No one else saw that third car."

For a moment Nick merely looked at his aunt. Then he said, "You didn't tell my father, did you?"

Marguerite didn't answer. Instead she turned and walked from the room. When Nick turned to Andie, his eyes were empty, flat. "You're right. She's hiding something," he said.

As she followed Nick from the room, Andie tried to think of something to say. Some way to comfort him. They were passing the staircase when she thought she saw something, a movement in the upstairs hall. She took the steps two at a time, but when she reached the top, the hallway was empty. "Nothing," she said as she turned to find Nick beside her.

"C'mon." He took her arm and led her down the stairs. "We'll talk some place more private."

THERE WAS SILENCE in Nick's office except for the sound of metal twisting into a cork. He was angry. Andie could see it in his short, jerky movements as he poured the wine. And she could feel it radiating from him. Still, she wasn't prepared for the raw fury in his eyes when he turned to hand her a glass. It took all her control not to step back. She'd seen the same kind of anger that day when she'd pulled the gun on him at the back of the library. He'd had a right to be angry with her then. There was an argument to be made that he had a right now. After all, hadn't she pushed him and prodded him into facing his past? And now...

"Why?" he asked.

He wasn't looking at her any longer, but at some space beyond her. So he wasn't angry at her, after all. The realization should have brought relief. It would have if she hadn't had such a clear idea of what it was he was seeing. Without thinking, she moved to him and put her arms around him. His body was tensed tight as a spring. She rested her head against his shoulder. "I don't know," she said.

For a moment Nick said nothing. All he could do was stand there as the simplicity of her gesture, the sweetness of it, poured through him. He wasn't sure of everything that he was feeling. All he was sure of was that the iciness of his anger was melting away. He pulled her closer. "You asked me once why I went along with her request to sign the winery over to Jeff. Part of it was because my family always treated her as an outsider. Being an outcast myself, I think I've always felt a sort of kinship with her. My grandfather was a proud man, proud of the Heagerty name. But the only way he could convince John Manetti to sell this vineyard to him was to agree to let Marguerite marry one of his sons. Once Manetti died, Marguerite was always having to prove herself worthy of being a Heagerty. It's a terrible thing to say, but I think my grandfather was secretly relieved when Uncle Mike died, and he could arrange it so that the winery would remain in Heagerty hands. When I accepted her offer, I thought it would be a hell of a revenge on the whole family if I turned the place back over to someone with Manetti blood."

Andie said nothing, but she continued to hold him.

"Now I'm not sure what to think. She's the only one who spoke to me after the accident. She assured me she'd speak to my father, explain what happened. And it was all a lie."

Andie stepped back and moved her hands up to frame his face. "You weren't to blame for what happened twenty years ago. You were sixteen, and she was the only one who offered you comfort. You shouldn't regret taking it. We'll find out the truth."

When he pulled her closer for a kiss, she felt his body soften against hers. His mouth softened, too. There was none of the passion, none of the fire that she'd come to expect from his kiss. There was none of the pressure, none of the demand she'd come to expect from his touch. Replacing everything was a tenderness that sent her emotions tumbling out of control.

"Andie..." He whispered her name, only her name, as he teasingly changed the angle of the kiss. But she knew exactly what he was asking, and she felt herself giving it as the drowsy warmth that filled her turned into an ache.

"Excuse me." The words were followed by a loud thumping noise.

Andie and Nick sprang apart to see Lieutenant Mendoza looking very pleased in the doorway to the office.

"Sorry, guys. I did knock." He demonstrated by pounding his fist on the doorjamb. "Several times," he added as he pulled out his notebook and settled himself in the nearest chair. "I have good news and bad. Mrs. Martinez died ten years ago in a state mental hospital. However, the restaurant mentioned in the letters no longer exists under that name. I talked to Nolan, and he's sending one of his people down there to see if he can track down Mr. Martinez." He put the notebook back in his pocket. "Once that happens we may even get a line on the older kid." Leaning back in his chair, he grinned at them. "Looks to me like the two of you are making progress, too."

"Actually, we are," Andie said, and she quickly summarized what they'd learned at the accident scene and from their interrogation of Marguerite.

"None of which brings us any closer to who is trying to kidnap Sarah," Nick commented when she was finished.

It was her own thought exactly, though she preferred not to give voice to it. Instead she said, "That means it's time to go back to the beginning and consider each suspect again." Suddenly she frowned. "I wish I had that album. I'm sure there's something in it that we've missed. C'mon." Rising, she led the way into the reception area and flipped on the track lighting so that the wall of Heagerty family photos was illuminated. "A lot of the pictures I saw in the album were ones I'd seen here." She pointed to one. "This appeared in the society column the day after the accident."

"The guy in the middle was the conductor of the Rochester Philharmonic," Nick said. "My parents are to his right. Patrick and Rose are next to Marguerite."

"What's so important about the picture?" Mendoza asked.

"I don't know," Andie said, staring at it. "I just keep thinking that we're missing something." Shoving her hands into her pockets, she began to pace. "We've got two things we know for sure. Someone is trying to kidnap Sarah. And someone tried to cover up what really happened on the night that little Juanita Martinez died."

"You don't think it's the same perp?" Mendoza asked.

"I'm not sure. Who would have a motive for doing both?"

Mendoza thought for a moment. "Conrad Forrester has no connection to the accident. Mr. Martinez or the older kid might have a reason for kidnapping Sarah—revenge. But why would they want to cover up what really happened that night?"

There was a moment of silence before Nick spoke. "Aunt Maggie might have a motive for both. The winery means everything to her. Kidnapping seems a stretch, but she feels very strongly that Heagerty Vineyards belongs to Jeff, and she's clearly threatened by the idea that I might change my mind and stay here to raise Sarah. Plus, she may have tried to cover up what really happened the night of the accident. What I can't figure out is why, or what that has to do with what's happening now. At that time, I wasn't in line to inherit the place. Unless..."

"She was driving the third car." Mendoza finished the thought out loud, then pointed to the picture. "But this looks like an alibi to me."

"And that brings us right back to square one," Andie said.

They were all standing, studying the picture as if it held the answer, when Nick's cellular phone rang. He flipped it open. "Sarah?" A smile lit his face instantly. "We're on our way. You got time for a fish dinner?" he asked Mendoza on the way out. "My niece caught it."

NICK CLIMBED UP the ladder to the deck of the *Nomad* and grabbed the towel he'd left on the railing. The last wispy, crimson streaks in the west struggled against the encroaching gray. Day was losing its battle with the night. And he couldn't get rid of the feeling that he was losing, too. Something. Even the brief swim he'd taken hadn't eased his restlessness.

The silence was broken only by the occasional drone of a motor as diehard fishermen finally headed their boats to shore. The smell of grilled fish still lingered faintly in the air. Above it Nick caught the scent of Rose's garden. And the thought came, sudden and unbidden, of walking there with Andie in the moonlight.

He hadn't been able get her out of his mind since she'd left with Sarah and Grady and Mendoza in the dinghy. Over and over, his thoughts had returned to that moment in his office when she'd simply held him. There'd been no punch of desire, no fire in his blood. All he'd felt was a sweetness, a steady warmth that was like coming home. And he hadn't wanted to let it go. Ever.

If he could just sail. But the air had remained still, and the lake lay smooth as a seamless sheet of black satin beneath the boat. Tomorrow, he promised himself. The weathercaster had predicted brisk winds, and he'd given his word to Sarah that she'd have her first sailing lesson in the morning.

Turning, Nick leaned against the rail and looked into the galley. He'd always been more comfortable on the boat than anywhere else. But tonight, with Andie smiling at him across the table and Sarah's laughter in the air, he'd felt at peace, as if he'd finally come home. The place seemed empty now. It struck him quite suddenly that he wanted them both here. With him.

And that was impossible. He looked up at the house. He didn't want to stay here, did he? He'd been running away from Heagerty Vineyards most of his adult life. Even if Marguerite had lied about the accident and somehow manipulated events to serve her own purposes, it didn't change anything.

He'd learned to live without trust and love. Love? No, loyalty. Why would the word *love* pop into his mind?

He'd stood in this same position less than a week ago and looked up at the rooms where his niece and Andie were sleeping. He'd been eager to be rid of them, anxious to be back running his charter sailing business. It seemed like months ago, not days.

Tonight he was looking at the same windows, but everything had changed. He had changed.

The sound of the small motor had him tensing, then relaxing as he watched the small dinghy move away from the shore. Even in the moonlight, he could see that it was Andie behind the wheel.

With her hand on the throttle, Andie concentrated on guiding the small craft toward Nick's sailboat. Only days ago she'd made this same trip. That time it had been for Sarah. She wouldn't lie to herself that her visit tonight had anything to do with the little girl. It had everything to do with the man she could see standing at the railing of the *Nomad.*

He'd stood in that very spot, alone on the deck of his boat, when she'd left earlier to take Sarah back to the house. She hadn't been able to rid her mind of the image. He'd spent so much of his life as a loner, wandering from place to place. And it shouldn't have to be that way. As soon as Sarah was tucked safely in bed, she'd felt the urgent need to return. Grady's offer to stay with Sarah and finish reading Nancy Drew's latest adventure had given Andie the opportunity she'd been waiting for.

With a quick turn of her wrist, she brought the dinghy parallel to the boat and cut the engine. She was taking a huge risk. Not that taking risks was anything new. But she couldn't remember ever taking one without carefully weighing the consequences. Never before had she thrown caution to the winds as she was doing tonight. And the worst of it was, she didn't have a plan. Once she climbed on that boat, she didn't know what she'd do. All she could be sure of was that Nick Heagerty wouldn't be spending the night alone. Reaching out, she grabbed the ladder, tied the rope to it and climbed onto the *Nomad.*

The moment she saw him, the fear began to seep in, pushing at the edges of her mind, making her fingertips tingle. He was wearing only the cut-off denims he'd been swimming in. Just looking at him was enough to stop her dead in her tracks. How many times had she imagined him just like this, standing on the deck of his boat with drops of water glistening on his skin? What she'd discovered that afternoon in the car with the sunlight streaming around them was only confirmed now in the moonlight. She loved him. Through the fear and the first stirrings of her own passion, she felt a quiet joy. She couldn't turn and run any more than she could stop the rapid beating of her heart.

She walked to him then, trying to appear confident. As she drew closer, what she saw in his eyes made the confidence real. Raising her hand to his cheek, she said, "I want you."

Nick didn't move, stunned by the ache he felt. He didn't know which was more seductive, those three words or the softness of her touch. He said nothing as he stared down at her, but what he saw in her eyes was everything he wanted, everything he would ever need.

She was so lovely. He'd thought of her before as an angel, both guardian and avenging. But tonight, with the moonlight spilling over her, she looked more like a witch. And she'd already cast her spell.

She raised her other hand to his chest, and it was enough to have his body coiling tight with desire, his mind swimming with needs. She was pulling so much out of him, and he couldn't seem to stop her. Before he gave everything, he asked, "Andie?"

She smiled. "I think it's time for Plan B."

"And tomorrow?" he asked.

She moved her hand to his lips to silence him. "Sarah is well guarded. Tomorrow we'll decide what to do. Tonight seems a perfect time to break some rules."

Her hand was so cool on his mouth, her eyes so warm and dark. The dull ache that had already begun to build turned suddenly sharp and stabbing. He wouldn't resist her. He couldn't. He'd never wanted anyone like this, and he never would, he realized as he pressed his lips into her palm. Then he lifted just a strand of her hair and rubbed it between his fingers. He couldn't get over how soft it felt. "I wanted to do this the first time I saw you at the train station." Gently, he tucked the strand behind her ear.

Keeping her eyes steady on his, she slid her hand to his

shoulder, then pulled him toward her so that his mouth was close. So close that she could feel his breath on her lips. "When Rose first asked me to check you out, she gave me a picture of you that I clipped to your file. Your mouth fascinated me. I dreamed of kissing you even then. Kiss me now."

For a moment he didn't do as she asked. He merely touched her, running his hands down her, gliding his fingertips over her throat, across her shoulders, then slowly down the sides of her breasts to her waist, reminding himself of her fragility, her strength. She was so slender, her waist so small he could span half of it with one hand. Pressing his fingers into her hips, he pulled her closer. Then he took her mouth with his.

He hungered. She hungered. Neither of them could get enough. He'd kissed her before with passion, with tenderness, and even with a friendly restraint. But this was new. She'd never known such devastating skill. His lips teased and tormented. His teeth tempted and aroused. Each sensation was so clear. The quick nip at her lower lip, then the soft brush of his tongue to heal the small hurt. Explosions of pleasure shot through her. Dimly, she recalled her fear of not having a plan. But she couldn't have foreseen this. There was no way she could have plotted a strategy for this. In her wildest dreams she couldn't even have imagined it.

Delighted, she wanted more. Digging her fingers into his shoulders, she pulled him closer. Once his body was pressed against hers, the fit was so right, so true. Instantly she felt his urgency, tasted his desperation. His greed fueled her own.

Then she was in his arms and the world spun and tilted as he carried her down the steps to the main cabin.

"I want to see you," he said as he laid her on his bunk. "All of you."

He took his time undressing her, drawing the T-shirt off,

then the jeans. When she was wearing nothing but a lacy bra and a triangle of satin riding low on her hips, he sat on the side of the bed and looked his fill. Moonlight poured through the porthole. Her skin was as pale as cream at her throat, as delicate as porcelain along her cheekbones. But it was her eyes that held him, mesmerized him. In their depths he could see everything she was feeling, including her trust. It was his for the taking. He reached out to her then, running only his fingertips up the long length of her leg, over her hip. Her body was just as he'd imagined it, straight and slim and supple. Her response as she reacted to his touch was everything he'd dreamed.

With the power drumming in his head, he traced his fingers over her stomach. She trembled, then sighed his name. Her breast filled his hand, small, fragile, and incredibly soft. Whatever he'd imagined, and he'd imagined quite a bit, this was more. She was more. When she murmured his name again, he ran his other hand up her thigh to the scrap of satin. The thin material slid under his palm, tempting him. Keeping his eyes on hers, he slipped his fingers beneath it and found her heat, then watched her eyes darken and cloud. Greed began to grow uncontrollably. He wanted more. He wanted everything.

*Magic* was the word that thrummed in Andie's mind. He had the hands of a magician, she thought as those long, clever fingers lit little fires along her skin. As they lingered, then pressed and then probed, she felt her body coil tight as a bowstring. Over and over, she struggled for a breath just to whisper his name. Fingers curled deep in the bedspread, she arched toward him even as he began to take his mouth on the same slow, torturous journey his hands had taken.

She couldn't think. She could only feel the scrape of his teeth at the back of her knee, the heat of his mouth on her breast. Each sensation ripped through her, catapulting her suddenly into a world of heat and pleasure and need. A place she'd never been before. Here there were no restrictions, no rules, and no need for them. Here there was no one but Nick.

Around him in the tiny cabin, the moonlight grew brighter. But Nick was aware only of Andie. He'd wanted everything from her, and there wasn't anything she'd denied him. Her generosity was endless, and now he was utterly lost, completely trapped in the hot, ripe passion they were creating between them. It surrounded them now. And she was his. He could feel it in the rapid fluttering of her heartbeat beneath his lips, taste it in the dampness of her skin, and smell it in the very air he breathed. She poured into him, filling him until he wasn't sure where she left off and he began.

She murmured his name, and just the sound was enough to push him closer to the edge. Then her hands were in his hair, dragging his mouth back to hers, and something snapped in both of them. Suddenly frantic, they fumbled together with the snap of his cutoffs and struggled to push the damp denim away. Then he dragged her beneath him.

He couldn't think. He could only feel as she wrapped her arms and legs around him and drew him inside. Though every muscle trembled, he rose above her to look into her eyes. Glazed and dark with pleasure, they were open and locked on his for one last moment. And he was hers.

"You." Just before his own vision blurred, he saw her lips form the word.

"Only you." He wasn't sure whether he'd said it or merely thought it as he buried his face in her hair. Then their bodies took over and they moved as one. Quickly, furiously. The ride was long and fast and climbed higher and higher. Her gasp of pleasure filled the small cabin seconds before his own.

AFTERWARD, Andie lay there, stunned, still holding him tightly, savoring the closeness. Had only moments passed?

She wasn't sure. Though she didn't know she had the energy, she ran her hand down his back for the simple pleasure of it. Then she tried her voice to see if it would work. "About those rules..."

He hadn't thought he had the strength to laugh, but the rumble started deep in his chest and erupted into the room. "Worth breaking, I'd say."

She ran her hand up his back, again for the pleasure of it. "That's one thing we can agree on, partner."

He managed to raise his head then and grinned down at her. "Let's just see how agreeable we can be."

And they did.

# 9

IT WAS A PERFECT DAY for a sail. Andie wondered if Nick had somehow magically conjured it up. The sun was a gold ball in the sky and as hot and soothing as a sauna. Earlier, when the wind had been up, Sarah had helped Nick steer while she and Grady had worked on the lines, adjusting the mainsail so the canvas would quiet, then stretch to its fullest whenever they changed direction.

The ride had been exhilarating; the feeling of power, seductive. With the wind whipping at her and the boat skimming faster and faster across the surface of the lake, Andie understood why Nick loved sailing. She could feel her worries and responsibilities melt away. All that remained was the sun and the water, and a feeling of utter relaxation.

Then suddenly the breeze that had been blowing quite steadily all morning had disappeared. Nick had Sarah on his lap, his head close to hers as he guided her hand on the tiller. So far he'd been skilled enough to capture every stray puff of wind. The movement of the water beneath the hull was quiet, and the mournful cry of a gull loud. Lifting his head from the deck, Brutus gave a sleepy bark before he drifted off again.

"Coming about," Nick said suddenly.

Ducking low to avoid the boom, Andie took the line Grady handed her and drew it in quickly as Nick brought the boat around. For a moment the sail ruffled and stilled before it puffed out once more. Then the boat moved forward slowly.

"He's good," Andie said as Grady secured the line.

Grady chuckled. "He's got the magic touch, all right. I'd have switched to engine power half an hour ago. But not Nick. Give him a sail and a deck beneath his feet, and he'd just as soon stay out here and go whichever way a stray breeze will blow him."

"A nomad." Andie smiled as she turned to watch Nick adjust Sarah's hand on the tiller. "Is that how the boat got its name?"

Grady joined her at the railing. "*Nomad* was his code name in the navy. Until I joined up with him, he always preferred to work alone. He doesn't like to have to depend on anyone but himself." He turned then to study his friend. "He's never told me much about his relationship with his family. He just says he doesn't want to be responsible for anyone else. But it's clear to me that he and Miss Sarah belong together."

And they did belong together. As she watched Sarah giggle at something her uncle whispered to her, Andie tried to ignore the band of pain that tightened around her heart. But she couldn't deny the longing that filled her. She wanted to be a part of their lives. But she didn't kid herself that she could. The one thing that she and Nick hadn't done during the night was talk. He was finding it difficult enough to accept Sarah, because he preferred to be alone. She could understand that. Life was safer that way. Simpler, she reminded herself. But there was something in Nick Heagerty's nature that wouldn't allow him to shirk responsibility. It was what had brought him back to the vineyard for the last five years. And she was betting that it would keep him from sending Sarah away.

He couldn't even turn his back completely on Marguerite. At breakfast she'd been noticeably distraught that Jeff had not returned, but she'd calmed down when Nick had offered to ask Mendoza to make some discrete inquiries.

As Nick steered the boat past a curve in the shoreline, Andie caught a glimpse of Heagerty House, and she felt her tension returning. Now they would to go back to the waiting game they were playing. Everyone was being watched, phone calls were being traced, and Jake Nolan might already have news from his Florida contacts. Something had to break soon, she told herself as she watched Grady grab the buoy and secure a rope to it.

In seconds Nick lowered the mainsail, and she and Sarah climbed up on the front deck to help him wrap the cover around it. When they were finished, Nick turned to Sarah. "So what did you think of your first sailing lesson?"

"I liked it best when we went fast," she said.

Grady laughed. "Next time the wind dies, you'll have to talk your uncle into using the engine."

Sarah looked around the deck. "Where's the engine? How fast can it go?"

Nick smiled as he ran a hand over her hair. "A speed demon, are you? C'mon, I'll show you. A good sailor should be familiar with every part of his boat."

"*Her* boat," Sarah said confidently.

The sound of his laughter filled the air as he led the way down the stairs into the galley. Then he and Grady lifted and set aside the stairtreads to reveal a large motor.

Even if Andie hadn't heard the quick whir that immediately faded into a low hum, the look that Nick and Grady exchanged would have alerted her.

"What is it?" she asked.

"Something that shouldn't be there." Nick pointed to a tangle of colored wires. "Let's go."

Grady moved quickly. Levering himself back up on the deck, he turned and extended his arms.

Nick was already lifting Sarah. "We're going to practice a fire drill now, sweetie. No one can talk until we're on the dinghy."

Andie's heart was in her throat as Nick boosted her onto the deck. A bomb. Thinking the word suddenly made it more real. The surge of panic propelled her halfway across the deck. Sarah. The little girl had just swung her leg over the railing, and Grady was waiting for her on the ladder.

Nick. She stopped short just as he grabbed her arm.

"Hurry," he said, pulling her with him.

Precious seconds ticked by as, one by one, they climbed down the ladder into the dinghy. Under Grady's skilled hands the motor sprang to life on the first try. Andie gripped Sarah's hand tightly in hers while Nick worked on the rope.

It seemed to take forever. Then, just as he freed them, they heard Brutus bark. The puppy poked his nose under the lowest rail and whined, then barked again.

In one smooth movement, Nick tossed the rope down and swung himself back onto the ladder. He paused only long enough to give the dinghy one hard push before he reboarded the *Nomad*.

"No!" Andie screamed the word, but it was lost in the roar of the motor as Grady opened the throttle and swerved sharply toward shore. Twisting around, Andie gripped Sarah tightly to her as she frantically searched for a glimpse of Nick.

He wasn't there. She knew a moment of pure terror. Frozen, she couldn't look at her watch. Desperately, she tried to calculate how much time had gone by. How much was left?

She wasn't aware of when the dinghy reached shore. Later, she wouldn't even remember getting out. With the fear tight in her throat, all she could think of was Nick, as if by will alone she could get him safely off the sailboat. He was going to be all right, she told herself. He had to be.

Suddenly she saw him. With Brutus tucked close under his arm, he swung himself over the railing and jumped. Andie saw the splash just as the first explosion ripped through the air.

She felt the scream tear through her throat, but she couldn't hear it. Nor could she feel her own heart racing, pumping against the fear. The light, blinding at first, gave way to a kaleidoscope of sensations. First, heat. In shimmering waves it raced toward shore, hitting with enough force to push them backward. Without taking her eyes off the water, she wrapped her arms around Sarah and held tight.

The mast crumpled as flames shot greedily up its length, then leapt for the sky. The smoke hit next. Thick with the smell of gasoline and burning wood, it clogged her throat and burned her lungs. Suddenly she couldn't see. Dragging Sarah with her, she ran forward to the edge of the water just as the second explosion hit. The force lifted the boat out of the water, splintering it into flaming pieces. A chunk of burning wood fell less than a yard away.

"Andie."

She jerked away from Grady when he tried to pull her back. "I have to see."

"Let me take Sarah."

She gave the little girl's hand to him, then moved further into the water, out of the next wave of smoke.

The wall of heat was less intense this time, but still it burned her eyes and seared her skin. She didn't even notice that it toppled her to her knees. Pieces of debris now littered the surface of the lake as far as she could see.

Had he been hit? Was he even now, unconscious, sinking to the bottom of the lake?

Ruthlessly, she pushed the image away and forced herself to scan the water slowly, methodically, searching for anything that moved. *He's all right. He has to be.* The words repeated themselves in her mind, over and over again.

Seconds became minutes. Terror gripped her with icy claws as she moved deeper into the water. How much time had gone by? How long could he hold his breath? She was vaguely aware of noises. Shouts from the cliff above, the piercing cry of the security alarm. Her vision was blurring. Frantic, she rubbed at her eyes, barely aware that she brushed away her own tears. Blinking rapidly, she walked further into the lake and began another thorough scan of the water.

She saw his hand first. Just his hand. Her feet lost contact with the bottom of the lake as she saw his head break the surface. Then she saw Brutus paddling smoothly through the water. She reached them in five strokes. And then she was holding him as if her life depended on it.

"You're all right," she murmured over and over as she ran her hands over him.

"I'm fine," Nick said as he stood and tugged her with him into shallower water. "Sarah?"

"With Grady. She's fine. I couldn't see you for so long..."

"I had to get as far away from the boat as I could before the gas tank blew." When they were both able to stand again with the water lapping at their knees, he turned to look at the spot where the *Nomad* had been. Where his home had been. Only pieces were left, some still burning on the surface of the lake. Turning back to Andie, he framed her face with his hands. When he'd first seen her in the water, he was sure he was imagining her. Even now he wasn't able to rid himself of the stark, raging terror that had filled him from the moment he'd heard the telltale whir of the bomb. The memory alone was enough to have his muscles trembling. As he'd jumped from the boat, he'd looked for the dinghy. He was sure it had reached shore. Almost.

"You're bleeding," Andie said as she touched his shoulder.

"I'm fine," he said. Very slowly, he lowered his mouth to hers. Her lips were soft, and as they heated beneath his, he felt his body relax, and very gradually, he let go of the fear. In its place came a slow, almost drowsy warmth that slid easily into an ache.

She was alive. She was whole. And so was he. When he stepped back, he looked into her eyes to reassure himself one last time. Then taking her hand, he pulled her with him toward the shore. Sarah was standing next to Grady, waiting for him. Brutus was barking and racing back and forth on the sand. They were all safe. He was going to make sure they stayed that way.

ANDIE SAT on the edge of her chair watching Nick pace back and forth behind his desk. Mendoza had taken the seat next to hers. Jake Nolan was leaning against the door with the leashed energy of a cat ready to spring.

The room was quiet. So quiet that they could hear the muffled sound of Sarah's laughter from the reception room next door where she was playing Monopoly with Grady.

Who, how and why? She'd had plenty of time to consider the questions during the past five hours while they'd waited for the state police and Jake and Lieutenant Mendoza to arrive and examine what was left of the *Nomad*.

When they'd first climbed up the stairs from the beach, Nick had refused any help from Marguerite or Sandra Martin, insisting, instead, that he and the others go directly to his office in the winery. Grady had brought clothes from the house, and Pierre had gone to the trouble of making them sandwiches and *pomme frites*. There'd been no opportunity to talk about what had happened because Nick had refused to let Sarah out of his sight.

But there'd been plenty of opportunity for reaction to set in. Andie found that her initial feeling of relief had faded. As she watched the light dim through the window behind Nick, she was reminded that time was running out.

Nick broke the silence. "You have to take Sarah back to Boston."

Andie folded her hands in her lap. "No."

"She's not safe as long as she stays anywhere near me. That bomb was meant for me." He placed both palms on his desk and leaned toward her. "Don't you see that? No kid-

napper in his right mind would try to blow up his victim before he could get the ransom. And no one could have predicted that I would take Sarah sailing today. I sail all the time
by myself. And when I go out in the morning, if the wind
dies, I use the engine so that I get to my office on time. Anyone here could tell you that. The only way to keep Sarah safe
is to take her back to Boston. I should have insisted you do
that the day you arrived."

Andie stopped herself from jumping out of her chair. Anger always interfered with logic. "The day I arrived, the
skinny chauffeur and the chubby nurse tried to kidnap
Sarah. If that was just some plot to get to you, then Sarah isn't
safe anywhere. But she's better off here where you can arrange the security."

Swearing, Nick walked around the desk. "I can't protect
her. Can't you get that through your head?"

Andie rose so that she faced him toe to toe. "I'll protect
her. But I can't do that in Boston. Her grandmother will write
me a check, and have me escorted out of the house. And
Conrad Forrester will have a judge giving him temporary
custody before I can walk down the front steps."

Nick turned to glare at Mendoza and Jake. "Tell her I'm
right. She has to take Sarah away from here. Away from
me."

"Tell him *I'm* right!" Andie said.

Mendoza directed a level look at both of them as he leaned
back in his chair. "You're both right. Sarah *would* be safer
away from Heagerty Vineyards. But Boston isn't the place. If
the kidnapping isn't connected to the bombing, Conrad is
still a suspect. I have no jurisdiction there, and Ms. Field
won't be able to protect Sarah once she's told her job is
done." He raised a hand to prevent Nick from interrupting.
"But I do have a compromise suggestion. Jake can arrange
for Sarah and Ms. Field to stay temporarily in a safe house."

"No—" Andie began.

"Fine," Nick said to Jake. "When can you arrange it?"

Andie opened her mouth and then shut it.

The look Jake Nolan gave her was sympathetic. "For the time being it's the only way I can guarantee Sarah's safety. I'll get on it as soon as I get back to my office."

"Take them with—"

Jake Nolan raised a hand. "Five hours have gone by. If I were to take them with me, I'm sure we'd be followed. And I have no intention of using your phones. The earliest I can promise is tomorrow morning. By then I should be able to arrange something so that no one here will know they've gone, at least until it's too late to arrange for a tail."

"Grady will go with them," Nick insisted. When Jake nodded, he continued. "What about tonight?"

"Get some rest. You'll be safe in the house. I've gone over the security from every angle. I've also had three of my men check the house from top to bottom. They're standing guard outside your rooms right now."

"Aunt Maggie let you get away with that?" Nick asked.

"She wasn't in much shape to protest. The Martin girl said she'd taken a sedative and gone to bed. Seems your cousin Jeff is still missing. He wouldn't have any experience with bombs?"

"Jeffrey?" Nick almost smiled. "He's the one person who doesn't want to get rid of me. He was upset yesterday when he learned that his mother had arranged for me to sign over the winery to him at our annual festival. He'll get over it."

Pulling his notebook out, Mendoza flipped through the pages. "I want to talk to him when he shows up."

"Waste of time," Nick said.

Mendoza shrugged. "It's my time. Now, about the bomb."

Andie said nothing as Mendoza methodically went over the methods he would use once he had some kind of report from the state police lab. It was standard police procedure. She couldn't find any fault with it, but it would take time.

And time was something they might not have. She knew exactly how Nick was feeling when he began to pace. Frustrated. She wanted to do something, anything, to speed up the investigation. But she had to go with Sarah. They were right. The little girl would be safer someplace else until they could arrest somebody.

That much she could accept. It was the look in Nick's eyes when he'd told her to go that had fear piling in on top of her frustration.

Not that she could fault Nick. He was trying to do what was best for Sarah. That had been his intention from the start. But the past few days he'd been growing closer and closer to his niece. Her plan had been working. She was sure of it.

But now he was withdrawing again. While she would be sitting in some safe place in Syracuse, playing Monopoly with Sarah and Grady, he would convince himself all over again that the best thing he could do for Sarah would be to send her away.

How could she blame him? Why would Nick Heagerty want anything to do with a family when all he'd ever learned to expect from them was rejection and loss?

"So basically what you're saying is that unless and until we get some startling information from the state police lab that points a direct finger at someone, we're no closer to figuring out who's behind this than we were a week ago," Nick said.

"What I'm saying is that we need a piece of hard evidence, something that links the vandalism here at the winery with the attempts to kidnap Sarah. The bomb may give us that." Mendoza shoved his notebook back into his pocket and rose.

"We're due for a break," Jake said. "I could get a call at any time from my operative down in Sarasota."

Before Nick could reply, there was a soft knock at the door, and then Sarah poked her head in. "Grady's bankrupt," she said with a giggle. "I'm supposed to tell you he needs a loan."

"A loan?" Nick repeated as he hurried to the door and lifted the little girl into his arms. "Why in the world would I want to throw good money away?"

Sarah kissed Nick's cheek. "Because I asked you to."

As Andie followed them out of the room, her heart twisted. She promised herself that she would do whatever it took to keep Nick and Sarah safe and together.

IT WAS GOING TO STORM. From the window seat in her bedroom, Andie could see faint flashes of lightning pierce the darkness. So far the thunder remained a distant rumble. But the wind had picked up, rustling the pine needles and pushing waves onto the shore. The air that blew in the curtains was still thick with the smell of charred wood and gas. The rain when it came would cleanse the air, and then maybe they could forget. Leaning her chin on her knees, she waited for the storm to come.

Marguerite had stopped by earlier when it was still light out. She'd looked exhausted. When she'd asked to see Sarah, Andie couldn't find it in her heart to refuse. She'd led Marguerite into Sarah's room and stayed in the doorway. For the first time since Andie had met her, the older woman had seemed suddenly at a loss for words. Then Sarah had asked, "Could you tell me the names of the roses?"

"Roses?" Marguerite had repeated.

"Grady said my mother knew the names of each one of the roses that she planted in the garden. But he couldn't remember them all. He said that you were the expert." Taking Marguerite's hand, Sarah had led her to the window. "What are the little white ones called?"

Much to Andie's surprise, Marguerite could name every flower. And before she'd left, Marguerite had even told

Sarah the story of how her father had proposed to her mother in the gazebo at the center of the garden.

Leaning her chin on her knees, Andie watched three quick flashes of lightning spike their way through the black sky. Marguerite was a puzzle. It was the second time she'd shown concern about Sarah, and yet she'd urged Nick from the beginning to send the little girl back to Boston.

Sarah had fallen asleep hours ago. But Andie felt wired. And not just because of the approaching storm. It wasn't even the day's events keeping her awake. She was thinking about Nick. She wanted him to come to her. And he wouldn't.

She'd come to know him so well. He would pull away from her now. The nomad. It was for the best, she reminded herself. If she was going to keep the promise she'd made to Rose, she'd better put to rest, once and for all, any idea, however fleeting it had been, that she could share a part of his life.

The one person she would not allow him to pull away from was Sarah. First, she would concentrate on keeping Sarah safe, and then she'd convince Nick that Sarah belonged with him. That would be the easy part because, in his heart of hearts, he believed it already.

And then she'd leave.

Lightning once more split the blackness over the lake, and thunder rumbled closer. Hugging her knees tight, she waited. Even as a little girl she'd loved the drama and the excitement of a thunderstorm. Tonight, it would take her mind off Nick. Perhaps for a little while she could forget how much she wanted him.

"Andie."

The one word had her rising from the window seat. Barefoot and wearing nothing but his jeans, he was standing in the doorway of her room. She walked toward him.

When he opened his mouth to speak again, she pressed her fingers to his lips. "Shh."

But he pushed her hand away. "You should send me away. I shouldn't have come."

"I wanted you to," she said as she raised his hand to her lips. After stepping around him to lock the door, she pulled him with her toward the bed.

"I told myself that I was only coming here to say goodbye."

She smiled at him then. "Liar."

Nick suddenly laughed. It was the first time he had since he'd discovered the bomb. Should he have known how much he needed to be with her? To laugh with her again. To make love with her.

But when he reached for her, she evaded him and instead urged him down on the bed. She was lovely, he thought as he looked up at her. Why did that still amaze him? An oversize white T-shirt just skimmed her thighs. Her hair was slicked back from her face, still damp from a shower. Her eyes were dark, and he could see her desire. Or was it his own reflecting back at him? He wasn't sure. What he was certain of was that he'd never wanted her more.

He would have reached for her then and pulled her beneath him on the bed, but she chose that moment to run a hand down his chest. When she slipped her fingers beneath the waistband of his jeans to pull the snap loose, the weakness seeped through him. And then she was straddling his waist. It seemed to take all his strength to reach for her hands, and the moment he did, she gripped them and pressed them into the pillow above his head.

With her eyes steady on his, she leaned over him and began to kiss him slowly, teasing his lips with hers, then going on to explore his face and his throat. When she finally returned to his mouth, she lingered briefly, offering a taste only. Not nearly enough to satisfy, only enough to arouse.

And then she took her mouth on a slow and thorough journey down his chest.

The coolness of her hair contrasted sharply with the heat of her mouth. Inch by inch, he felt his skin dampen then burn. When she released his hands, he hadn't the strength to use them.

When she slowly dragged down the zipper of his jeans, his breath backed up in his lungs. He opened his mouth to beg her to stop. To go on. But the only sound he heard was a moan.

And then she was pulling his jeans down. When her teeth scraped along his thigh, he felt the flame sear across his skin and the smoke move through his brain. He heard another moan, but wasn't sure it was his.

Suddenly he was trembling. She had the power to make him tremble. Positioning herself above him, she looked into his eyes. And what she saw was more than enough. There was need, as desperate as her own. He belonged to her, at least for tonight. And there was desire, too. Their bodies were vibrating from it. And the heat. She thought she might melt from it. But not yet. First she had to have more.

She lowered her head and pressed her open mouth to his. Then his hands were gripping her waist and she was suddenly beneath him on the bed. Her gasp of pleasure mixed with his cry of her name.

They were still mouth to mouth as they joined and began to move quickly, almost furiously as one.

Outside, the skies opened and the storm burst, but it was no greater than the one that raged between them. They made their own lightning, their own thunder. And as their storm finally reached its peak, they were holding each other so tightly that they might have been fused as one.

THE DICE CLATTERED across the game board and rolled to a stop. "Seven." Andie kept her face expressionless as she moved her token noisily down the properties. "One, two, three, four, five, six, seven." Setting it with a final smack between two hotels on Boardwalk, she sighed and threw up her hands. "I'm dead meat."

"Gimmee, gimmee!" Giggling, Sarah extended both her hands.

Andie aimed a narrowed-eyed look at the little girl as she passed over her pitiful pile of money. "It's not nice to gloat at another person's misfortune."

"Especially when that person's had a steady run of bad luck," Grady added as he scooped up the dice.

"I like to win," Sarah said as she added Andie's bills to her already large stacks.

"Don't count your chickens yet," Grady warned as he rolled the dice. "I think they're getting ready to fly the coop."

Sarah merely smiled.

Resting her elbows on the table, Andie continued to fake interest in the game. Across the room, Ms. Markham was patiently working a crossword puzzle while her partner stared at the TV.

They were bored. She was practically catatonic herself.

Nearly forty-eight hours had gone by, and there was no news. The worst part of it was that even if something broke, they'd be the last to know. To ensure Sarah's safety, Jake Nolan had completely cut off any communication with them. They couldn't call out. Nick couldn't call in. She thought about him constantly. She was worried about him. She hadn't seen him or talked to him for two days, and it had created a void in her life that she didn't even want to think about. No, she wasn't going to think about it, because she had a plan. Pretending to stifle a yawn, she slid out of her chair. "I'm going to take a nap. Call me if you hear anything," she said to the room in general as she moved toward the door to her bedroom.

Once inside, she quietly slipped the lock into place and

hurried to pull the duffel bag from underneath her bed. It had taken less than twenty-four hours for her to make the decision. Another twenty-four to plan her escape.

She'd informed Sarah of her plan and had the little girl's unqualified support. That hadn't required much effort, Andie thought grimly. In Sarah's mind, Andie Field was "Nancy Drew," perfect and unstoppable. No one knew better than she that the real Andie was far from that.

Pausing at the window, she checked the street. The tan sedan was parked down the block as it had been off and on for two days. At times, there was a blue station wagon in its place. That meant that in addition to the team of four operatives who rotated twelve-hour shifts in the suite, Jake had also assigned guards to watch the hotel itself. His thoroughness made her wonder if he'd assigned even more people to the lobby.

The suspicion had caused an extra twelve-hour delay while she'd arranged for a disguise. Opening the duffel bag, she pulled it out. The young maid she'd bribed had brought her brother's coolest gear. Quickly, Andie stripped off her jeans and shirt and donned a pair of oversize shorts. Even with the belt, they settled low on her hips and bagged below her knees. Opening the drawer in her bedside table, she zipped her gun into the pouch and fastened it around her waist. The T-shirt was oversize, but at least it hid the fact that the shorts might fall down at any minute, and it completely camouflaged the pouch. The baseball hat came next. She put it on backward, just the way she'd seen kids wear theirs. Then she stuffed her hair beneath it. Last, she pulled on socks and the high-top shoes.

Hunching her shoulders over, she practiced her walk one more time, stopping when she reached the full-length mirror on the bathroom door. The high-tops were at least two sizes too big. Luckily, the young maid had brought two extra pairs of ribbed socks. Pulling the hat lower on her forehead, Andie surveyed herself critically. One thing she was certain of. Nancy Drew wouldn't be caught dead in an outfit like this. But if her luck held, it just might get her out of the hotel without being busted by one of Jake Nolan's operatives.

Turning, she stuffed her own clothes into the duffel bag and kicked it under her bed. Then she arranged pillows and blankets so that it looked as though someone was napping.

When she heard Sarah's triumphant laugh from the other room, she sauntered to the door that led to the hallway. The little girl was doing her part by keeping everyone busy and distracted. It was high time she did hers. She pulled open the door and found herself face-to-face with Grady.

"Going somewhere?" he asked, stepping into the room.

"How did you—"

"In my experience, when people cheat at Monopoly, it's usually to win. That last roll of dice should have landed you clear of Boardwalk." Pausing, he gave her outfit an amused glance. "Got a hot date?"

Andie took a deep breath and gave him the same lecture she'd given herself. "I'm going to do what I do best. Investigate. It's a waste of my time to be here when I can help." She raised a hand to stop him when he would have spoken. "I'm not going anywhere near the vineyard. I just want to use the public library for a while."

"The library?" Grady asked with a puzzled frown.

As quickly and concisely as she could, Andie explained about the album that Mrs. Mabrey had given her, how she'd shown it to Nick and then how it had mysteriously disappeared from her room. "Why would someone take the album? It's been bothering me ever since it happened. And the only explanation I can figure out is that there's something there. Nick and I have already seen it. We just haven't made the right connection yet. And someone was afraid that we would. But if I can get to a library, I can use microfilm to refresh my memory of the newspaper articles that were in the album."

Grady studied her. "You think that will help?"

Andie began to pace. When her shorts began to slip lower on her hips, she automatically hitched them up. "I don't have any proof, just a feeling, call it a hunch if you will, that there's something in the album that could help us link the accident twenty years ago to what's happening now." She turned to face Grady then and met his eyes levelly. Everything depended on her argument. "I can't fault Mendoza. In his place, I'd follow the same procedure. Analyze the evidence and wait. But time's running out. And if the lab report on the bomb doesn't give us the connection we need, maybe the microfilm will."

Leaning against the wall, Grady rubbed his chin. "The thing is, I promised Nick I'd watch out for you. Sarah's safe here, and so are you."

Andie walked toward him. "But Nick's not safe. And if I'm right, he's in more and more danger with each passing moment."

Grady smiled. "You're in love with him, aren't you?"

"Of course..." She intended to say "not," but the word hadn't come out. The last thing she'd meant was to tell anyone. She'd only admitted it to herself that one time. On some level she'd known instinctively that thinking about it, talking about it, would only make it more real. What she hadn't realized was that admitting it out loud would also make her feel relieved—and joyful.

"Okay," Grady said. "I'll let you go on one condition."

"What?" Andie asked.

"Your legs are a dead giveaway. Can you pull those shorts down a little without losing them completely?"

She tugged them lower on her hips, then pulled her belt tighter to secure them.

"Better," Grady said.

When she reached the door, he spoke again. "Andie."

With her hand on the knob, she turned back.

"Don't do anything I wouldn't do."

She was smiling as she slipped into the hallway.

THE DISGUISE had definite drawbacks, Andie thought as she waited impatiently for the librarian to crank his way slowly through a roll of microfilm. Faster, she wanted to shout in his ear. Instead she hitched up her shorts, which were once more on the slide.

Left on her own, she would have had the information she was after thirty minutes ago. But there was no way the young man with the button-down collar and neatly pressed pants was going to trust his precious microfilm to someone dressed as she was.

Even the man at the budget rental car agency had been slightly nonplussed at her request for a car. But her driver's license and credit card coupled with his greed had overcome his initial reservations.

"There." Andie pointed at the screen. "You passed it. Go back a few pages."

Suddenly it was there on the screen: the obituary she'd first seen in the scrapbook Mrs. Mabrey had shown her. Digging into her pouch, she found some loose change. "I need a copy."

Once the machine had spit it out, she continued. "In the same issue, there's a society column..."

When the young librarian turned to stare at her, she reached for the knob and began to crank it herself. In seconds she was looking at the picture of Nick's family that had been taken on the night of the accident. Shoving coins into the slot, she pressed the button. Just before the librarian sent the microfilm spinning back into its case, she read the byline on the column. Loretta Glass.

Fifteen minutes later she was driving the speed limit on

the New York State Thruway, headed toward Rochester. It had taken two phone calls to the *Rochester Democrat and Chronicle* to get a home address for Loretta Glass. The straightforward approach had gotten her the information that Ms. Glass had retired from the paper to breed Siamese cats and company policy prevented the release of home addresses or phone numbers.

Plan B had involved a direct phone call to the society desk. A brief but heartrending story about newly orphaned Sarah Heagerty's dream of having a Siamese kitten had gotten her detailed directions to Loretta Glass's cattery. She'd rejected the idea of phoning Ms. Glass and asking for an appointment. The outfit she was wearing was simply not conducive to the direct, straightforward approach she usually preferred.

The thought had her frowning. Could it be that she was actually beginning to prefer Nick Heagerty's style of detective work? *Never.* Pushing the idea out of her mind, she concentrated on what kind of a story would best fit her disguise and help her get the information she needed from Loretta Glass.

NICK WAITED for Andie to park her car before he stepped from behind the stone pillar that marked the entrance to Loretta Glass's driveway. It had been two hours since he'd concealed his own car in a turnaround area a short distance up the road. And two hours since the knot of anxiety that had settled in his stomach two days ago had turned to ice. He was betting on Andie's predictability. After two hours of worrying, he'd almost convinced himself that it was a mistake.

The moment he saw her climb out of her car and pause to hitch up the baggy shorts she was wearing, he felt his tension flow away. "Don't tell me. Let me guess. That outfit's some kind of Nancy Drew thing."

She whirled and swallowed the lump of fear that had

lodged in her throat. For a moment she couldn't move. The pleasure, the relief of seeing him was so intense. She was almost giddy from it. The moment she could, she replied with as much dignity as she could muster, "Nancy Drew wouldn't be caught dead wearing this outfit." Then keeping a tight grip on her pants, she strode toward him. "What are you doing here?" She grabbed his T-shirt and yanked. "How can Jake protect you if you don't at least stay on the estate?"

"How can Jake protect you if you don't at least stay in your hotel?" Nick countered.

She couldn't ignore the question because he had a point. But she might have been able to think of a better explanation if he hadn't been smiling at her that way. "I couldn't stay there."

"And I couldn't stay on the estate once I figured out that you'd fly the coop the first chance you got. As soon as I convinced Jake of that, he cut me loose to take care of you."

Andie drew to her full height. "I don't need—"

Laughing, Nick cupped her chin with his hand and kissed her lightly. "I'm beginning to think you need a caretaker full-time."

There were bees buzzing busily in a nearby field, a bird chattering in a tree above. Their sudden noise as they filled the silence convinced Andie that she hadn't heard Nick correctly. She probably hadn't heard him at all because the moment his mouth had touched hers, her mind had shut down. Or maybe he'd been teasing. He still had that smile on his face. Ruthlessly, she gathered her thoughts. "You followed me here?"

"No. If I'd gone anywhere near that hotel, I would have put both you and Sarah at risk. I just pretended that I was a private investigator obsessed with procedure and asked myself who I'd need to talk to next."

Her mind racing, Andie studied him for a moment. Would he have remembered Loretta Glass's name from the brief glance he'd had of the scrapbook? She'd had to go to the library to refresh her memory. Suddenly, she dropped her hands to her hips. "You went to Mrs. Mabrey for help."

Nick shrugged. "I just asked myself what a procedure-obsessed—"

"Yeah, yeah, yeah," Andie said, but she had to fight the urge to laugh as she pulled the photocopies out of her pants' pocket and went to spread them out on the hood of her car. "I got hard copies of the articles. And the answer's got to be here." She glanced up then. "Unless Mendoza's found out something?"

"Skinny and Chubby are in custody. The Rochester police picked them up yesterday. The nurse has been cooperating fully, but she claims they never saw their employer. All contacts were made by phone, and the voice was electronically distorted. Maps, money, and instructions were dropped at John Manetti's fishing cabin. Neither admits planting the bomb."

"Has Mendoza had any luck locating Mr. Martinez?"

Nick shook his head.

"Then it's up to us. We've got to find something here."

Nick watched her as she studied the two pieces of paper. Should he have known how much he'd miss simply seeing her? Hearing her voice? He'd even missed the tiny frown that appeared on her forehead when she was totally focused on something. And if he'd missed her this much in two short days....

"Andie..."

Suddenly she slammed her fist down on the hood of the car. "It's right here, staring us in the face! What is it?"

He took her fisted hand in his, and lifted her chin so that her eyes met his. Once again, he saw his own feelings reflected there. Frustration, almost desperation. What he needed was time and a better place to tell her what was in his heart. For now he said, "That's why we're here. To see if Ms. Glass can tell us what it is."

Andie took in a deep breath as she returned the grip of his hand. "Okay." She even managed a smile. "You've got a plan, I presume?"

Nick's brows shot up. "I assumed we'd do it your way. March up to the front door and ask."

Andie glanced down at her clothes. "I've found that this disguise does not exactly inspire confidence. It has several limitations, including that the pants are constantly on a downward slide."

"Can I help in any way?"

Andie laughed as she swatted his hand away and started toward the house. "I can just imagine how you'd like to help. You've got the length of this driveway to figure out some kind of story that will explain...." She hitched up the pants again.

"What are partners for?" Nick asked as he followed her up the drive. The house was a low-slung, sprawling, stone ranch. Behind it at the edge of the woods was an outbuilding that resembled a small barn. Mrs. Mabrey had filled him in on the cats. He quickly improvised a story as he climbed the two steps and rapped on the door. Though he heard nothing, he could feel himself being sized up through the one-way glass. Then the bolt slid back, the door opened, and he found himself looking into a pair of wide-set, bright blue eyes.

Although he knew she had to be somewhere in her eighties, Loretta Glass was still a very striking woman. She wore a man's plaid workshirt over pale denim jeans. One kitten slept snuggled beneath her chin and another purred at her ankles. The only clues to her age were the silvery-gray hair she wore pulled back in a neat bun and the spray of wrinkles around her eyes. It was the intelligence he saw in those eyes that made him change his mind. "I don't think I have a chance of getting you to believe the story I was going to tell you," he said.

Loretta Glass smiled. "Probably not, Mr. Heagerty." At his surprised expression, she continued. "I may be retired, but I still read the newspapers avidly. That was quite a nice picture of you the other day. But it's a pity you've decided to leave Heagerty Vineyards. We also met briefly twenty years ago, though you probably don't remember."

Then she turned to Andie. "Let me guess. You're the young woman who talked with my old editor at the *Chronicle*. And I *did* believe the story you told him. I even selected two kittens from my latest litter for you to choose from. But then, I don't suppose Sarah Heagerty really wants one, does she?"

"She would if she could see them," Andie said as she leaned over to pick up the one at Loretta's feet. She grabbed a handful of her shorts as she stood up again.

"This is Andie Field," Nick said. "She's the private investigator my sister-in-law hired to bring Sarah home."

Loretta Glass's eyes brightened. "A private investigator." She shifted her gaze from Andie's face to her clothes. "Interesting. You've got me curious now. Come in." Turning, she led the way to a bright, airy room with a view of a stream. She waved them into a love seat and sat across from them on a wide overstuffed ottoman. "I've come to believe that curiosity is in the genes. I was this way long before I became a reporter and a columnist. And it's not something I've outgrown since my retirement." She settled the sleeping kitten on her lap. "Why are you really here? And what does it have to do with that explosion that happened in front of your place the other day?"

Nick exchanged a quick look with Andie. Then he said, "We're not sure yet that what we're here about has any connection. But you wrote a column twenty years ago about a fund-raising party that my family gave at the winery to benefit the Rochester Philharmonic."

"Your aunt Marguerite gave a lot of parties," Loretta said.

Shifting the kitten to her other arm, Andie pulled the photocopies from her pocket and rose to hand them to the older woman. Loretta glanced at them briefly before setting them down on the table. Then she shook her head sadly. "I remember that night very well. And the column. I was the first person to arrive at the scene of the accident."

"You were there?" Andie asked.

"I didn't see the crash. I was following Marguerite and Mike. The concert had run late, and Marguerite was anxious to be the first to arrive back at the house. It was to be a late supper with the visiting guest conductor, and only the very biggest contributors had been invited. She wanted to get home before any of the guests arrived. I remember having to drive very fast to keep their taillights in view. You know how those roads are, full of twists and hills. I'd lost sight of them temporarily when I heard it." Raising one hand, she pressed her fingers briefly against her temple. "I'll never forget it, the squeal of tires, glass breaking. I thought it wouldn't stop. When I reached the top of the hill, I saw two cars in the ditch. I thought for sure that one of them belonged to your aunt and uncle. I checked the car with the children in it first. The mother was screaming, rocking the child back and forth in her arms. There was blood all over the dashboard. The father and the little one in the back seat...they seemed to be in shock."

She turned to Nick. "Then I went to your car. It had rolled over, and you'd been thrown free. Of course, I didn't know it was you. I checked for your pulse, and it was strong. There was nothing I could do, so I went for help.

"The closest place was Heagerty House. I knew that from the directions I'd been given. Marguerite was there, and your family. When I told them about the accident, they called the police and an ambulance. I went back to the intersection to wait for them to arrive. I couldn't stay at the party. Not with the image of that little baby in my mind."

"But my family stayed at the party. I'm sure it wasn't a problem for them," Nick said.

"They didn't know that you were one of the victims. It wasn't until later when I got back there that I learned the police had called and you'd been identified."

"Let's go back a little bit," Andie said. "You said that you were sure at first that Mike and Marguerite might have been involved in the accident. If they were that close, why didn't they stop when they heard the crash?"

"There wasn't really much of a crash. The tires were the worst of it. Some breaking glass. The tall grass must have muffled the sound once the cars rolled into the ditch. But I did ask Marguerite about it." Loretta smiled briefly. "Curiosity can be a curse. She was quite offended. She said she and Mike hadn't heard a thing."

Andie pulled the copy of the column around so that she could look at it. It was then that she saw what she'd overlooked before. "Mike isn't in this picture. Where was he?"

"He wasn't there." Loretta frowned as she glanced down at the photo. "I remember when we took that picture, Marguerite said he wasn't feeling well. But earlier... Now that I think of it, he wasn't there when we phoned the police, either."

"Nick remembers seeing a third car, one that ran the blinking red light seconds before his car overturned in the ditch. Did the police ever ask you about that?" Andie asked.

Loretta shook her head. "I told them exactly what I've told you. They took my phone number, but they never contacted me again." Eyes narrowed, she looked from Andie to Nick. "Do you think that your aunt and uncle were driving the third car?"

"What I remember is that I overturned in the ditch because

I was trying to avoid a collision with a car that speeded through the stoplight. I think the Martinez family ended up in the ditch because they tried to do the same thing."

Loretta thought for a moment. "It's entirely possible. Mike and Marguerite hadn't been out of my sight for very long when I heard the noise." Suddenly her eyes narrowed. "Is there some connection between the accident and that explosion that occurred near your place the other day?"

"It's a strong possibility," Andie said as she settled her kitten on a nearby cushion and gathered up the photocopies. "I'm sorry about the story I told your editor. I'm sure Sarah would love one of these kittens, but Nick just got her a puppy."

"Think nothing of it," Loretta said as she rose and followed them down the hall. "I've told much worse when I was after a story. And Hank doesn't give out my address easily."

At the door, Nick turned back and took Loretta's hand. "Thank you. You've been a big help."

"Don't thank me," she said. "Just come back and fill me in once you've solved the case."

Nick smiled. "You've got yourself a deal."

They didn't speak until they reached the end of the driveway. Then Andie reached for Nick's hand. "You could let Mendoza handle this," she said.

"No. This is my family. I'll handle it."

When he tried to pull away, she tightened her grip on his hand. "*We'll* handle it, partner."

# 10

IT WAS A FAST RIDE. Just keeping Nick's car in sight took all of Andie's concentration. She didn't have time to think about what he must be feeling. There was every reason to believe that Marguerite's betrayal had gone much deeper than they'd suspected. As she pressed on the brake and guided the car through the next set of hairpin curves, she reminded herself that the truth hurt. But not nearly as much as lies.

And if they were right, Nick's entire life for the past twenty years had been based on a lie. On the final turn, the back wheels skidded onto the shoulder. She jerked the steering wheel to the right, then took her foot momentarily off the gas pedal.

*Concentrate on the driving, Field.* For a while she did. Her rental car needed all the help it could get to keep up with Nick's. But every time the road straightened, her thoughts returned to Marguerite. Was a lie told twenty years ago a strong enough motivation for murder? On the surface, it didn't seem to be. One thing Andie was sure of was that Marguerite wanted Heagerty Vineyards for her son Jeffrey. If she *was* desperate enough to engineer a kidnapping attempt and blow up a boat, then Andie couldn't allow Nick to confront his aunt alone. The instant his car disappeared around the next curve, she gripped the steering wheel and floored the gas pedal.

It wasn't until they reached the gate to the vineyard that she caught up, and when the guard waved him through, she stayed close on his tail. By the time he opened the door to Heagerty House, she was at his side.

"No!" Sandra Martin was talking on the phone in the hallway. She'd nearly shouted the word into the receiver, then the moment she saw them she turned away and spoke in a low voice. Her tone was urgent, angry almost, but Andie couldn't quite catch what she was saying. When Sandra turned back to them, she was perfectly composed.

"Where's my aunt?" Nick asked.

"In the parlor. Lieutenant Mendoza just arrested Jeff and dragged him off to jail. Mrs. Heagerty has asked me to call the family attorney." She glanced at the phone, then turned and began to climb the stairs. "I'll use the extension in my room."

Andie hurried after Nick. Marguerite was seated in the wing chair beneath her father's portrait, her shoulders slumped. As they reached her, Andie could see that behind the designer glasses, her eyes were red and her cheeks damp. But the moment she saw Nick, she straightened, gathering herself.

"You have to do something. They've arrested Jeff."

"For what?" Nick asked.

Marguerite waved a hand. "For trying to destroy Heagerty Vineyards. He called that lieutenant up and told him to meet him here. He confessed to all of it right in this room." She let her gaze move around the room. "So that I would know."

"What did he want you to know, Mrs. Heagerty?" Andie asked.

"He doesn't want it. Not any of it." She met Nick's eyes then. "My father wanted a son. He didn't believe that a woman could run a winery, so he sold it to your grandfather. He told me if I wanted Manetti Vineyards back, I would have to marry a Heagerty and produce a son. So I did. And now my son is going to leave. He said all along that he didn't want to run the winery. I didn't believe him."

"Neither did I, Aunt Maggie," Nick said. "I still don't believe that he would give all of this up."

"You didn't see him. He was so angry with me. He blames me for sending you away. Please..." She reached out a hand. "I know that he didn't mean you any harm. Can you do something?"

Nick took her hand and sat on the ottoman next to her chair. "Did Mendoza arrest Jeff for setting off that bomb?"

"He read him his rights. He took him..." Marguerite's voice broke.

Nick squeezed her hands. "If I'm going to help Jeff, you have to tell me everything you know about that accident twenty years ago."

Stiffening, Marguerite tried to pull her hands away, but Nick held on.

"What does that have to—" She stopped suddenly and studied Nick. Then she seemed to shrink even further into her chair. "You know, don't you?"

"I want you to tell me," Nick said.

Marguerite shifted her gaze then, beyond Nick, to something only she could see. After a moment she spoke. "Michael drove that night, and I was urging him to hurry. That's why we took the shortcut. It was the first party that your grandfather had allowed me to arrange by myself, and I was so anxious for everything to be right."

Closing her eyes, she drew in a deep breath. When she let it out, she seemed smaller. "You don't know how often I've gone over and over it in my mind. If we'd just taken a different route. If I hadn't been so eager to prove myself to your family. If we'd only left the concert a few minutes earlier or a few minutes later." She opened her eyes then to look at Nick. "Can you understand that?"

When he nodded, she seemed to find the strength to continue.

"Michael drove fast up that hill. I was talking about the party, what I'd planned. Maybe I distracted him, or maybe it was just the speed, but suddenly the light there, flashing in front of us, and the cars were almost in the intersection." Marguerite closed her eyes again. "I've pictured it so many times in my mind. Like a movie. If he'd put on the brakes...perhaps the accident would have been even worse. That's what I've told myself sometimes. Or maybe he was trying to put on the brakes and his foot hit the gas pedal instead. At the last minute, I closed my eyes, and then I heard the tires squealing. The sound seemed to go on forever. But I didn't hear any crash."

Opening her eyes, she looked from Nick to Andie. "If we'd just heard a crash, we would have turned back. Then maybe everything would have been different. But there was nothing. We even laughed about it, how lucky we'd been to avoid a collision. I'd almost forgotten the whole incident when Loretta arrived at the party. She was horribly shaken up about an accident she'd seen. Even then, I told myself it had nothing to do with us. Until she described the intersection and asked me if I'd heard anything." Marguerite looked at Nick. "I didn't lie then. We hadn't heard a thing, so I convinced myself that the accident must have happened later."

She paused for a moment, then glanced down at her hands, which were still clasped in Nick's. "That was the first lie, and I told it to myself. But then I lied to you. When you told me about the third car you'd seen, I was almost sure it was the one that Mike and I were in, but I didn't tell you that. And I didn't tell your father, either. The police told him that you'd been drinking, and I convinced myself that you were mistaken. You hadn't seen our car. I tried to convince Mike, too. Once Loretta arrived at the party, he wanted to tell the police everything. I told him it was too soon. We couldn't be sure it was our car. Later, I told him it was too late to step forward. What good would it do? Nothing he could say would change anything. If he admitted we'd driven through that red light, it would only hurt him and his future at the winery. Your grandfather would have been furious with him. He hated scandal of any kind, and he might have decided right then and there to disinherit Mike. I argued that you were a child. No one would blame you. He was an adult with much more to lose. I urged him to think of our son's future.''

Marguerite sighed again. ''In the end I convinced him. But he was never the same. Especially after your father sent you away to school. He wanted to tell the truth then, but I convinced him once again to keep silent. I don't expect you to believe me. But I did think that if you spent some time away, you and your father might find a way to mend your fences.'' Drawing in another deep breath, she shook her head. ''But it was a very self-serving justification for a lie. And it didn't fool Mike for a minute. He started drinking then. He never forgave me or himself, and it wasn't long before he wanted nothing to do with the winery.'' Her hands tightened on Nick's. ''It all started with such a small lie. I convinced myself that I was doing the right thing for the family. And it's destroyed everything. Your life and Mike's and now Jeff's. I'm sorry.'' Gathering herself together, she rose. ''I'll leave as soon as I can find a place to stay. And unless you object, I'll ask the family attorney to represent Jeff.''

Nick rose and put his arms around his aunt. ''The lie ruined your life, too, Aunt Maggie.''

For a moment the older woman stiffened, and then she seemed to collapse in Nick's arms. As Andie watched, she felt a tightness in her throat and tears slipped down her cheeks.

Keeping his arm around his aunt, Nick began to lead her

out of the room. "Why don't you go upstairs and rest while I see what I can do about Jeff?"

"You're still going to help Jeff?" Marguerite asked. "I don't understand."

"Someone planted a bomb on my boat yesterday," Nick said. "I don't think you did it, and I don't think Jeff did it, either. But I intend to find out who wants to hurt this family. Andie—" he turned back at the foot of the stairs "—see if you can reach Mendoza."

While Nick escorted Marguerite to her room, Andie picked up the phone in the hall and started to dial the number when she heard a voice. A man's, speaking in a foreign language. Glancing down at the lit-up button, she saw that it wasn't the kitchen extension. And it wasn't French, either. Then a woman's voice interrupted, angry, in the same language. Spanish, Andie realized as she quickly tried another line.

Just then, Jake Nolan pushed through the front door as Nick descended the stairs. "I have a message for you from Mendoza," Jake said. "He figures you'll want to see Jeff, arrange for bail. I'm going to drive you to Syracuse myself."

For over an hour, Andie had been watching Mendoza question Jeff Heagerty through the two-way glass. With his sleeves rolled up and his arms resting on the table, he looked perfectly at ease, as though he were drinking coffee in a restaurant instead of an interrogation room. He'd even gotten Jeff to laugh at one point. And that was making it easier for the young man to pour out his story.

"He's very good," Andie said. It was the first time she'd spoken since Jake had left them in the small observation room.

Nick's only reply was a sound that communicated his frustration as well as his agreement. Twisting in her chair, she looked at him. For the past hour he'd been pacing back and forth in the limited space with all the patience of a caged lion.

For the life of her, she couldn't think of what to say to him. She could only imagine what it might feel like to listen to the voice coming through the speakers, your cousin's voice, describing in great detail how he'd used a hypodermic syringe to inject ipecac through the corks of Chardonnay bottles. Another betrayal from a family that had betrayed him before. But Jeff's lack of loyalty seemed to be limited.

Though he was willing, eager even, to confess to doctoring the Chardonnay and to sabotaging the refrigeration tank, he vehemently denied any involvement in the attempts to kidnap Sarah or in the bombing of the *Nomad*.

"You believe him, don't you?" she asked.

He stopped and turned to her. "I want to."

"I believe him. It makes sense if you think about it. Marguerite was pressuring him into assuming his responsibilities. He thought if there continued to be problems at the winery, you'd postpone leaving, and he'd have time to change your mind."

"If only I'd—"

Rising, Andie moved quickly into his path. "Hold it right there. None of this is your fault."

"I didn't listen to him," Nick said.

"His mother is the one who didn't listen to him. You just didn't believe him when he claimed he didn't want to run the winery. And do you know why you didn't believe him? I'll tell you why." Andie tapped a finger into his chest. "Because deep down inside, *you* want to run the vineyard. It's a part of you, just as it's part of Marguerite. That's why you understand her. You both love Heagerty Vineyards so much that it's hard for you to imagine someone walking away from it if they didn't have to."

The sound of the door shutting had them both turning to face Mendoza. "I couldn't help overhearing the last of that." He sent Nick a pointed look. "And I couldn't have summed it up better myself. I told you right from the start she was a good detective. And—" he looked through the two-way glass to where Jeff was still sitting at the interrogation table "—I'll bet my badge that your cousin had nothing to do with the kidnapping attempts or the bombing."

"I agree," Andie said. "Sarah's arrival was the answer to Jeff's prayer. And the more interest Nick showed in her, the more hopeful Jeff became that he would change his mind and stay."

"And the more nervous that would make Aunt Maggie," Mendoza confirmed.

Frowning, Nick shook his head. "I can't believe she would have planted a bomb on my boat. Jeff and I sailed a lot together. She would never have endangered him." Shoving his hands into his pockets, Nick began to pace again in the cramped space. "I got a call from Conrad Forrester's lawyer today. He encouraged me to voluntarily grant his client temporary custody of Sarah. He seems confident that a judge will grant Forrester's request just as soon as he hears about the bomb that went off on my sailboat."

"What did you tell him?" Andie asked.

"That Sarah was currently under protective custody, and that my attorney would ask the judge to postpone any hearing until Lieutenant Mendoza felt it was safe to move her."

"If Forrester thought an explosion would cause a judge to favor his custody suit—" Mendoza began.

"No." Andie raised a hand. "Think it through. Conrad wants custody of Sarah because he wants control of her money. Trying to kidnap her for ransom or to make Nick look bad as a guardian is one thing. But a bomb? That could place Sarah in danger, too. Conrad needs Sarah alive to get the money."

Mendoza looked at Nick. "She's got a point."

It was Andie's turn to pace. "Let's take it one step further. We've been assuming that the bomb on the boat was meant for Nick. But if we're right in what we're thinking now, no one could really know for sure that it would only kill Nick. They would have to know there was a risk someone else could be killed, too. Sarah. Or Jeff."

Leaning against the wall, Mendoza pursed his lips thoughtfully. "Could be they don't care."

"Or they could be out to destroy the whole family," Nick said. "That eliminates Marguerite and Jeff."

"And probably Forrester," Mendoza added.

There was a knock at the door before Jake entered.

"We're just reviewing the suspects," Mendoza explained.

"Well, the Martinez family is moving their way up on the list. My operative in Florida finally located the father. He's working as a chef in a hotel in Miami. He hasn't had more than an occasional weekend off in years. But his older kid moved away, came up here to attend college. The father couldn't—or wouldn't—remember the name of the school."

"So this older kid, Santino or something, sees his little sister die and then watches his mother literally lose her sanity because of the grief. Twenty years later, he comes back to upstate New York to go to college, and decides to get his revenge on the Heagerty family," Andie said.

"Put that way, it sounds like the movie of the week. But most of my case files would never make it to a movie because they're too unbelievable." Mendoza pushed himself away from the wall and reached for the door handle. "I'll get someone to start calling colleges and universities."

"Wait," Nick said. "If we do it your way, it's going to take too much time."

"We could get lucky," Mendoza said.

"Or our luck could run out," Nick replied. "I'm tired of waiting for that to happen."

"What's your plan?" Andie asked.

"Don't encourage him," Mendoza warned.

"He's right. We've been lucky so far, and that could change," Andie argued.

"Jake?" Mendoza appealed to his friend for help.

Jake shrugged. "She's got a point."

"Okay," Mendoza sighed as he sank into a chair. "I know I'm going to be sorry for asking. What's your plan?"

"Going along with the theory that someone, the Martinez kid, if you will, is out to destroy me and perhaps the whole family, I'd say he's pretty much succeeded. It's been in the papers that I'm leaving the vineyard. Tomorrow night at the annual wine festival, I'm supposed to officially announce the transfer of power and ownership to Jeff. That will be a little hard to do since he's in jail, and he plans to leave town as soon as he's free. When that becomes common knowledge, there will be a loss of confidence in Heagerty Vineyards and a huge dip in sales. I could, of course, announce that I'm staying on, but the question in everyone's minds will be how long? This Martinez person could afford to sit tight and bide his time before he makes his next move."

"If he's succeeded, why would he necessarily make one?" Mendoza asked.

"Because of the bomb," Andie said. "He wants more than to destroy the vineyard. It's personal."

"I agree," Nick said. "And that's why I want to move quickly. So far, he hasn't made any mistakes. I want to tempt him into making one. Tomorrow night at the festival I'll announce that contrary to rumor, I'm going to make my home at Heagerty Vineyards, and Jeff and I are going to run the

winery together. I'll also announce that Jeff has been cleared
of all suspicion in the bombing incident.''

"Hold it right there." Mendoza turned to Andie. "Ms.
Field, talk some sense into him."

"I think he's right," Andie said. "If we follow Plan A, and
do it your way, we have to sit and wait and play right into
this nutso's hands. I vote for Plan B."

"Right or wrong, setting a trap in the middle of a wine festival with three possible targets! It's a crazy idea! Jake, back
me up here," Mendoza said.

"The plan has a certain appeal," Jake began. "With the
proper precautions…" He began to enumerate them.

The whole idea was crazy. Risky, too. But for the next fifteen minutes Jake and Andie added their persuasive argu-
ments to Nick's, and together they changed Mendoza's ada-
mant refusal into a grudging acceptance of the inevitable.
Point by point, the lieutenant alternately poked holes and offered solutions until it was something he could live with. Almost.

In the end they agreed unanimously that Jeff had to be
fully informed so that he could cooperate, and that they
would only fill Marguerite in at the last moment. For the
time being all she would know was that the festival was to go
on as scheduled.

"The damn house has too many ears," Mendoza grum-
bled.

"I want to tell Jeff," Nick said.

"He's all yours," Mendoza replied.

"I'll start making the arrangements," Jake said as he followed Nick out of the room.

"I don't like it," Mendoza said as he watched Nick join his
cousin in the interrogation room.

"Neither do I," Andie replied. "But you've known him
longer than I have. If we hadn't agreed to it, he'd have put an

equally risky alternate plan into effect. At least this way, with Jake's help, we have a chance to protect him.''

Mendoza's sigh echoed her own feelings of frustration. Even with the modifications they'd hammered out, their plan was risky. She didn't like it one bit. What she *did* like was what she saw through the two-way glass. Whatever Nick had said when he'd entered the room was enough to have Jeff out of his chair. And then the two men were holding each other. Andie felt the prick of tears behind her eyes. She'd protect them, no matter what.

ANDIE HAD TO HAND it to Marguerite. She'd created a fantasy world at Heagerty House. The porch and front yard were strung with hundreds of Chinese lanterns, their lights flickering in the gentle breeze from the lake.

Colorful tents housed a band and a dance floor, plus several tables laden with food. Jake Nolan had insisted on keeping the wine and the reception line inside the house. Guests entered through the front door and were directed into the parlor. Marguerite's job was to greet them and inform each one personally of the new partnership that her son and her nephew had formed.

From her position near the foot of the stairs, Andie could see Sandra Martin pouring wine and handing out brochures. Mendoza was mingling with guests. Even Jake Nolan had a job, passing out hors d'oeuvres. He'd chosen it to give himself maximum flexibility. Andie couldn't help but notice that he was providing some of the female guests with an opportunity for maximum pleasure. Yet the moment that one of them became too clingy, he would move on, leaving them smiling.

Marguerite looked perfectly at ease as she performed her duties. Though she hadn't been fully informed of the plan until early that afternoon, she had certainly risen to the occasion. From where Andie was standing, she appeared thrilled to be telling everyone of Nick's change of plans. Jeff seemed a little nervous, and Nick looked tense. He hadn't been pleased at all to be confined to the reception line. But it was the only way to convince everyone that the story Marguerite was telling was true.

Andie turned her attention back to the front door, scanning the guests as they entered. She sympathized with Nick's frustration. More than anything, she wanted action. She wanted to get her hands on the person who was behind everything.

During the next half hour the flow of people through the front door increased, and Andie moved up to the stair landing for a better view of the parlor. Two men in white catering jackets stayed close to the reception line. More of Jake's men.

From outside, she could hear the band begin to play. Almost immediately the guests who were lingering at the wine table began to move toward the French doors.

"It looks like a fairy tale," Mrs. Mabrey said, climbing the three stairs to take Andie's hands in hers. "We're just missing the little princess, but not for long, I hope."

"No, Sarah is—"

"You needn't bother to explain. Nicholas told me everything when he stopped by the library yesterday." At Andie's amused expression, she continued. "He needed some advice about tracking you down."

"How did you know that I would go to Loretta Glass?"

Mrs. Mabrey beamed a smile at her. "I just asked myself where I would go if I were Nancy Drew. He's much handsomer than Ned Nickerson, don't you think? I told him when he found you, he'd better not let you get away again." Without missing a beat, Mrs. Mabrey turned her attention to the parlor. "My, this is quite a gathering. And I see that John Manetti is still presiding." She gestured to the painting. "Nice enough man, but he had a very narrow view of what a woman's role should be. He certainly wouldn't have approved of a woman private detective. Oh, my."

"What is it?" Andie asked.

"If I didn't know better, I'd think I stepped into a time warp. That young woman over there handing out the brochures is the spitting image of Lucia Martinez."

Andie followed the direction of Mrs. Mabrey's gaze and found herself looking at Sandra Martin. "Sandra Martin." She spoke the name in a whisper. "Of course."

"Who is she?" Mrs. Mabrey asked.

"She's been Marguerite's personal assistant for the past year," Andie said, then quickly added, "but I think she's Juanita Martinez's older sister, Santina. We assumed she was a he. This would explain why Father Murphy believes that a young Mrs. Martinez has been visiting him lately." Even as she talked, Andie's mind was racing. Should she tell Lieutenant Mendoza? A resemblance to Mrs. Martinez was something. But it wasn't proof. She doubted it was enough to make an arrest.

The parlor was still crowded. Sandra Martin was busy, and Nick's family was well protected. She turned to Mrs. Mabrey. "Don't tell anyone about this. Just go through the reception line. I'm going to try to find some proof."

"Go to it," Mrs. Mabrey said. "I'll keep everyone distracted just like Nancy's best friends would do."

Andie climbed the stairs slowly until she was sure she was out of sight. Then she took them two at a time. Sandra's—Santina's—rooms were on the third floor. There were two doors opening off the narrow hallway. Betting that Pierre had the one with the view of the lake, Andie tried the one that faced the front yard. It was locked. She fished a safety pin out of her pocket and went to work. Thirty seconds later she was inside.

The room was dark, lit only by pale moonlight slanting through the window. Praying that the reception line was still occupying everyone's time, Andie risked a light. A dress lying across the foot of the bed told her she'd guessed the right room.

A quick glance around revealed nothing. The dress was the only clue that the room was even occupied. She pulled open the closet door. Shoes formed a row across the floor, clothes hung from hangers, the shelves were empty.

The dresser top held a brush and a mirror. Nothing else. No photos. No books. She discovered an appointment book in the top drawer of the nightstand. Flipping to the latest date, she turned the pages backward. Most notations, written in a cryptic shorthand, chronicled Marguerite's heavy social calendar.

Scattered through the references to lunches and board meetings were reminders to make calls. A garage, a florist and a *D*. A dentist? A doctor? There didn't seem to be any corresponding appointments. The fourth time Andie saw the note to call *D*, she flipped the pages forward to check the regularity of the calls. Once a week. She began to pace. If *D* stood for Santina's father.... She recalled the phone conversation in Spanish she'd accidentally punched into the day before. Mendoza could get the records from the phone company.

After replacing the book in the nightstand, Andie glanced at her watch. She'd been gone ten minutes. Too long. She had a quick mental image of Nick leaving the reception line to look for her. Halfway to the door, she turned back, then dropped to her knees to check beneath the bed. Her hand was on the album Mrs. Mabrey had given her when she heard the sound of the key turning in the lock. In an instant she rejected the option of hiding under the bed. If she was found, she'd be trapped. Andie rose to face the enemy.

Santina Martinez stepped into the room and aimed a gun at Andie's heart. It was small and equipped with a silencer.

"Don't even think of it," Santina said as she circled the bed. Andie felt the cold metal press into the back of her neck as Santina reached under her jacket and removed Andie's gun from her waistband.

Outside in the hall, a floorboard creaked. Andie prayed it wasn't Nick, prayed that Santina didn't hear it. Then it was her own gun that she felt against her spine as the door swung open and a white-jacketed security guard stepped into the room. He had his weapon raised, but Santina fired first. There was only a puff of sound before the man fell silently to the floor.

Andie took a quick involuntary step forward and felt Santina's fingers clamp on her wrist. "Leave him."

"There are others," Andie said.

Santina laughed softly. Cold and mirthless, the sound sent an icy shiver up Andie's spine. "If you want to keep them alive, you'll come with me quietly."

They moved forward, stepping over the body of the dead guard.

"To the right," Santina said, prodding her with the gun. "We'll use the back stairs."

At the top, Andie stumbled. Santina jabbed the gun into her back. "Don't try anything. If I have to shoot you here, I'll put a bullet in your spine. If you live, you'll never walk again."

Several plans raced through Andie's mind as they hurried down the wooden staircase. By the time they reached the bottom, she'd discarded all of them. There were two white-jacketed men in the kitchen. Neither was Jake. They didn't even glance up. Once outside the house, Santina urged her toward the rose garden.

"Sit," she said once they reached the gazebo. Then she settled herself on the bench facing Andie. "Now we'll wait for your lover to come to the rescue."

Andie sat perfectly still while an image formed in her mind of Nick running down the path, calling her name. Then the gun that was now aimed at her would shift, there would be a puff of sound.... There was a sudden buzzing in her ears, an iciness in her veins. She'd felt the same way the night she'd faced death in that alley. Only it wasn't rotting garbage she smelled now. It was the scent of roses. Bloodred roses. The buzzing grew louder. And then suddenly she thought of her angel charm.

"You've caused me a lot of trouble," Santina was saying.

Concentrating on the weight of the small angel pressing against her throat, Andie pushed away the panic and focused her attention on the woman sitting across from her. In the light from the full moon, she could see Santina Martinez quite clearly. Her eyes were cool, calculating, the madness quite hidden.

"He'll watch you die before I kill him," Santina said. The words were spoken in the same tone she'd heard Sandra Martin use when speaking to Marguerite about her schedule. The young woman might have been a robot for all the emotion she showed.

But it was there. That much Andie was sure of. Hadn't someone once said that revenge was a dish best eaten cold? Perhaps, but it required a lot of hate and anger. And if she was going to rattle Santina Martinez, she would have to set those emotions loose.

"I was disappointed when the bomb didn't work, but this will be even better," Santina said.

"Did you plant it yourself?" Andie asked.

"Hardly. The whole idea was Barstow's. He was desperate for the money I'd promised to pay him once he had Sarah."

So, it had been Skinny, Andie thought, "When did he do it?"

"The same day that he set off the alarm at the state fairgrounds. He didn't want to risk it with Nick around."

Andie thought of the fishing boat that had been hovering close to the shore that day.

"The only problem with the bomb was that Nick wouldn't have any time to suffer. So I insisted that Barstow continue to try and kidnap Sarah. But this will be even better. Before Nicholas Heagerty dies, I want him to know what it feels like to lose someone he loves."

"It must have been hard, losing a sister," Andie said.

Santina's hand tightened on the gun. "You think this is about Juanita? It has nothing to do with her. I was glad when Juanita died. Once she came, my mother never had time to read me stories, she couldn't take me to the park. All she had time for was my sister. Juanita took my mother away from me. After the accident, I thought everything would change."

Muscles tensed, Andie watched Santina Martinez. The emotions were beginning to surface. Though the hand holding the gun remained rock-steady, the other one had begun to clench and unclench. And her voice had become tighter, more high-pitched, almost childlike. "But my mommy didn't forget about Juanita. She forgot about me. She even called me *Juanita*. She'd take me in her arms and rock me. And she made me sleep in Juanita's bed. My father said it was just a pretend game, that I had to do it if I wanted Mommy to get better. But she didn't. And then they came and took her away."

Santina took a deep breath. Her eyes had filled with tears. One had escaped to roll down her cheek. But when Andie glanced down, she saw that the hand holding the gun was still steady.

"I wanted my mother!"

The sudden shout made Andie jump.

"Don't move," Santina said.

A twig snapped then. Startled, Santina glanced around quickly, but when her eyes met Andie's, they were clear and focused. "Your lover is coming. It's almost time."

Andie swallowed and tasted the metallic flavor of fear.

"Maybe I'll just kill you. Then he'll know what it's like to wait and wait for someone you love to come back."

"Santina!"

It was the moment Andie had been waiting for. The instant she heard the word, she sprang forward. Then everything seemed to happen at once. As her fingers closed around Santina's wrist she saw the flash of light, felt the fire tear through her shoulder as she and Santina tumbled off the bench.

Then it was all a blur. There were shouts, footsteps running. But her world was quickly narrowing to the pain in her shoulder, the pressure of Santina's weight as the woman straddled her and aimed the gun at her head. Shots cut through the night. Andie saw blood blossom on Santina's chest at the same instant a bullet burned past her cheek. Then blackness swallowed her.

SHE'D SLEPT around the clock. Andie's first reaction when she looked at her watch was anger. The smiling resident who had stitched up her shoulder in the emergency room had lied to her. He'd assured her that the shot he'd administered was for tetanus, standard procedure for a gunshot wound. Minutes later she'd been floating, and she couldn't recall anything beyond Nick carrying her to his car.

Where was he now? She sat up in bed, then winced and raised one hand to gingerly touch her bandaged shoulder. She'd been very lucky. That's what the resident had said. And she agreed. Santina's bullet had just torn the flesh. The young woman hadn't been as fortunate. Just before she'd drifted off, Andie'd made Nick confirm what she'd already known. She'd seen where the bullet had hit Santina Martinez.

Very carefully she swung her legs over the side of the bed. She needed to find Nick and talk to him. She was halfway to her feet when the knock came at her door.

"Come in."

"*Non! Non! Non!*" Pierre burst into the room with Marguerite close on his heels. Muttering in French, he set a loaded tray on the window seat and urged her back into bed. "Please," he finally managed in English as he settled the tray on her lap. "We are under orders to keep you in bed, Ma'm'selle."

"The only way I'll do that is if you bring Nick here."

"He went to pick up Sarah," Marguerite explained as she set a vase of roses on the nightstand. "But he did ask me to bring you these. They're from Rose's garden. He wanted you to have them as soon as you woke up."

Pierre fluffed out a napkin, tucked it in the neck of her T-shirt, then whipped the covers off plates. Andie was afraid he might offer to feed her when he finally drew himself to attention and said, "Will there be anything else?"

"No, thank you," she managed. Then she found herself alone with Marguerite.

"He's never brought me breakfast in bed," Marguerite said. "But then, a lot of things have changed since you arrived."

Andie glanced down at the tray. The scrambled eggs were hot and tempting, the coffee, irresistible. There were two cups. "Would you like some?" she asked.

"If you're not too tired." Marguerite took a step toward the bed, then hesitated.

"No, I'm okay." Andie smiled as she offered a cup.

"I came here to thank you for giving me my family."

"I didn't..." Andie began.

Marguerite raised a hand. "Please let me finish. I realized as I was cutting the flowers that I owe Rose a great deal, too. For sending Sarah here and for sending you."

Andie studied the older woman for a moment. As always, Marguerite was exquisitely dressed, immaculately groomed, but something was different. The strength was still there, but it had softened.

"It's Nick you should be thanking," Andie said.

"I've tried. But I need your help."

"How?" Andie asked.

"I realized when I was standing in that reception line last night that I wanted what I was saying to be true. More than anything." Taking a sip of her coffee, Marguerite sat on the edge of the bed. "I've done Nick a horrible injustice. I'm not sure he can forgive me. I'm not even sure he should. The only thing I'm really sure of is that Nick belongs here. I think Rose knew that, and that's why she sent Sarah to him."

Andie reached out to cover Marguerite's hand with hers. "Tell him how you feel. Tell him you want him to stay."

Marguerite sighed. "I don't think he'll believe me. Why should he? Jeff won't be able to convince him, either. He's been trying to for years." Setting her cup on the tray, Marguerite faced Andie. "The only person who has a chance of persuading Nick to stay here at Heagerty Vineyards is you."

"I've been trying. And I think that he will, now that he's come to love Sarah." Andie frowned. "Of course, I'll talk to him again."

Rising, Marguerite smiled. "You do that."

"But I can't promise anything," Andie said as Marguerite started toward the door. "I mean..."

When Marguerite turned back, she was still smiling. "My

dear, you'll only have to tell him that you'll stay, too, if you really want to persuade him."

SHE'D LEFT. It was the first thought that raced through Nick's mind when he stepped into Andie's bedroom. With one sweeping glance, he took in the empty, perfectly made bed, the vase of roses on the table. Pushing back the panic, he forced himself to check the bathroom and Sarah's room. But the raw fear didn't subside until he found that her clothes were still hanging neatly in the closet.

Marguerite was presiding over a tea party in the parlor. Pierre had made cupcakes to celebrate Sarah's return. The aloof chef had certainly defrosted since Andie had brought Sarah to Heagerty House. And so had Marguerite. She was even teaching Sarah how to pour the tea.

Where could Andie be? he wondered as he hurried back to her room. He spotted her from the window. She was sitting in the gazebo on the same bench she'd sat on last night. Only then, Santina Martinez had been pointing a gun at her heart. Terror, rage, helplessness, all the emotions that he'd felt as he'd stood there watching threatened to overwhelm him again. Ruthlessly, he reined them in. He didn't want to recall those few endless minutes when he'd thought he'd lost her. Taking a deep breath, he turned away from the window and hurried out the door.

As he took the back stairs two at a time, a sense of urgency overtook him. Pierre called a greeting as he hurried through the kitchen. Nick waved a hand.

*She's still here.* The words formed a chant in his mind as he ran down the path to the gazebo. When she turned and rose to greet him, he forced himself to slow down. *Plan A*, he reminded himself. He was determined to do it her way—this one time, at least. The breeze off the lake was heavy with the scent of roses. Flowers. Mentally, he added them to his list.

Sally Ann would have the candles; Grady, the champagne. Moonlight would provide the right atmosphere. Without the *Nomad*, privacy might be hard to come by, but there was time to solve that problem, too.

He stopped two feet away from her. More than anything he wanted to touch her, to hold her. If he did, he'd never stick to his plan.

"Sarah?" Andie asked.

"She's stuffing herself with Pierre's cupcakes."

Andie's brows rose. "Cupcakes?"

"He even decorated them with clown faces."

Andie smiled. There was a moment of silence. Then she said, "I'd better—"

Nick took her arm as she moved forward. "I have something—" He broke off the second she winced. "Your shoulder?"

"I'm fine. You heard the doctor. It's nothing." She thought of the way Nick had insisted on staying with her, holding her hand while the young resident in the emergency room had cleaned the flesh wound, then stitched it up. "I heard him, too, until he drugged me."

"He was young," Nick said with a frown. "Inexperienced."

"And very clever." Andie smiled again. "He prescribed rest and then made sure I got it. I'm fine. Really." More than anything she wanted to be in his arms. But he'd dropped his hand to his side as soon as she'd winced. "Or at least I will be fine when you tell me what I want to hear about your plans for Sarah."

"She'll stay here with me, of course."

"You won't be sorry." Andie focused on the relief she felt, ignoring the little band of pain that tightened around her heart. "Have you told her?"

"Yes. She wants you to stay, too," Nick said.

"Of course." Twisting her hands together, Andie began to pace. "That was the deal we made. I would stay for two weeks until she felt comfortable here. And I don't think we can count the last two weeks. I mean, who can get comfortable with a kidnapping threat and a bomb?" She was babbling. She couldn't seem to stop. "I'll call my ex-partner back. He offered to handle my clients while I did this favor for Rose. He says he misses me, but everything's going fine. He's great. I'm sure it won't be a problem."

Nick snagged her hand. "I'm your partner, too."

When she stared at him silently, he said, "What I mean is...oh, to hell with it!" Nick dragged her close and kissed her. His tension dissolved in a heartbeat, in the instant it took to taste her again, to feel her body mold itself to his. He'd almost lost this, he reminded himself as he pulled away. He forced his voice to be calm. "I don't want you to go back to Boston. I want you to stay right here with me and Sarah."

His grip on her arm was so tight that it sent pain singing up her arm to her shoulder. She hardly noticed it. "Nick, I..."

"No." He barely stopped himself from shaking her. "I wasn't going to talk about it. Not ever. But I can still see it. I had to stand not twenty feet from here and watch while you talked to that madwoman. She had a gun pointed at your heart, and I couldn't do a thing. And when I heard the shot and saw you tumble over that bench with her.... Why didn't you tell Mendoza or Jake instead of going off like that?"

"All I had was Mrs. Mabrey's memory. I went with Plan B."

"I thought you were dead." He was gripping her arms too tightly. He couldn't seem to stop.

"I'm not dead. I'm right here," Andie said.

"I won't allow you to leave. Not now. Not ever."

When she simply stared at him, saying nothing, Nick felt the panic bubble up. "Damn it, I love you. I wanted to do this properly with candles and moonlight." Suddenly he released her and dropped to one knee. "Marry me."

Andie drew in a deep breath and dropped to her knees in front of him. Very carefully she raised both hands and framed his face. "Yes."

He let out the breath he'd been holding and rested his forehead against hers. Quite suddenly he wanted to laugh. "Yes? Just like that?"

"This was Plan B, right? It always gets quicker results."

He did laugh then, and for the first time the disturbing image from the night before began to fade from his mind. Cupping her face in his hands, he began kissing her cheeks, her eyelids, the tiny pulse that beat fast at her throat. "More," he murmured as he brushed his lips against hers.

"I love you, I'll marry you, I'll share your life."

Then he kissed her lips, and the horror melted completely away. In it's place came a peace and a contentment that he'd never hoped to find. Rising, he took her hand. "Let's go in and tell our family."

# _____Epilogue_____

ALL BRIDES had the jitters, Andie assured herself as she paced back and forth in her room.

"Brutus!" Sarah's muffled shout from the next room was followed by a fit of giggles and a series of short, staccato barks. "Come back here!"

But not all brides had a ringbearer who was a puppy. Andie pressed a hand against the nerves fluttering in her stomach. She took one step toward the door that led to Sarah's room and then thought better of it. Instead, she paused to check herself in the mirror one last time.

Andie barely recognized the woman staring back at her. She was pale, with a smooth fall of dark hair, swept back on one side and fastened with a single white rose. The slim, ivory sheath that dropped in an unbroken line to the floor was elegant. It looked like something a princess would wear. Certainly not Andie Field.

Turning, she moved quickly to the window to convince herself that she wasn't dreaming.

A soft breeze carried the sound of violins, and above it the hum of conversation. Rows of chairs circled the gazebo. Jake Nolan, looking as if he had been born to wear a tuxedo, was escorting Sally Ann Tanner to one of them. Grady was just starting down the path with Mrs. Mabrey on his arm, while Lieutenant Mendoza waited to lead Marguerite to her seat. The preacher was already in place with Jeffrey at his side.

Suddenly, Andie frowned. Where was the groom? He should be standing with his best man. The preacher had been very clear about that at the rehearsal. Her gaze shifted immediately to the lake, but the *Nomad II* was still tied to its buoy.

Suddenly, Brutus burst into the room, barking.

"He keeps getting away," Sarah said breathlessly as she raced after him.

Andie grabbed for the leash and missed. She and Sarah, after several unsuccessful attempts, had the puppy backed into a corner when the knock sounded at the door. Grady stepped into the room. "Need some help?"

"Tie the leash to Sarah's wrist while I tidy her hair," Andie said. A few minutes later they were done. Sarah once more looked like a picture-book flower girl in her pale blue dress, and for the moment Brutus sat quietly at her feet, looking innocent.

"Be good." Andie shook a warning finger at the puppy. "Without that ring, your uncle Nick and I can't get married."

"Let's go." Grady took Sarah's free hand.

"I'll be right down," Andie assured him. After shutting the door, she drew in a deep breath.

"Andie."

With a gasp, she whirled around and saw Nick standing in the doorway to the bathroom. In his tuxedo he looked so handsome that for one moment he literally took her breath away. The moment she found her voice, she said the first thing that came into her head. "You're not supposed to be here. You're breaking all the rules."

Shoving his hands into his pockets, he said, "I decided to start this marriage the way I intend it to continue."

She could hear the trace of nerves in his voice, see it in the way he shifted his weight. Curious, she walked toward him.

It was the first time she'd ever seen Nick Heagerty nervous, and quite suddenly her own nerves disappeared. "I thought we agreed we were going to do this wedding strictly by the book. Plan A all the way."

"I got tired of waiting for you." Nick found that just saying it out loud eased some of his tension. Her smile sent the rest flowing away.

Outside, Brutus began to bark again, loud enough to compete with the violin music. Moving to the window, they watched the puppy break free from Sarah and tear across the lawn. Lieutenant Mendoza was hot on his tail with Jake Nolan and Grady splitting up to run in wide circles, hoping to head the puppy off. Arms spread, Pierre stood in front of a table laden with food. It was Jake who finally made the successful interception while the wedding guests cheered.

"I don't think Brutus understands the concept of Plan A. If he breaks loose during the ceremony..." Andie began.

"Not to worry." Nick patted his pocket. "I have some backup rings right here."

She laughed then. "I should have known." Linking her fingers with his, she turned to face him. "I've been thinking. Do you suppose it would be all right if we bent the rules a bit more and walked down the aisle together?"

Nick's eyebrows rose. "What happened to doing this by the book?"

"You did say something about starting our marriage the way we intend it to continue. I'd like to do it together, partner."

He raised their joined hands to his lips. "Forever."

# 4 FREE

## books and a surprise gift!

We would like to take this opportunity to thank you for reading this Mills & Boon® book by offering you the chance to take FOUR more specially selected titles from the Temptation® series absolutely FREE! We're also making this offer to introduce you to the benefits of the Reader Service™—

- ★ FREE home delivery
- ★ FREE gifts and competitions
- ★ FREE monthly newsletter
- ★ Books available before they're in the shops
- ★ Exclusive Reader Service discounts

Accepting these FREE books and gift places you under no obligation to buy, you may cancel at any time, even after receiving your free shipment. Simply complete your details below and return the entire page to the address below. *You don't even need a stamp!*

**YES!** Please send me 4 free Temptation books and a surprise gift. I understand that unless you hear from me, I will receive 4 superb new titles every month for just £2.30 each, postage and packing free. I am under no obligation to purchase any books and may cancel my subscription at any time. The free books and gift will be mine to keep in any case.

T8XE

Ms/Mrs/Miss/Mr..................................Initials ........................................
BLOCK CAPITALS PLEASE

Surname ...............................................................................................

Address ...............................................................................................

..............................................................................................................

.........................................................Postcode....................................

**Send this whole page to:**
THE READER SERVICE, FREEPOST, CROYDON, CR9 3WZ
(Eire readers please send coupon to: P.O. BOX 4546, DUBLIN 24.)

# This month's irresistible novels from

### THE BLACK SHEEP by Carolyn Andrews

Nick Heagerty was a loner, a rebel *with* a cause. Ten years ago he'd been accused of a crime he didn't commit—and he'd left town without a backward glance. Now he was back—but not for long. Then *everything* changed when he met gorgeous P.I. Andie Field and realized that his wandering days were numbered...

### WISHES by Rita Clay Estrada

When Virginia Gallagher found a wallet full of cash, it would've been the answer to her prayers, *if* she hadn't been so honest. When Wilder Hunnicut came to pick it up, *he* would've been a wish come true, *if* he hadn't been out of her league. And when her reward was a lamp with three wishes, she started hoping wishes really could come true...

### AFTER THE LOVING by Sandy Steen

*It Happened One Night*

To claim her inheritance, Isabella Farentino must find a husband—fast! The only man around is the arrogant, infuriatingly sexy Cade McBride. Belle's counting on his love-and-leave-them attitude to get him out of her life, but after one incredible wedding night with Cade, she's having second thoughts...

### BRIDE OVERBOARD by Heather MacAllister

*Brides on the Run*

Blair Thomason was about to take the plunge—into marriage, that is. But when she found herself on a yacht, about to marry a crook, she plunged into the sea instead! Luckily, Drake O'Keefe was there to rescue her... She'd barely escaped marrying one man, only to be stranded with another!

Spoil yourself next month
with these four novels from

## ROARKE: THE ADVENTURER by JoAnn Ross

*New Orleans Lovers*

Shaken by an attempt on his life, journalist Roarke O'Malley
returned home. But he was thrown into more danger when
beautiful Daria Shea turned to him for help. Without her
memory, she had no idea who was trying to hurt her or why...
And as they investigated together, the sultry days turned into hot,
passionate nights...

## NOT THIS GAL! by Glenda Sanders

*Brides on the Run*

Keeley Owens was in a tacky Las Vegas wedding chapel, about
to marry her drunken boyfriend, when she realized it would be a
fate worse than death. So she stalked off into the desert—only to
be rescued by a gorgeous stranger. He wined her, dined her and
loved her all night long. But Keeley had only just left one groom
at the altar...

## ONE ENCHANTED NIGHT by Debra Carroll

*It Happened One Night*

The man Lucy Weston found on her doorstep was half-dead from
the winter storm outside. She kept him alive with the warmth of
her body, and reacted to him as she never had to any man. He
was a strong, sensual lover. But he had no idea who he was...

## ONE HOT SUMMER by Suzanne Scott

Jillian Sanderson had just inherited half an inn—but the other
half was a problem. Because that half belonged to sexy-as-sin
Kit Malone...and the fever that raged between them was
uncontrollable. Would Kit stay around if they could make those
hot summer nights last forever?

**On sale from 6th April 1998**

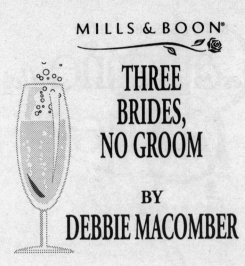

# MILLS & BOON®

# THREE BRIDES, NO GROOM

## BY

# DEBBIE MACOMBER

We are delighted to bring you three brand-new stories
about love and marriage from one of our
most popular authors.

Even though the caterers were booked, the bouquets
bought and the bridal dresses were ready to wear...the
grooms suddenly got cold feet. And that's when three
women decided they weren't going to get mad...they
were going to get even!

On sale from 6th April 1998
Price £5.25

*Available at most branches of WH Smith, John Menzies,
Martins, Tesco, Asda, Volume One, Sainsbury and Safeway*

# Catherine Coulter

## *Afterglow*

Chalk-and-cheese lovers Chelsea Lattimer and
David Winter finally find happiness after a series
of disastrous relationships—thanks to their
match-making friends.

*Afterglow* is a wonderful romantic comedy from
*New York Times* bestselling author Catherine Coulter.

1-55166-472-0

**AVAILABLE FROM MARCH 1998**

# JAYNE ANN KRENTZ

# *Lady's Choice*

Travis Sawyer has a plan for revenge. Juliana Grant has a
plan too—she has picked Travis as Mr Right. When
Travis takes over the resort in which Juliana has invested
her money, Juliana takes matters
into her own hands.

*"Jayne Ann Krentz is one of the hottest writers
in romance today."*—USA Today

1-55166-270-1
**AVAILABLE FROM MARCH 1998**

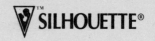

# SPECIAL OFFER £5 OFF

FLYING FLOWERS

**Beautiful fresh flowers, sent by 1st class post to any UK and Eire address.**

We have teamed up with Flying Flowers, the UK's premier 'flowers by post' company, to offer you £5 off a choice of their two most popular bouquets the 18 mix (CAS) of 10 multihead and 8 luxury bloom Carnations and the 25 mix (CFG) of 15 luxury bloom Carnations, 10 Freesias and Gypsophila. All bouquets contain fresh flowers 'in bud', added greenery, bouquet wrap, flower food care instructions, and personal message card. They are boxed, gift wrapped and sent by 1st class post.

To redeem £5 off a Flying Flowers bouquet, simply complete the application form below and send it with your cheque or postal order to; **HMB Flying Flowers Offer, The Jersey Flower Centre, Jersey JE1 5FF**

**ORDER FORM** (Block capitals please) Valid for delivery anytime until 30th November 1998 MAB/0298/A

Title ............... Initials ............... Surname ...............

Address ...............

............... Postcode ...............

Signature ............... Are you a Reader Service Subscriber **YES/N**

Bouquet(s) **18 CAS** (Usual Price £14.99) **£9.99** ☐   **25 CFG** (Usual Price £19.99) **£14.99** ☐

I enclose a cheque/postal order payable to Flying Flowers for £ ............... or payment b

VISA/MASTERCARD ☐☐☐☐☐☐☐☐☐☐☐☐☐☐☐☐☐ Expiry Date ......... / ......... /

**PLEASE SEND MY BOUQUET TO ARRIVE BY** ......... / ......... / .........

**TO** Title ............... Initials ............... Surname ...............

Address ...............

............... Postcode ...............

Message (Max 10 Words) ...............

Please allow a minimum of four working days between receipt of order and 'required by date' for deliver

You may be mailed with offers from other reputable companies as a result of this application. Please tick box if you would prefer not to receive such offers. ☐

**Terms and Conditions** Although dispatched by 1st class post to arrive by the required date the exact day of delivery cannot be guaranteed Valid for delivery anytime until 30th November 1998. Maximum of 5 redemptions per household. photocopies of the voucher will be accepted.